ESTONIAN SHORT STORIES

Writings from an Unbound Europe

■ □ ■ □ ■

ESTONIAN SHORT STORIES

Edited by Kajar Pruul and Darlene Reddaway

Translated by Ritva Poom

NORTHWESTERN UNIVERSITY PRESS

EVANSTON, ILLINOIS

Northwestern University Press
Evanston, Illinois 60208-4210

Printed in the United States of America

ISBN 0-8101-1240-X (CLOTH)
ISBN 0-8101-1241-8 (PAPER)

Library of Congress Cataloging-in-Publication Data

Estonian short stories / edited by Kajar Pruul and Darlene Reddaway ;
translated by Ritva Poom.
     p. cm.—(Writings from an unbound Europe)
   ISBN 0-8101-1240-X (cloth : alk. paper).—ISBN 0-8101-1241-8
(pbk. : alk. paper)
     1. Short stories, Estonian—Translations into English.
   2. Estonian fiction—20th century—Translations into English.
   I. Pruul, Kajar. II. Reddaway, Darlene. III. Poom, Ritva. IV. Series.
PH671.E5E874 1996
894'.54530108—dc20   95-40096
                                                           CIP

The paper used in this publication meets the minimum requirements of
the American National Standard for Information Sciences—Permanence
of Paper for Printed Library Materials, ANSI Z39.48-1984.

CONTENTS

■ □ ■ □ ■

Tiit Hennoste, Kajar Pruul, and
Darlene Reddaway

INTRODUCTION

ESTONIAN SHORT PROSE OF THE 1960S THROUGH THE 1980S explores the sometimes troubled, sometimes playful Estonian consciousness as it emerges from an artificially imposed Soviet culture, and as it subsequently enters a dialogue with a Western model of civilization that leaves one with more questions than answers. The stories in this anthology trace the development of this dialogue through the vigorous return of modernism to Estonian prose fiction during the 1960s as well as its subsequent evolution, both thematic and stylistic, during the following two decades. The stories represented here are boldly written, infused with a quiet, individualistic response to the small joys of life and the subtle complexities of an unrelenting dual Soviet/Western reality. It is this same undaunted individualism that has enabled the Estonian people to perpetuate their unique culture despite the political and cultural invasions they have experienced over the centuries: by the Swedes, the Germans, the Russians. And it is this stalwart individualism that has enabled them to produce a group of world-class writers that, due to the obscurity of the Estonian language, has until now escaped the notice of even the keenest Western literary critics.

During World War II, the Soviet Union "annexed" independent Estonia and began to restructure its economy and society to render the Estonians dependent on Moscow. This dramatically changed the face of Estonian literature. During the Stalinist period, the Soviet Writers' Union adopted the literary doctrine of Socialist Realism, and Soviet officials now demanded that Estonian writers forsake their "bourgeois decadence" and adhere to this doctrine. The Socialist Realist formula enjoined authors to "realistically" portray the "utopian" struggle to secure the "bright Communist future." In Estonia, Socialist Realism was more prevalent in the development of academic theories and literary criticism than it was in literature itself. Only after Stalin's death and the "thaw" that followed Nikita Khrushchev's liberalizing measures at the end of the 1950s did official literary history and criticism begin to slowly reject the accepted opposition between realism/good and nonrealism/bad.

There were Estonian writers who conformed to the Socialist Realist formula, but most did not submit to the official doctrinal line. These nonconformists either wrote stories that were hidden in desks and dark closets for years before being published or they emigrated. In volume as well as quality, the most significant Estonian literary works during the 1940s and 1950s were written by Estonian writers in exile, primarily by those writers who had fled to Sweden. Postwar modernism first entered Estonian literature through the writings of these Swedish-Estonian authors during the 1950s.

Not until the end of the 1960s were Estonian authors permitted to publish their own modernist works in the Soviet Union. With this new freedom, the literary world revived and began to flourish. More traditional short stories that employ the techniques of social or psychological realism, characteristic of Estonia in the 1930s, figured in Estonian literature during this period, but it was the rediscovery of modernism that revitalized the literary process and inspired the development of a rich and original Estonian literature.

In the Russian Republic, emerging modernist authors were more strongly censored than they were in Estonia, and they developed an unofficial, underground literary movement on the strength of samizdat, that is, of literature passed from hand to hand in manuscript form. There was a smaller Estonian underground, but Estonian authors were not under the same political constraints as their Russian compatriots. Estonia was, in a sense, the "Soviet abroad," its "display window" to the West, and this afforded Estonians a margin of freedom not known to Russian writers. Although many Estonian authors were unable to publish their works immediately, and although some of these authors were not far from being "dissidents," most published openly and were publicly acknowledged from the beginning of their careers. Two of the stories included in this anthology even received the Tuglas Short Story Award for Estonian short prose writers in their year of publication: Toomas Vint's "This So Unexpected and Embarrassing a Death" and Mari Saat's "Elsa Hermann."

As ideological reins slackened in the 1960s, Estonian writers won the right to generalize about all aspects of life without having to frame their work around political issues, as had been imperative under Socialist Realism. For example, poetry concerned purely with love and nature reemerged, as did stories about the quests of youth. Initially, both poetry and prose followed the format of traditional realism; then a few modernist parameters were slowly introduced, among them free verse in poetry, internal monologue and multiple points of view in prose.

THE 1960S AND EARLY 1970S: LIVELY DIVERSITY

Estonian culture in the 1960s was in a genuine state of flux. During the latter half of this decade, authors and artists alike pursued active, avant-garde experiments and turned to modernist means of expression. In painting and graphics, pop art, constructivism, and surrealism became influential. "Happenings" and "performances" were organized. In the theater and in dramatic literature, P. E. Rummo's *The Cinderella Game* (1969) caused a sensation; it was performed a few years later at La Mama in New York. A theater of metaphor influenced by J. Grotowski and A. Artaud developed in the Estonian university town of Tartu. Modernism in music first appeared in those pieces composed by Arvo Pärt. Often one individual would become an innovator in a number of areas simultaneously. Mati Unt, whose stories are represented in this anthology, was not only a writer but a pioneer who reformed the theater with Western avant-garde theories. Toomas Vint, also included in this anthology, has become well known in Estonia as a metaphysical, naive painter.

If by the end of the 1960s modernism had begun to permeate Estonian poetry and short prose, at the beginning of the 1970s the innovative techniques of modernism began to be employed in novels. The worldwide counterculture movement and a certain new "openness" in the Soviet Union vis-à-vis the West were the central factors that precipitated these modernistic innovations. In the early 1970s, a great many classics of twentieth-century literature were translated into Estonian, including works by such world-renowned authors as Camus, Salinger, Hesse, Mroźek, Kafka, Beckett, Butor, Bellow, and Hemingway. Consequently, psychoanalysis, existentialism, and the absurd became particularly significant for young Estonian writers of this period.

The literary trends that defined Western literary practice from 1920 through 1960 were compressed and telescoped together with the 1960s' counterculture of rebellion to yield a literature in Estonia that was quite distinct from that which developed organically in the West. Angst, lack of motivation and commitment, and the absurdity of existence are key themes of the late 1960s and early 1970s. The young intellectuals at Tartu University became interested in modern sociology and Freudian Marxism. These interests were no doubt characteristic of those prevalent throughout Eastern Central Europe at this time. Estonian literature was especially marked by the popularity of and emphasis on the absurd.

In order to understand more fully the Estonian literary establishment of that time, we must take into account the fact that ideological requirements were more stringently enforced with regard to theoretical writing and literary critical interpretations of published texts than with regard to literature itself. For example, although modernist prose pieces were published early on, the first Estonian translation from the Russian of a collection of theoretical articles by the Tartu structuralist-semiotician Yurii Lotman could be published for the first time only in 1990. For this reason, during the 1960s and 1970s, openly published criticism could only refer to modernism as a negative phenomenon. This created a topsy-turvy, carnivalesque situation in which literature itself was quite free in form and relatively free in content, whereas public theoretical discussion of this very same literature was rigorously censored.

At the end of the 1960s, for instance, a polemic developed in which politicians as well as critics close to the center of power accused Arvo Valton of having exhibited existentialism in his stories. Such an accusation could have led to a ban on Valton's fiction. In order to prevent the eradication of modernism, the critics who supported Valton denied that even the faintest hint of existentialism could be gleaned from his work. Modernism thus had to enter Estonian literature in a nameless fashion. This situation prevailed for many more years, and although writers enjoyed relative freedom in their treatment of individual mores, a great number of forbidden themes remained: questions of Estonian nationalism, the true state of Soviet society, and recent Estonian history among them. To express these themes, writers learned to use more and more allegory, as Valton has masterfully done in his short story trilogy "The Snare I–III."

The leading figures of Estonian modernist literary reform were Arvo Valton and Mati Unt. Both had made their writing debuts at the beginning of the 1960s. Valton began with short realistic pieces characterized by a melancholy humor and an interest in the "man on the street." Unt's early stories were lyrical and realistic, and were either very long or very short. They generally concerned a young man of the 1960s who was confronted with spiritual and ethical choices. Unt himself later characterized this genre as "naive."

In the middle of the 1960s, both of these authors began using modernist techniques. Valton developed a grotesque, absurd type of short story with an objective, neutral narrator. "Vernanda Bread" falls into this category. The allegory in Valton's short stories has a great deal in common with the antitotalitarian prose found throughout Eastern Europe at that time, for instance, that of S. Mrożek and V. Havel. On the whole, Valton wrote absurd and allegorical stories until the mid-1970s, gradually embellishing them by adding dream symbolism and mythological motifs.

For Unt, the breakthrough to modernism came with the long short story "Murder in the Hotel" (1969), an in-depth, Kafkaesque stylization, which was the most provocative manifestation of the new modernism in Estonia up to that time. Depiction of the intricate workings of the psyche play a much greater role for Unt than they do for Valton. For this reason, Unt's stories seem to be driven by a halted stream of consciousness, relying on the strength of chains of association and types derived from literature, mythology, and history.

On the one hand, Unt describes immediate and concrete sense perceptions (smells, sights, sounds, touches); on the other hand, he presents the unreal, wanton world that exists alongside us. In "The Black Motorcyclist" we sweat with the cheerful farmers, squish mud between our toes with the journalist's wife, but the larger significance of the sinister and unacceptable reality coexisting with these simple human pleasures strikes us squarely in our psyches when we see how the journalist's wife returns after having naively responded to a chance call. Psychoanalysis, particularly that of Jung, and existentialism are the key to understanding Unt's work during this period. In "Tantalus," Unt tries to discover several possible explanations for Tantalus' guilt, and we experience a kind of gestalt shift with each version as we try on different psychological hats. Unt is the kind of avant-garde writer for whom the creation of each new work simultaneously means posing and solving a new technical problem. Unt's prose became the model for those Estonian writers who continued the process of modernistic innovation in the 1970s.

NEWCOMERS IN THE 1970S

At the beginning of the 1970s, many of the prose writers who first appeared on the literary scene were the same age as writers from the 1960s' generation, or a bit younger. They had drunk in the intellectual atmosphere created by those writers, and by the end of the 1960s they were participating in avant-garde events. Representatives of this group included in here are Toomas Vint and Mari Saat.

These newcomers largely continued in Unt's footsteps. However, their works began to reflect new social problems, which they expressed in the altered, detached tonality characteristic of the 1970s' worldview. This detached tonality permeates the cold and calculated murders committed in so many of the stories by Mari Saat. In "Elsa Hermann," the death of parents and sister are accepted matter-of-factly by a distanced Elsa, who is too drawn into her immediate practical concerns to register these events on an emotional scale.

The problems of living space, work, and sheer survival over-shadow her humanity, which can be regained only by yielding to the black despair of a countryside lake and its beckoning call.

In Estonia as in Eastern Europe at large, the 1960s' hope for an open, tolerant discussion of socialism with a "human face" had been completely abandoned. The desire to change society had been replaced by a turning inward, by a skepticism about continual progress toward either the utopian Soviet future or its "liberating" Western variant. This myopia rendered Marxism so inconsequential that it was dropped from any dialectic consideration. Toomas Vint's "The Swan-Stealing" is almost a parable that illuminates this turning inward away from the socialist ideal. Instead of sharing the swans in the park with "the people," the heroine opts to steal a swan for her own private enjoyment in a closed-in world she has created for herself alone.

This turning inward resulted in a peculiar "psychomodernism," a prose style abounding in the very psychoanalytic motifs that the official Socialist Realist stance condemned as anti-Soviet, anti-Marxist. Although Estonians had been aware of classical psychoanalysis since the 1930s when psychoanalytic models were taken "seriously" as a branch of science, the relationship between the psychomodernism of the 1970s and classical psychoanalytic theory was ambivalent. Like all else, psychoanalytic patterns in the literature of the 1970s had become subordinated to a grotesque and skeptical worldview, as in Vint's "This So Unexpected and Embarrassing a Death."

One of the new social problems that conditioned this psychomodernism was Estonia's emerging modern urban culture. The capital city, Tallinn, was the first to be transformed by the construction of bleak city districts composed of nondescript, concrete-block apartment buildings of obvious poor workmanship. These eyesores stood in stark contrast to the graceful stone structures of the medieval old city at the center of town and the two-story wooden homes of the more recently built suburbs. The Soviet-erected concrete matchboxes evoked new feelings of alienation and ugliness, which are expressed in many stories by Unt and Valton. This alienation and the dehumanization that accompanies it are aptly expressed in Vint's "This So Unexpected and Embarrassing a Death," where the city is insensitive to the atrocities that are committed within it, and where the characters dance about the disenchanted cityscape like marionettes choreographed by vacant agents of their lost inner worlds, crossing each other's paths as though on the whim of malicious chance and scrupulously driven to obtain their own dishonorable ends at the expense of those around them.

NEW PHENOMENA OF THE MID-1970S

By the mid-1970s, Estonian modernism had become an established practice. Even many writers of more traditional, realistic prose had adopted its literary devices and textual structure. To a significant extent, these devices and structural principles shaped the literary development of the entire period. Nevertheless, some writers did not stop here, but came to realize that the same modernist extremes that so aptly expressed their own alienation had in fact alienated their readers. And, in the meantime, paradigms had shifted in the world at large. It was time to find a new language that could respond to the day's global challenges.

Two main literary movements developed during the 1970s: experiential and historical. Experiential prose is characterized by a detailed depiction of everyday life, above all, urban life with its sense of alienation. It is a Socialist Realism that has been subverted by modern psychology and elements of popular mass fiction. These experiential works were primarily novels. Historical prose made possible the reintroduction of a logical story line, adventure, and story closure, attributes characteristic of premodernist, realist prose. These premodernist characteristics were undercut, however, by the author's sly manipulation of narrative time on various levels and by manifestations of an altered human psyche. An increase in the use of historical material was also related to a search for roots as well as to the actualization of a sense of ethnicity and tradition in Estonian culture.

Many authors turned to historical prose at this time. Valton ventured into this realm in the early 1970s, writing collections of short stories on historical topics, including *A Courtly Game* and *The Messenger,* and later writing a novel about Genghis Khan, *The Path to the Other End of Infinity.* At the beginning of the 1980s, Mati Unt wrote dramatic works in this same vein. Jaan Kross stands out as the most startling representative of this group, with his many short stories and novels based on historical subject matter.

After a decade or so of writing poetry, Kross began writing historical prose at the beginning of the 1970s, centering on events that took place in the fifteenth to the nineteenth centuries. The main character in these works is usually a historical individual of known or putative Estonian heritage who must overcome the bounds of nationality and status to wend his way through power intrigues. In his award-winning *The Emperor's Madman* (1978), Kross details one Estonian's refusal to compromise with the autocratic regime of Russian Emperor Alexander I in the early 1800s and the consequences he faces for making this choice. The choice of a more distant time period afforded Kross the opportunity to offer oblique commentary on contemporary technical and social issues. His historical work thus dovetails with the trend toward allegorical, or Aesopian, expression in literature.

From the beginning of the 1980s, Kross began to focus upon his own historical experience, initially in his short stories. He completed a series of stories set in Estonia during World War II and its aftermath. Later stories focused on his experiences in Stalin's labor camps. They center around an individual skating on the razor's edge, in danger of being crushed by the totalitarian cogs of German might, Russian might, or both. "Hallelujah" and "The Day His Eyes Are Opened" fall into this category.

Both "Hallelujah" and "The Day His Eyes Are Opened" depict the irony inherent in the suffering of the individual in post–World War II times, and can be seen as Kross's critique of Western literature that takes the Second World War as its main theme. In these stories, Kross investigates the gray, altered area of the human psyche that lies between normalcy and insanity, kindness and malice, that surfaces to enable the individual to change shape and slither through the violent attack of those impending totalitarian cogs. Kross also plays with the strands of narrative time and shifts the perspective by telling his story through the eyes of two, or even three, unreliable narrators. In so doing, Kross toys with the reader's sense of certainty and belief in "facts," and undermines the very nature of the historical genre itself, turning history into the questionable reconstruction of disturbed minds that see and hear only those things they want to see and hear as they seek to make sense out of an absurd, senseless reality.

THE CRISIS AT THE BEGINNING OF THE 1980s

The end of the 1970s was a period of aesthetic crisis for Estonian literature. The majority of the "sixties' generation" authors had exhausted their creative output and were publishing collected works. Many of the prose modernists had reached a barrier in their worldview or a stalemate in their creative work. This is particularly apparent in the work of Unt and Valton. By the beginning of this new decade, both faced a disintegration in the relationship between language and reality. Valton's works from the early 1980s consist of a variety of marginal genres, such as aphorisms and scripts. His crisis was resolved at the end of the 1980s with a return to the relatively traditional-classical story genre, represented in this anthology by "On the Church Step" and "Photosensitivity." Unt, however, resolved his personal crisis early in the 1980s and turned to the postmodern novel.

Few interesting new writers emerged during the 1980s. A general feeling that "the rooms were full" prevailed, that is, that all modernist devices had been exhausted. Many of the young eschewed any participation in the already "official" modernist culture that writers like Unt, Valton, and Kross had struggled to establish. By this time, a new Estonian youth culture independent of and disaffected with other forms of cultural life had evolved.

If the 1960s had been dominated by an attempt to fit cultural quests into the system, and even to improve that system and make it more human, and if the 1970s had been dominated, to a certain extent, by an escapism into the depths of history or the individual psyche, the 1980s' generation desired not to fit into or deny the existing culture but to overcome it. It was within the parameters of this newly created culture that so many young people realized their artistic potential, above all, in writing lyrics for rock and other kinds of music. When examining this movement, tensions within Estonian society during the 1980s must be taken into account: a wave of pressure to Russify, letters of protest written by intellectuals against this pressure, and the brutal suppression of these protests.

NEW NAMES IN THE 1980S

The most significant among the authors who made their literary debuts in the 1980s and who continued to develop the modernist tradition in the short story genre were Ülo Matteus and Toomas Raudam. Matteus is important above all for his Borgesian mythological references and intertextual links. His story "Our Mother" grows out of an ancient Estonian myth in which people and trees merge in soul and body. Raudam writes microscopically detailed autobiographical "psychological history." This history courses through his language as well, establishing a semantic game in which meanings attributed to certain words shift at various times. For instance, in "Drooping Wings," the phrase "drooping wings" is subjected to a series of semantic shifts so that it functions as a kind of "mantra"; plot and character are transformed by its very mention. These phrases sometimes function on the purely aural level, spawning a multitude of associations or recalling references to strange texts.

The third important newcomer, Maimu Berg, had already published stories in journals during the 1970s, but she went relatively unnoticed until she began publishing short novels on historical themes in the mid-1980s. In some of these novels, it was already possible to discern a polemic between Jaan Kross's "male-centered" historical writing and a highly contrastive woman's point of view on the same subject matter. Some critics have cited the short story "The Mill Ghost," included in this anthology, as the seminal work and starting point for feminist issues in Estonian prose.

THE RUPTURE AT THE END OF THE 1980S

The nationalistic struggle for freedom, the disappearance of the censor, and Estonia's regaining its independence radically altered the circumstances, potential, and requirements of Estonian prose at the end of the 1980s. During perestroika and glasnost, a revelatory novel evolved. This novel began to describe the crimes of the Soviet regime and attempted to rethink the historical experience of the Estonian people after World War II. Perestroika also forced Estonian authors to reconsider and search for their own role within the context of a changing European culture. A central theme of the most significant of these novels is the growing relationship of Estonia, and in a broader sense the relationship of all of Eastern Europe, to the West.

Contemporary, so-called "dirty" prose began to pervade the short stories of the younger writers, shocking the more conservative readership with its dispassionate, open portrayal of violence and eroticism. This younger late-1980s generation of writers is represented in this collection by Jüri Ehlvest. The primary theme of his stories is an individual's tragicomic adventures in a strange and uncertain world where text and reality can change roles at any moment, as they do so poignantly in his short story "Disintegration of the Spiral."

FUTURE PROSPECTS

As Estonia continues to fight for its own cultural identity and to grapple with issues of worldwide concern, it will no doubt continue to produce writers of the caliber found in this anthology. And as it is a small nation, disinterested in global political gains, we might do well to listen to the dispassionate truth that sounds through the voices of these authors.

■ □ ■ □ ■

Ritva Poom

TRANSLATOR'S NOTE

IT HAS BEEN THE CHALLENGE OF THIS PROJECT TO RENDER into English the voices of nine different authors. Ranging from the straightforward prose of Mari Saat and Toomas Vint to the terse irony of Arvo Valton and the opaque, highly nuanced style of Jaan Kross, each of these writers has his or her own distinctive rhythm and style.

Adding to the challenges inherent in literary translation has been the structure of the Estonian language itself. Estonian is one of the few non-Indo-European languages spoken in Europe. It belongs to the Finno-Ugrian language family, which includes Finnish, Hungarian, and approximately a dozen related languages found in the former Soviet Union. Structurally, Estonian is as different from Russian, German, or Latvian as English is from Japanese, for instance. Estonian has fourteen cases. Gender and future tense are not marked. There are no articles or prepositions. It has a preponderance of vowels rather than consonants.

In an agglutinative language such as Estonian, linguistic structures of varying complexity can be created within a word. For example, the word *majas,* when translated into English, becomes "in a/the house" while *majasse* becomes "into a/the house." Translated literally, the phrase *ôuest majasse pakiga* is "from a/the yard into a/the house with a/the package." In each case, it is up to the translator to choose the definite or indefinite article or to exclude the article entirely. The rhythm of the original Estonian text is radically altered when it is rendered into English, and the pitfall of having string after string of subordinate clauses in the English translation is always imminent. To give another example, the particle *gi* is often added to a word for emphasis or to achieve the effect of irony. *Majagi* could be translated into English as "even the/a house." The wordiness of this phrase in English slows down the text considerably and may have quite the opposite effect from that sought by the author. Therefore, although every effort has been made to remain as faithful to the original as possible, it has been necessary at times to depart somewhat from the text in the attempt to render into English the spirit intended.

In addition to the structural differences between Estonian and English, during recent years many new words not yet included in dictionaries have entered the Estonian language. I am indebted to Kajar Pruul for his comprehensive responses to questions about vocabulary and also for information contained in the notes, which was impossible to pin down on this side of the Atlantic. I am also indebted to a number of stalwart research institutions in New York City, including Butler Library at Columbia University, Goethe House, and the Research Department of the New York Public Library, and to the compassionate staff of Northwestern University Press. My thanks to my family and friends for their patience and support throughout. Without them, the project could never have been completed. This translation is dedicated to the memory of my father.

■ □ ■ □ ■

Arvo Valton

VERNANDA BREAD

THE TRAIN REACHED VERNANDA STATION. THE CONDUCTOR announced that there would be a ten-minute stopover. Ramon took an empty briefcase off the luggage rack and stepped onto the platform of the unfamiliar station. In the distance there was a counter with refreshments and a green stand with stale pirogi; Ramon wanted to buy a loaf of black bread. He walked through the railway station toward a square on the city side of the tracks. The early-morning city was almost empty. Pelicans idled in the middle of the square, possibly they were made of plaster. The street that began at the square glowed with night-weary neon lights. One of them spelled "Bread." Ramon looked at the clock and then headed toward the bakery. Lazily, clumsily, a pelican rose into flight. It was difficult for the plaster bird to fly.

The bakery was closed. Ramon rang the bell, but no one came to open the door. Ramon quickly returned to the station. When he stepped onto the platform, the train was no longer there.

Ramon looked around, everything was unfamiliar. It wasn't possible, was it, that he might have chanced into another railway station? Ramon went into the station building, saw an attendant, and asked, "Pardon me, is this Ver-nanda Station?"

"Seems to be," answered the sleepy attendant.

"Is that possible?" marveled Ramon.

"If you don't believe me, ask someone else."

The attendant wanted to leave. Except for the two of them, there wasn't a single soul in the railway station. Ramon seized the attendant by the sleeve.

"But there's no train here!"

With passive interest, the attendant observed how the man was kneading his sleeve.

"It left."

"When?"

"About half an hour ago."

Ramon grew angry.

"It only pulled in eight minutes ago!"

The attendant shrugged his shoulders.

"Well, maybe five minutes ago then. What difference does it make?"

"How come it left early? It was supposed to stop for ten minutes," lamented Ramon.

"The engineer felt obligated."

"And what's to become of me now?"

The attendant sized him up with a glance.

"And what's supposed to become of you?"

"When does the next train leave?"

"At night. The timetable is on the wall."

"Is there a ticket available?"

"You can get a ticket anytime, if you want to ride out of Vernanda."

"Of course I do."

"Very good!" said the attendant and left.

Ramon scurried after him.

"Why's that good?" he asked.

"Some are hard to get rid of."

Ramon halted and shrugged his shoulders.

Now he had time to go look for bread.

The bakery door was still closed. Ramon rang. A fat, tousle-headed man appeared from the back room. He stared at Ramon for quite a while through the door windowpane. He pressed his broad forehead against the glass and scowled. When he had had his fill of looking and had nodded a few times, deliberating, he opened the door and stepped behind the counter.

Ramon looked around. As is typical of a bakery, bread, macaroni, and washtubs were sold here.

"One loaf of bread," he said to the shopkeeper.

The fat, scowling man thrust forward a loaf standing on the counter. Ramon examined the bread closely, touched it with his finger: it was soft and well-baked. Ramon paid the money and put the loaf into his empty briefcase.

The scowling shopkeeper locked the door behind him. People had appeared on the long, neon-lit street, but they were solitary, each of them, and they did not fill the emptiness.

Ramon turned onto a cross street. He wanted to break off a piece of the loaf in his briefcase, but a woman came striding toward him, looking at him sleepily. Ramon pressed the briefcase under his arm, looked around, and slipped beneath an archway leading into a courtyard. He picked at the recalcitrant briefcase lock. Through the archway came a whistling schoolboy. Ramon made himself appear to be scrutinizing apartment numbers, which aroused the little boy's curiosity. Not finding the necessary number, Ramon walked back to the street.

Finally he chanced into a little park beside the street. He sat down on a bench and opened the briefcase lock. On the neighboring bench, a young woman sat nervously eyeing a watch. A dubious business this early in the morning, thought Ramon, and thrust his hand into the briefcase. He wanted to break off a piece of bread—it was hard as plastic and not bread at all.

Ramon opened the briefcase wide. Instead of the bread it

contained an unfamiliar, dark brown object of some sort, a bit smaller than a loaf of bread. Ramon tilted the interior of the briefcase toward the distant streetlight. Besides the unknown object, it contained nothing. Ramon took out the object: a hard, plastic box with a knob and some marks on it. Ramon sniffed, held it to his ear. From inside came the sound of barely audible ticking.

It was a bomb with a clockwork. Ramon had seen others like it sometime during his stint in the army. It had yet another name or designation of some sort, and they had to memorize its destructive force, but he had forgotten that long ago.

Ramon eyed the briefcase. That same worn corner, torn lining, the handle repaired with black cobbler's thread. His own.

In the bakery he had thrust a soft loaf into the briefcase with his own hand, it had been under his arm the whole time, he hadn't let it out of his hand for a second. How could a bomb have gotten in there?

What sort of mixed-up city is this Vernanda, anyway? Ramon wanted to ask, but the woman had disappeared from the neighboring bench.

The spot was empty. Ramon did not dare go buy a new loaf of bread; one couldn't be sure of anything in this city anymore.

Ramon respected justice. Where to put the bomb? Where would it be possible to exchange it for a loaf of bread? In some other city, perhaps? But Ramon didn't have the slightest desire to keep the bomb in his possession for long! Of course, everything is determined by fate. If Ramon was meant to meet his end by means of a bomb, then, though he might throw it down right here and flee, there would still be no escaping fate. And the bomb had cropped up in place of the loaf of bread, so that Ramon had every right to be reimbursed in either bread or money. Ramon wasn't stingy, but he did have principles.

It was senseless to go back to the fat man, he scowled suspiciously. If he were to go anywhere at all, then to another store.

Ramon got up from the bench and went back toward the main street of the strange city. Approaching him came a woman with a loaf of bread visible in her shopping bag.

"Pardon me, I'd like to offer you some barter."

The woman looked in amazement at the stranger who had stopped her. Ramon fumbled with the briefcase lock.

"I have here a mine with a clockwork. Would you like to exchange it for a loaf of bread?"

The woman looked at the mine with interest.

"Children don't eat that, do they?" she judged.

"Nor grown-ups, either," admitted Ramon, but he tried further persuasion: "Considering the fact that there's a clockwork in here, it wouldn't be a bad deal."

"That's certainly true," agreed the woman. "But the children are expecting bread and . . . "

The woman rushed off.

Ramon thought that trading a bomb to a private individual might be entirely illegal.

On the main street there was another bakery. Ramon stood in line. When his turn came, taking the bomb out of his briefcase, he said, "Please exchange this bomb for a loaf of bread for me!"

"We haven't exchanged bread for bombs since I don't know when," responded the salesgirl with a glance that sought the customer's approval.

"You see, I was given this bomb in place of a loaf of bread here in your city; therefore I have the right to exchange it," explained Ramon.

"If you don't have money to buy bread, I can give you some," promised an older man on the line.

"It's a matter of principle. I want bread, not a bomb," Ramon said to the man.

"Then buy it!" a woman devoid of principles simplified the matter.

VERNANDA BREAD

"If you'd buy this bomb for the price of a loaf of bread, I'd gladly accept your offer."

"What'll I do with a bomb?" the man shrugged his shoulders.

The salesgirl was already distributing bread rolls to the next customer. Ramon announced throughout the store, "Would someone want a bomb, perhaps?"

The response was silence. Ramon shut his briefcase lock and walked out angrily. A natural trade hadn't succeeded. The only recourse was to try to sell the bomb somewhere.

Ramon asked the first person to come toward him, "You know, I have a bomb, I'd like to sell it, where could I do that?"

The passerby thought and responded, "I haven't seen bombs for sale anywhere, but perhaps a thrift shop of some sort—or an antique store would take it."

Ramon said thank you and moved on. The kindly advice-giver ran after him and said, panting, "You can also offer it at the market."

The other's helpfulness set Ramon thinking.

"Wouldn't you like to buy it yourself?" he asked.

The kindly person departed without saying a word.

The main street was a good location. In fact, Ramon soon came to an antique store. He placed the bomb on the counter silently. The salesman put on his glasses and pondered what was being offered for a long while. Then he shook his head.

"We take only used articles," said he.

"This is, namely, a bomb, and it is not possible to sell a bomb in used condition," said Ramon, sighing politely.

"Why are you offering it to us then? We are not permitted to accept new things."

Ramon walked on. Out on the street he could feel the bomb growing constantly heavier. This made him irritable. All around him, it was a normal morning, the sun was shining, people were taking care of their essential and significant matters in the city. But he, Ramon, was walking about, an infernal apparatus in his briefcase. He wanted to get rid of it as fast as possible.

He had to wait in line for quite a while at the thrift shop.

"How much are you asking?"

The appraiser was rummaging through his papers and didn't look over at the bomb.

"The price of a loaf of bread," responded Ramon. He wasn't greedy or a speculator—he offered it at the price he had paid.

"Are you joking or what!"

The appraiser now looked at the bomb.

"What is this?"

"A bomb. With a clockwork and timer."

"A bomb? We've never accepted those."

"Perhaps you haven't been offered any?"

The appraiser began flipping through the price list. He ran his finger down the columns and muttered, "A bomb . . . a bomb . . . "

"Look under—mine!" advised Ramon.

The appraiser leafed backward.

"Not here," he announced. "It's not on the price list, can't take it. Next!"

Ramon hid the bomb in his briefcase and walked on.

After receiving numerous directions, he reached the marketplace. It was a typical bartering area consisting of small stands and open-air counters. Behind the counters, merchants stood and called:

"Fresh bananas!"

"Salted polar bear!"

"Donkey milkbutter, buttermilk donkey, milkdonkey butter, donkey buttermilk!"

"The cheapest frog meat in Vernanda. Anyone who tries it, buys it!"

"Live leeches! Over here, all ye oppressed! Into every man's groin, a leech!"

The bidding was lively. Ramon put the bomb on a bit of empty shelf and waited for a buyer.

The bomb was scrutinized with inexpert interest. Only one doleful-looking man inquired about its price: "So how much do those bombs cost nowadays?"

"The price of a loaf of bread," answered Ramon, full of hope.

The man shook his head and sighed.

"Yes, they've become cheap," and then he added in a whisper: "It's the fault of the city government's politics!"

Another who spoke was a white-smocked market inspector who commanded that a sales permit be purchased.

"Type of merchandise?" he demanded, in order to fill out a receipt.

"A bomb," answered Ramon.

The market inspector wrote the word "bomb" on the receipt and then remained there, wavering.

"Only foodstuffs are sold here!"

"But the sheepskins?"

Next to Ramon an old man was selling sheepskins.

"An agricultural product. For nonindustrial use," the inspector knew from memory.

"Likewise, for nonindustrial use," Ramon pointed to the bomb.

"What's it used for?" the overseer was curious.

"To create a detonation, to wreck," explained Ramon.

"Selling bombs is not permitted at our marketplace!"

"I'll buy two coupons," Ramon offered the market inspector a deal. He thought that he would add their price to that of the loaf of bread.

"Leave, if you don't want trouble!" threatened the official.

Ramon put the bomb in his briefcase. The old man selling the sheepskins whispered to him, "Sell things like that only on the sly."

But before Ramon could leave, a customer came.

"What do you have?" whispered the person who wanted contraband.

Ramon opened his briefcase again, tore open the compartment flaps, and displayed the bomb.

"What is that?"

"A bomb. With a clockwork and a timer."

"How much are you asking?"

"The price of a loaf of bread."

"And how much will you give it away for?"

"For the same price, in fact!"

The buyer made a disappointed face.

"Well, actually you're supposed to be able to bargain things down at a market!"

The surreptitious display had enticed others to come over as well. There was whispering.

"A bomb . . . The price of a loaf of bread."

An old lady with a pouting expression scolded, "They're going crazy nowadays. The price of a whole loaf of bread for a worthless bomb!"

"I call your attention to the fact that a bomb is complicated to construct," argued Ramon with accentuated politeness.

"Pshaw!" said the old lady. "Do you think loaves of bread grow on trees or what?"

She turned her back on the merchandise emphatically.

"People have gone to the trouble of constructing it," Ramon defended himself weakly.

"Who told them to?" remarked a middle-aged, tired woman.

A man with an economic cast of mind argued for establishing the truth.

"Those bombs are manufactured in large series, now don't you go believe that their cost of production is so great!"

"It's greater than that of bread, in any case," Ramon supposed.

"So why are you selling it at the price of bread, then?" rebuked a scandal-hungry, gnarled old man. "Fake stuff, it's clear that's no bomb if you're selling it so cheaply!"

Ramon was in a fix. He didn't know how to talk with these people.

"Understand this, I was given the bomb in place of bread, and this is a matter of principle!"

"Come to the marketplace with goods, not with principles!" one of the shoppers summarized, and the cluster of people dispersed.

Ramon hid the bomb in his briefcase and snuck away. He opened his coat, put the open briefcase under his coat flap, and went over to a cucumber vendor. Ramon watched him to see whether he was trustworthy enough, and then with a swift motion, he thrust open his coat flap.

The cucumber vendor glared and waved his hands.

Ramon had no luck in selling. He repeated, "A bomb. With a clockwork and a timer," but there were no takers to be found.

Selling illicitly, longer explanations could not be risked. And in fact Ramon didn't know anything more; he himself had added the clockwork and the timer. He could not even say for sure whether the inside of the bomb was ticking or not. One shopper put his ear to it, but he might have been deaf.

Ramon wouldn't even have been able to swear, with his hand on the Bible, that it was a bomb at all. Thinking about that, he began to feel lousy, as if he were advertising merchandise with an intent to swindle.

Hungry and tired, Ramon left the marketplace. The bomb had grown heavy as lead. The stupid Vernandans had lost touch with life; they didn't want to buy a bomb.

Ramon gave up the idea of getting money for the bomb. But he had to put it somewhere so that the trials people had experienced in inventing, designing, assembling, and keeping accounts for the bomb would not have been for naught.

A beauty came toward him. On a sudden impulse, he stopped the woman.

"Pardon me, may I give you a present?"

The woman laughed coquettishly.

"Oh, what for!"

Ramon quickly took out the mine.

"This is a bomb. With a clockwork and a timer. I'd like to give this to you as a present."

"But what will I tell my husband?"

"Tell him the truth: that a total stranger, a man on the street, gave it to you as a present for being Vernanda's most beautiful woman!"

The flattery had to have an effect.

"Oh, you don't know my husband, he's so jealous he won't believe that . . . No, no . . . "

Ramon put the bomb back in his briefcase disappointedly.

The main street, which began at the railway station, ended on a grandiose scale in a tasteless square at the center of which stood the city hall, wreathed in flags.

Ramon was fed up and indifferent. He went into the city hall with his bomb, which was growing constantly heavier, as if this were a daily errand for him.

"Where is the mayor?" he demanded.

He was directed into a large room full of insincerely polite, conceited secretaries.

I want to speak with the mayor," Ramon let his request be known.

"What problem do you have?" demanded the young ladies of the bureaucratic guard.

"I'm passing through," recounted Ramon. "In one of your city's bakeries, a bomb was palmed off on me in place of a loaf of bread. . . . " Ramon patted his briefcase.

"Department Three," announced a young lady giving herself a manicure. "The eighth door to the left."

There was a sign on the door: "Institute for the Scientific Study of Science."

Ramon knocked. The door opened of its own accord. Behind the sole desk in the large office sat a man who was wearing a uniform with insignia unfamiliar to Ramon. He rose and extended his hand. Ramon thought this was a greeting, but the uniformed man gestured impatiently and said, "A bomb!"

Ramon was surprised at the man's level of information. The briefcase lock did not want to open. When Ramon finally gave the bomb to him, the official turned the knob to a certain position, and the lid of the plastic box sprang open. Inside the box were chocolate candies. The man thrust the box under Ramon's nose, smiling morosely. Ramon looked at him and, as if hypnotized, took a candy. The uniformed man slammed down the lid with a click, pulled open the door of a tremendously large closet, and placed the bomb on the shelf beside others of its ilk.

"Eat it!" ordered the morose smirker.

Ramon put the candy in his mouth. It had a bitterish taste.

"So-o-o," said the uniform, as if an important task of some kind had been completed.

"I thought that it was a bomb," said Ramon, smiling doltishly.

"Being excessively principled will not be beneficial to you. Keep that in mind," instructed the official with a frighteningly expressionless smile.

Ramon recovered from his bafflement. He narrowed his eyes obstinately and said, "What about the loaf of bread? I paid for it."

"The candy you ate costs exactly the price of a loaf of bread."

Ramon moved his bullish neck.

"I want black bread, not bitter-tasting candy that has been forcefully palmed off on me!"

"While staying in Vernanda, one must take into account local customs, not one's own wishes."

Ramon glowered at the persistently smiling, uniformed man and demanded, "What's the meaning of all this, then?"

The man looked at the clock and said, "Hurry to the station, your train is leaving soon."

The man motioned toward the door with his hand and didn't wish to talk any further.

Ramon went to the station hungry and feeling very confused. He bought a ticket and sat down in the evening train. The strange city, Vernanda, was left behind.

–1968–

■ □ ■ □ ■

Arvo Valton

THE SNARE (I)

WHEN THE MAN CAME FROM THE WINDING BIRCH GROVE trail to a broad expanse, the trail forked into many. The man stopped, hesitating, but he soon grew convinced that all these trails led in the same direction. They were merely some twenty tracks of road running parallel on the steppes, as usual: here any vehicle could trample down a road for itself wherever it liked, and, during periods of rain or thawing snow, this multiplication of tracks was inevitable.

The man began going down a road. All around lay a bare steppe. Up ahead, somewhere near the horizon, groves of birch and aspen began again; there must be a settlement behind them. The level expanse was enlivened only by solitary gray clumps of sagebrush and dried, lumpy pieces of clay that had been churned up in the springtime by tractor treads and by automobile tires that had sunk in the mud. Then up ahead, on one track of road, an incomprehensible apparatus of some sort emerged into view.

The man looked up ahead intently to discern what it could be here on the bare steppe. As he drew nearer, his eyes distinguished a ring and, on two sides of it, stakes. The man began to make conjectures about the function of the contraption. It could be an animal trap, except that it would most likely have been too large for an animal of any kind.

The matter began to interest the man. There was still some distance to the apparatus. If it actually were a trap, then its placement in the middle of the bare plain was absolutely incomprehensible. In addition to the track of road on which the snare was located, there existed nineteen other roads with which to bypass it. What a stupid and blind animal it must be that would stay on that single road and climb into the snare.

The man began to eye the land before him sharply in order to find an animal track of some sort. Except for the tire tracks, tractor treads, and boot tracks, however, there was nothing there. Half-sideways, he walked to the next parallel road across a narrow bit of steppe covered with sparse grass, but he did not see anything new there, either. He examined almost all twenty of the roads, but there wasn't a single track to be seen anywhere, not even on the path where the snare had been set up.

And yet there it stood up ahead, and nineteen completely unobstructed roads led past it. Something is indeed awry here, thought the man. Why is a snare standing in the middle of the bare steppe when there isn't even a single animal track? The man moved toward the snare to examine the apparatus more thoroughly. Who had carried out so purposeless an act as to set up an animal trap on tractor tracks in the middle of a bare plain? There must be a hidden meaning to this. Why had all the other nineteen roads been left unhindered? What was the meaning of this?

The air was hazy and warm. As the man moved toward the snare, he was reminded of visions from fairy tales heard in childhood. An immense spider stood at the gate of an underground cave filled with treasures, and asked someone who had chanced into its web the answers to riddles. The snare in the middle of the steppe was itself a riddle. Outwardly it was a snare, but it undoubtedly served some completely different purpose.

THE SNARE (I)

Visions passed before him. Apparent evil was good and just, while that which was reasonable proved foolish or even destructive. This was a fairy tale, vast, all-encompassing. Whoever looks back turns into a pillar of stone. At night, in the dark, goblins lurk everywhere, especially behind one's back, especially there. Whoever can crawl through the snare untouched gets the princess. Who knows whether a princess is something sweet, in fact? In order to obtain her, at least three heroic deeds must be performed: you must herd a wild reindeer all day long, guard a golden apple from being stolen by a witch's birds, and battle a giant. And crawl through a snare. Then you get half the kingdom and the princess. Ruling a country isn't easy, pleasant work in the slightest, and, by and large, women are malicious, harmful creatures. But then again, not everyone can obtain half a kingdom and a princess; that's the secret. If it's difficult to obtain, then you want it badly. Because it's difficult for others, too, and who wouldn't want to be better than his peers? Might as well accept the princess too; she could turn out to be a good person.

These were strange visions indeed, and the man shook his head. He had reached the snare. He walked around it, scrutinizing. At the center stood a threatening noose with two running knots. On two sides, a few yards away, were strong posts. From them, through powerful roller springs, fine cables led to the noose. The man measured the noose opening with his eyes. If you wanted to, you could climb through it without touching a single cable. What a strange thing people—or the Devil knows who, but in all likelihood, people— had set up here in the middle of the steppe. What could its function possibly be? After all, purposeless things don't exist, do they? In all likelihood, the person who crawled through this would not obtain a princess. But what would he obtain, then? Furrowing his brow, the man walked around the snare, which was, in a word, a dubious contraption.

The man touched one of the cables cautiously. It was just taut enough. Nothing happened. The man looked around.

He got down on all fours in front of the noose; he stood so that neither his head nor any of his limbs traversed the noose's plane. The man squatted down on all fours in the parched tractor trail, and directly before him yawned the threatening noose. The man blinked his eyes repeatedly and thrust his hand through the center of the noose opening, ready at any moment to pull back his hand, which was taut with nervousness. His hand was in the center of the noose and nothing was happening.

The man flinched at his next thought. What would happen if he were to jump through the noose at lightning speed? Somewhere deep down inside him something was astir and trembling wildly. But the thought was enticing and drew him along despite his fear. The man gauged his position relative to the noose precisely; he wrenched his knees from the ground, leaned over on his hands, bent himself forward, and gave a sudden thrust with his legs. He flew through the snare dexterously, only slightly grazing its cable. The cables leading to the posts whined barely audibly. Nothing else happened. The man had passed through the snare without its having closed. No one offered him a princess, and that wasn't even necessary, in fact, because he had already forgotten the fairy tale. His interest in the technology and meaning of the apparatus had also waned before an inexplicable athletic fervor. The man grew bold. He walked around the apparatus and stepped into the noose on all fours. The threatening cable was somewhere at the height of his chest. The man turned his head toward both poles with a superior and, for some reason, mocking air. But his body was still taut and anxious. However, the sparks of fear soon vanished, and, like an unruly child, the man began stamping with his knees. Still nothing happened. The ground thudded a bit and the noose cables remained in place.

Then, on the other side of the noose, the man began pounding the ground with his hands. Like a little boy, like a fool. Who knows what kind of childish urge overcame him?

He stamped with his hands and feet, and howled shrilly, intending to sing a toddler's song of some kind.

But suddenly, a powerful whack against a sod lump with his right hand—and something snapped there. All at the same time, springs rattled, the cables pulled taut, and the noose drew shut, seizing the man forcefully around his body. The man went rigid with fright, and then his face turned chalk-white. Apparently a trigger had been hidden under the sod lump.

It turned out, however, that this was merely the most ordinary type of snare. The cable lightly scraped his chest. The man tried to free himself with his hands, but the powerful springs did not yield. This enabled him to breathe more freely, but as a result his fingers hurt. He could not reach the stakes or the spring mechanisms with his hands. Exerting his entire body, the man tried to yank and tear, but that only caused excessive pain. In the truest sense, he was in a snare. For what purpose, now that he didn't understand. To be alone in the middle of a steppe in a noose—it seemed completely senseless. Not even a large spider appeared there to pose riddles. If he had at least done this to get a princess! Why had he done it anyway? Out of idiotic curiosity? The impulse to take a chance? Out of fervor, the desire for an intense experience?

This must serve a purpose of some kind thought the man wearily. For nothing exists in the world without a purpose or a function. Not even a noose in the middle of a steppe, on one of twenty parallel roads. For once it exists, someone must also crawl into it.

And this is how the man was left in the snare, and he is there to this day if the driver of a passing car or tractor hasn't rescued him.

But the latter is entirely likely, in fact. If only because good must triumph over evil and every tale must have a happy ending.

—1966—

■ □ ■ □ ■

Arvo Valton

THE SNARE (II)

IN THE MIDDLE OF AN EMPTY PLAIN, A MAN HAD CRAWLED into a snare. The snare stood on one of twenty parallel tracks of road and there were opportunities enough to bypass it. But the man had chosen the road that led him into the snare. Perhaps out of curiosity, perhaps on a chance, idle impulse. Or perhaps the opposite is true. Perhaps it is inevitable that once such an apparatus has been constructed on a steppe, then it necessarily has a function, and it is a given that someone must crawl into it. And the man had felt his calling. To verify the universality of order and to confirm that senseless things do not exist. Perhaps.

Now he was squatting in the snare, a powerful iron cable around his thorax, and he was ashamed of his situation. To a possible savior—the driver of a passing car or tractor—a man in a snare in the middle of an empty steppe might look embarrassingly absurd. What kind of expression would he face them with? How would he explain his having chanced into the snare?

The warm afternoon sun shone down on top of his head, and the knowledge that he was unable to get a drink anywhere made him thirsty. The vicious iron cable squeezed his chest; it was painful to breathe deeply. The man crooked his legs. The cable yielded, his feet touched the ground again. The pressure around his chest grew more intense. The roller springs drew the noose together. They could also yield to a certain extent, but such that, as the cable lengthened, the pressure in the noose increased. If the man were of a technological bent, he could have pondered the construction's craftiness. That might even have helped him out of the snare, although it's hardly likely. It might have helped to pass the time while waiting for escape, but the man preferred a game: he inclined himself forward, pressed his feet against the ground, and moved three progressively more difficult steps forward. Then he let his feet free of the ground, and the cable thrust him back forcefully, his body outstretched in a horizontal position, his chest moving near the ground. The man repeated the ride, again and again. The game was painful, and it was fun, and maybe it wasn't a game at all, but rather hope and an exercise, anger and self-punishment. The man moved backward, his body taut, his heels on the ground. He raised his legs, the cable moved him forward, and his backside thudded painfully against the ground. He then tried to move toward the pole that held the cable; but that proved impossible—the cables could unwind from the springs only in equal lengths. Technology was in harmony with function: after all, capture would make no sense if the captive could get close to the pole and free himself.

During the struggle the cable had cut into him deeply, and bit by bit the man edged it up higher. The principle discovered—the less cable unwound from the reel, the less the pressure—foreordained his position. The noose was fixed so that for the cable to be at its least taut, the man had to descend to his knees. Hadn't even this been maliciously premeditated: to force a man down on his knees in parched tractor tracks so that he might receive the full measure of his humiliation? Understanding increased, even more, his ignominy before a possible savior.

His body did not in the slightest want to grow used to

the cable. Apparently many generations are required for changes to become hereditary. In order to breed insects unable to live without DDT. In order to breed men for whom a cable squeezing their chest would be as natural as a tie around their neck.

The man stuffed his pipe stem under the cable. The pain would be that much less the greater the surface over which the pressure could successfully be dispersed. The man took off his pants, rolled them into a tube, and somehow stuffed it, bit by bit, between the cable and himself.

That took time, made the man impatient. Excessive practicality, pursuit of one's own personal comfort. When he got the pants under the cable, the pain should have decreased, but that didn't happen. Apparently this action sufficiently lengthened the cable, the pressure increased, and the result of the effort proved negligible. Here, too, is a stanza of life's wisdom: you win the most if you don't go into battle.

The possibility of thirst tortured him. Activity was no help in banishing thoughts. The shame of escaping haunted him, images came, his head drooped, the sun shone on the nape of his neck.

Perhaps the battle, in fact, lay in escaping? At least from images. For every proverb there is an opposite proverb; one is no more foolish than the other. The man raised his head. The experience with his pants had taught him that, were he a thinner man, the pressure on his lungs would also have decreased. If he succeeded in squeezing through the cable with his hands, it would draw shut around his neck. . . . But the man didn't get as far as actions; he didn't have the strength.

Action on his part was futile. The man submitted, that was smartest thing he could do.

He was disturbed only by the ridiculousness of the situation. Even if the snare were a perfectly logical thing on the steppe, there was nevertheless no respectable explanation for why he was squatting in it. His head drooped. If only the content of all his thoughts merged into a desireless state, but that was not up to him.

No, it was not his calling to squat in a snare. This was not his sole and proper station in life. He had never striven for this.

And even if chance were to lead him astray here in the harmonious world, life should immediately rectify this deviation.

When an animal chances into a snare, it struggles until it strangles itself. The unnaturalness of the snare forces it to chew up the paw that has chanced into the noose. It is unlikely that this urge toward freedom is smart—in the harsh law of the jungle, the animal won't survive for long on three paws. Nature's crowning glory, a man of experience, remains quietly on his knees.

It would be good to sit in front of a fireplace now wearing furry slippers, to puff on a pipe, and to read about momentous and distant politics in the newspaper, to chuckle smugly over one's own conclusions: how everyone is out for his own interests, the larger consumes the smaller. These conclusions are concealed by words and expressed with particular joy as their direct opposites. But he himself sees through everything, stands apart, and scratches himself with his pipe stem.

Or he'd be sitting at a soccer match, his heart pounding, he'd wave his hands, bellow, not noticing at what. Awkward men would be chasing a ball around a field, they'd get in each other's way, but inside his own clumsy body, he would feel skill and limberness, and, in his mind's eye, he'd strike the ball with more precision than any of those little boys, and directly to where it was needed.

Or at the very least he would be gathering potatoes, once again he'd bend and take a potato, bend and take a potato, bend and take a potato.

He knelt senselessly in the snare. Were he even given the chance to become a crooked old witch and blacken everything with his tongue—he was ready, the present situation saddened him so greatly. Or should he consider being in the snare not so very terrible after all? Taking extremes into account, he represented the average and would have to reconcile himself to the infuriating status quo. Catching himself in a lie struck a crack in the images. The man adjusted the cable, his rolled-up pants remained dangling by two ends. It would have made sense to put them on, but he wasn't ripe for a practical effort. Even though the sun rolled on into evening, and the steppe had grown cool.

He squats in a snare, his head drooping, and he is ashamed before the world at his own inactivity. At a time when bombs are falling, when red deer are crying out, children are starving, buds swelling, and the larger sits on the smaller one's nape sucking lymph through a cocktail straw. A wizen face, an eternally gray skirt, two immensely large hands towering toward the heavens, despair and desperation like a caravan of mirages and screaming before him. He is in debt to the world, in debt, in debt. And he has nowhere to hide his shame. He simply cannot escape the circle of his own stupidity and inadequacy. Why has he been born like this, why isn't he an absorbent sponge of another kind which, with every squeeze of the cable, squirts what it has absorbed back into the world as rainbow-gleaming droplets? He is indebted and idiotic-comical in his puerile indebtedness. Oh why was he born into this world stupid, to kneel in a snare, to reek of shame, to drown in puddles of shame?

Then came the saviors, the first, a second, a third. They puttered about the cables with elegant, calculated movements and raised him up from his knees. He smiled, embarrassed, and looked down. There was red in his cheeks; he picked at his apron strings not saying a single word to the suitors.

And again shame billowed over the drooping man and cold-hearted night crept along the disconsolate steppe.

. . . The thirsty man hanging in the snare is left behind us

THE SNARE (II)

there in the flaring wind of the bare expanses. But we know for certain and sentimentally hope that jackals, hyenas, or wolves will do him no harm during the night as he, an Andromeda chained there, awaits the monster. He will come, it is certain that his Perseus will come sometime and free him from those bonds, and ask not a single explanation for his stupidity.

Because evil must be punished and a story must have a happy ending.

–1969–

■ □ ■ □ ■

Arvo Valton

THE SNARE (III)

THE NIGHT WAS A BARE PLAIN, AND IT HAD NOT A SINGLE protuberance or jagged edge. There was no memory of the bleeding sun that had set behind the earth, naked. The stars were indifferent, and there was no solace in them. Somewhere in the midst of the darkness knelt a drooping man, a noose's steel cable squeezing his chest. On the day the earth had become inhabited, he had made his choice and entered the snare. Or had chance chosen him, or had he felt obliged? Now it was night and that soul throbbed in the midst of a plain with no supports. Shame at thirst and thirst for shame weighed mockingly, and apathy spread its veil.

Mechanically, the man shifted the cable upward a bit, and the pants he had stuffed between the cable and himself fell down. His bare knees rested on the sharp angularities of the parched tractor trail and they had grown numb. The man pulled his pants beneath his knees. And again he sank, drooping. The cable held him in balance and his long hands hung down. Dozing, he sank onto all fours, but the growing pressure on his thorax forced him to assume the half-falling posture anew.

The man groped at the cable, it had a certainty and nearness. His torpid knees touched the ground, but they felt nothing. The man hung in the air, his only contact with the world was the steel cable that squeezed and supported. Steady, but sufficiently yielding; comprehending, but aware of its role every moment and eschewing excesses, the cable was for the man a hold on reality; it was truth, religion, hope, love. It could be touched, the sole thing in the night, perhaps; when his hands wanted to grope for the tractor trail in the strapping earth, the cable warned the man; it was his sole tether and support, contact and explanation, reality and consolation; not a miracle, it was a smooth, steel cable from this century and palpable to the hand. The man could stretch out his hands; grasp, at the furthest point possible, the branches of the cable flowing into the night and, in this way, diminish his own incessant feeling of perishing. But he could also thrust his hands through the cable from behind, remain hanging by the fissures, and by extending his shoulders fly to the stars. He and the cable belonged together, perhaps one did not exist without the other. The union was voluntary: the man gave the cable life and a meaning; the cable kept the man from falling into the fathomlessness of night, maintained for him a worthwhile reality.

The dimly flickering sentinel light of consciousness grew faint from time to time, and the habitual cable was unable to keep it lit.

The night was one and boundless; there was nothing at all to grasp, and his feet did not reach the bottom. Did he have strength enough to paddle to the twinkling stars, to rise to the surface, to breathe the air? And when no hope existed any longer, the cable came, seized hold of him, and held him, and night's currents flowed over him and beneath him, and he was in contact with something that could form a circle, fastened end to end.

The night was empty, its walls droned, cavernous, and the small, struggling man was there inside. But through him coursed the droning cable, its telephones called him to distant lands; he slid along the main cable, and through all the windows one and the same night was visible.

A thousand years passed this way, no dawn or cock's crow to be found anywhere. The steppe was uninhabited, a cold wind snooped about without any joy of encounter. And only upon the man kneeling in the noose could it subvert its passions. Here it rallied its confused emotions, which grew denser from time to time, took on shapes and then scattered again.

A thin rider floated toward the man, his horse's long, pliant legs trembled and writhed from contact with the invisible earth. The rider paid no attention to the man; the horse jumped over the cable, its jellylike leg grazed the kneeler's shoulder. Serpentine derelicts raced toward the snare, but before reaching the man they parted to two sides, and he felt only their cold breath. And the man feared that these nonexistent forms would force themselves into his comfortable home, would rust his cables with the dampness of their breath.

The man stretched his hands along the cable, seized it in his palm as redemption, and shook it. At the end of the cable was the world, and it was unlikely that the world would yield to his shaking. But it did indeed seem to shift from its position when he strained hard and with both hands simultaneously. As a result of this unexpected sensation, the man awoke to consciousness of daily existence, the rotation of images was interrupted, and objects took on sharp contours despite the fact that they were invisible in the night. The pressure on his thorax decreased; it was now shifted to his throbbing hands. A practical and cheerful daytime thought passed through his head: if he had a great deal of strength, he could loosen the cable so much that he would be able to get out. But that wouldn't be logical—practical thoughts could not evade logic. And the idea of freedom only frightened him: where would he go on the bare steppe in the midst of impenetrable darkness? He had no moral right, in the name of liberating his own inconsequential person, to shift the whole world from its position at the ends of the cable, to tear apart that which formed a circle somewhere far off, intertwined end to end.

And in fact his hands, quaking from exertion, would not have been capable of this. He let go of the cable, and this feverish moment of activity left his hands feeling a pleasant tremor. That feeling soon also subsided into the cheerful indifference of existence when the man let his able hands drop and trustingly leaned on the cable. And the shadowy figures born of the whistling night wind's clumps of soil were replaced by clear images.

Green lights flashed and a complicated apparatus arrived; out of it spilled men with grave faces. They set up powerful floodlights that obliterated night near the snare. The brutal light robbed the man of solitude. Useless strangers bustled around the snare; they were probably saviors. Perhaps someone had called them. The man did not feel ashamed, but he did feel an antagonism precipitated by the matter-of-fact activity of those who had come and now carried on as though they knew why the night and the steppe needed them.

The man wanted to protest, but he had no voice. He was ready to fight for his home and his rights. He had entered the snare voluntarily; that now gave him vast rights and in fact no one had the right to save him against his own wishes. He had already been here a thousand years. How could these greenhorns be allowed to take his cable from him? What did they want from him? What did they have to offer in place of the sure cable? Must he begin again to echo along the empty steppe like a unsaved soul? Must he begin again to see perils everywhere before him, to wander about haplessly, longing for his home snare, which, though it might indeed be slender, was sufficient for him, a man of modest demands? What did they intend to offer him in place of his shattered home, where he was comfortable and content?

What did it matter that the cable pressed on his chest? At least it was of steel you could touch with your hand, not the incurable oppression experienced by a soul with no supports. For a thousand years his heart had been at peace; only at first had the pressure seemed strange, it had never been too intense for him. Why must he now suddenly plunge into emptiness, to fear getting caught in a new snare that might be much worse, unyielding, and merciless? His existence was settled, all the possibilities were of equal worth, he was at the bottom. Why must he again begin to fear drowning?

That is what he wished to say to his saviors, but he had no voice.

Perhaps they would offer him the easy chair and green newspaper about which he had once dreamed. But that had been so long ago, the dream now crumpled and moldy. It was unlikely that these strangers' fur slippers were better than his comfortable snare.

Or would they offer him the soccer ball and earth-covered potatoes on green plains that used to console him? The green stuff was a strange and frightening illusion.

The man had no voice, and he was heroically silent. The strangers soon dragged their floodlights back to their vehicles and rode off. They hadn't managed to touch him, he was protected by the world cable. The man felt a power and connectedness, he could not be saved if he himself did not wish it. Or had those strangers even wanted to save him? Perhaps they had come only to film him?

Once again it was night, and at the bottom of it, a man. We, who now know so much about him, are seriously concerned. We might perhaps have managed to keep him from entering the snare in the morning, we might perhaps have been able to save him from shame in the evening, but how are we to cope with him, himself, now, with his nocturnal joy and song of praise to the cable? For we are not permitted to tolerate the kneeler's peace of mind. An endless road on an endless steppe is what we hope to awaken him to in the morning, because a story must have a happy ending, as we understand that to be. The trampled and the slain must attain peace within a man's heart—we sense this without explanation and without substantiation. Although restlessness makes a person unhappy, although evening follows day, written tales have their own rules: love must conclude in meeting, perils in survival, deaths in moral victory.

That is why we know for certain that morning will dawn on the steppe and a wanderer will liberate our thirsty sufferer from the fetter into which he has chanced. And our drawn-out tale will finally have a happy ending.

–1969–

■ □ ■ □ ■

Arvo Valton

PHOTOSENSITIVITY

THE PEOPLE FROM PAIDE,[1] JAANUS AND ÜLLE, CAME OUT OF A large church. Their senses reverberated with mass in a foreign language and the imperious strains of an organ. Their curious glances had slid along the arch of the vault to a fathomless height, and at its apex had encountered Him, Himself. He most likely accompanied the married Estonian couple to the door, where the vault's opening expanse permitted Him to return to the sacred chamber and to His more basic responsibilities.

It was raining outside.

"Let's wait here under the arch, maybe it will pass," Ülle suggested.

People bustled through the lateral portals; the large main door was closed. Others seeking shelter also huddled beneath the magnificent arch of the portal.

The Estonians pressed themselves into the mass of people and found that it was pleasant to observe Paris reality from there as well.

Because of the rain, that reality was rather niggardly. A thousand people usually stood in the plaza in front of the church and carried out their tourist rituals; today only a few solitary umbrella owners defied nature. The rain had unexpectedly intersected a sunny week and only the particularly cautious carried with them the equipment to counter it.

The downpour slowly began to subside, however, and became a drizzle. Most of the people left the shelter of the vault. Jaanus studied the team of saints on the portal arches. He discovered quite a few things there in fact, but even more remained undiscovered because his background knowledge proved scant. Why did one stone man, stretched out to a considerable height, have a sword in his hand? Why did another have a scroll? Why must the soles of venerable feet, along with a sly grotesque face, rest upon the backs of simple folk? Entirely more comprehensible was that sparrow which hopped on a stone book and chirped as much as its throat was able. It appeared that all the bird's scant energy was being spent on erroneous information; this book belongs to me, let not a single other sparrow set its foot down here.

The tourists were not so intolerant; they let anyone at all step on their feet.

The area beneath the arch had emptied; those waiting had disappeared into the restive tumult. In fact, the two of them were the only ones left. Jaanus contemplated the sculptures and Ülle did not hurry him. Then a black man stepped in front of the portal and took a picture. He was no doubt interested in the stone men who had stood there for many centuries and not in the fair-haired Nordic couple who, together with the sparrow, had also been included in the African's picture.

This lasted a second, then mundane disregard led them separate ways. The Estonians tramped along the ancient Parisian cobblestones on their own. Through their feet they experienced the vastness of the world capital, whereas the black man, whether he was a tourist or gathering information about arrogant Europe for his native land, went off to take care of his own matters.

After a while the Estonians' Paris days came to an end,

and along complicated roads, they drove back to their hometown, Paide. There they patted the children, displayed objects purchased at a discount store, and roused themselves to enthusiasm when they talked about noble and sinful Paris. But they did not recount how their feet had shot off sparks as they traversed the distance from the few remaining fortress stones of the Bastille to the Little Corporal's Arc de Triomphe. Bus tickets were expensive, and you only truly experience a city by foot. Men of yore had heaped great stone blocks into a wall. Looking at them, Jaanus had been reminded of distant ancestors, and, upon returning to his monotonous construction job, he might also have considered the eternal nature of his own handiwork, but he didn't think about that particularly. In order to more fully experience her own elitism, Ülle enriched it with crumbs of jealousy elicited from her girlfriends when she recommended to them that they too visit Paris.

Scarcely a month had passed since the trip when one evening Jaanus and Ülle looked at each other with a strange glance. After considerable hesitation, the man asked, "Do you feel something?"

"I was just about to ask you that," the woman confessed.

Meanwhile, something unknown to the Estonian couple should be mentioned, something they could have intuited only by letting their fantasies run wild.

The black man, Combo, had also taken many other photos in Paris, and he had them developed for precious French currency. The pictures had been placed in a multicolored envelope. Combo had thrust them into his travel bag and taken them with him when he journeyed back to his homeland. Following his trip to the seventh cradle of civilization, Combo immediately had a great deal to do in his own office. Trips from the former French colony to its motherland, with which ties had been preserved, were nothing unusual, and so there was no need to show the glossy colored pictures either to co-workers or to those at home, insofar as the latter had gone to visit relatives in the so-called jungle. Local festivities were about to begin there, and Combo hurried to take care of work obligations in order to be able to join his tribe for the culmination of the festivities.

And in fact it was there that, for the first time, Combo took out the pictures shot in Paris and talked about his trip. This included the Cathedral of Notre Dame in Paris where the statues standing at the portals were no larger than those of the Africans. The craftsmanship was different, true enough, and the significance of their long epoch of standing there differed from that of the local African deities, who could be produced more quickly and, if necessary, also more quickly destroyed.

These children of nature, less spoiled by industrial worlds, took a lively interest in the people who had chanced into the photos. They asked Combo those people's names, and it took patience for the urbanite to explain that there were a great many people in Paris, and that it was not customary to ask their names, except upon being introduced, and then, too, names tend to slip from memory.

The festivities, which lasted for many days, took their own course, and one evening the village elder decided to revitalize the ritual next in sequence. He recommended that a symbolic ingestion be performed at the sacrifice ritual. For this purpose he chose, from among Combo's pictures, the very one upon which stood Ülle and Jaanus, fair-haired and with a slight tendency toward stoutness.

For the sake of historical accuracy, it must be noted that cannibalism has in fact never been practiced by this or by any other tribe. Stories of such practices had been precipitated by the fear and evil intent of erstwhile European travelers. As everywhere amongst witless mankind, wars had been waged here since time immemorial. Adversaries had been slain with lesser or greater brutality; fortitude and bravery had been drawn from fantasies. In writing about the ancient Estonians, Henry of Livonia[2] also describes how they are said to have eaten a priest's heart. Similar activities were no doubt carried out elsewhere in the world as well: sea monsters were fed beautiful Greek maidens, the blood of innocent young men was shed upon the altars of Indian gods.

This ancient custom of Combo's relatives also necessitated that the gods be placated and that ancient adversaries be destroyed, even those enemies who had wandered off into other civilizations for a while or had otherwise met their end. This was done to the accompaniment of dances and no doubt embodied more enjoyment than threat. Customs are customs, they must be fulfilled. It had filtered into the Africans' consciousness that a great many of their woes had been precipitated by the white man who had forced himself upon the land or had manipulated them from afar. That is why there was nothing unusual about Jaanus and Ülle being, so to speak, included in the program.

There in far-off Paide, however, those two looked at each other with a strange expression and felt a peculiar tickling sensation in many parts of their mortal flesh. But, oddly enough, this didn't cause their eternal souls the slightest discomfort.

—1991—

■ □ ■ □ ■

Arvo Valton

ON THE CHURCH STEP

THE MEETING TOOK PLACE IN WEST BERLIN, WHERE I SPENT A few hours as a through passenger. I went to look at a church that had stood in ruins for almost fifty years near a zoo. The German people apparently wished to have a long memory and to preserve this witness to historical misfortune, perhaps as a specific reminder of their own guilt, as a warning against possible recurrence. Today the area around this profound memorial had been usurped by protesters with their heads painted in many colors, by bums, street musicians, buffoons, hawkers, and beggars.

Among the latter, I spotted a gray-haired gentleman who was reading Immanuel Kant. I observed him for a few minutes, because I thought this must be a mistake: had he perhaps dropped his hat on the street accidently?

An older lady who in a novel might have been the beggar gentleman's love in youth tossed a few coins into the hat alongside the others. The gentleman rose and made a gallant, dignified bow.

My German was quite poor; nevertheless, I dared to address the unconventional beggar. I began by gathering my few pennies together and, with a guilty smile, held them out to the Kant enthusiast. Extended them, precisely that: I did not toss them into the hat with an air of superiority.

The gentleman looked at me in surprise and perhaps even a bit reproachfully: why did I wish to disturb him?

"Why are you here, my good man?" I asked.

He pointed to his hat, motioned broadly, and responded, "This is my profession."

"In what sense?"

"Literally. During my childhood we had beggars for neighbors. They were very wealthy. Father placed me with them to study."

The beggar gentleman uttered those words with singular affability. Apparently he had nothing against talking about himself. Perhaps he had to do so repeatedly.

I looked over at the other beggars, who were pitiful and traditional.

"You mean to say that I differ from my colleagues. Regrettably, I have always wanted to be original, despite good teaching. This is my innovation, if you will. All my neighbors here are wealthy enough to wear as good a suit as mine. They don't want to shatter the notion that if they did no one would give them anything. Although they see that I earn no less than they."

"Perhaps you have an advantage in that you differ from them?" I attempted to apply the principles of a psychology primer.

The gentleman shrugged his shoulders.

"It is possible that my contingent of donors differs from those who give to them. In the final analysis, everyone has their own favorite ploy."

"At any rate, yours is noteworthy," I bestowed the recognition.

Nearby begged colorful little old ladies, children in tatters, men with obvious deformities that had been put out on display. I imagined them well-dressed, yet I did not know how to compare them to my partner in conversation. I said, "Nevertheless, they probably wouldn't be able to understand Kant's philosophy."

"Me either, for the most part," the gentleman admitted, laughing. "Are you able to read him with ease?"

In German, definitely not. I've tried to read him in Estonian, but I didn't find in him the appeal one might assume based upon interpretations. In any case, I didn't force myself to like him. I feared that if I became fond of philosophy, it would have primarily been because I'd taken great pains to master it.

"No," I answered briefly.

"I can tell from your accent that you are a Finn," said the beggar.

"No, an Estonian."

I had once written an article in which I accused Estonians of begging. Fortunately, it had not been published. After all, any accusation whatsoever is unjust to the extent that it deals with phenomena narrowly. Nevertheless, there was no similarity between the activities of my interlocutor and his colleagues, and the people's representatives toying with their misfortune and demanding the world's attention. These people here supported themselves robustly, theirs was a profession of vast traditions. In the Russian imperium, Estonians were among the last to know how to milk the big cow. Instead they implemented, with German precision, Russian law, even though that law wasn't meant to be implemented at all. Such a people could definitely never support itself by begging in the West. A long history has hardened Europe's heart; the Estonian, however, remains in his spasm of dignity.

"Interesting," said the beggar gentleman. He would no doubt have used the same tone in discussing Africa's exotic animals.

With a sure motion, he pressed the coins I had given him back into my palm and said, "If it wouldn't offend you, I'd offer you even more. I know that it will take you some time yet before you obtain actual money."

So this was the effect of recalling the article. I smiled as nicely as I knew how, and shook my head.

"May I sit by you for a moment to rest my feet?" I pointed to a place beside him.

"Please do. You are a stranger and bold," he said indifferently.

I sat down on the step.

We were silent.

I like to collect headgear of unique shapes. Women collect hats in order to put on airs with them. I, likewise, except that I keep them at home on the study wall. Very rarely do I put one on except, occasionally, upon having just obtained it.

I had also bought a German-looking hat in West Berlin. It may have been the symbol of huntsmen or chief foresters and, no doubt, presently it was more of a souvenir. I was wearing the hat because I wanted to see whether I would be noticed. A person with a hardened Western temperament doesn't pay attention to anything; he allows all the world's eccentrics to feel themselves his equals. Even if he himself, in fact, looks down upon them.

The weather was hot. I took off the woolen hat, put it on my knees.

The beggar gentleman indicated that I should place it on the asphalt. Perhaps he wanted to put my tolerance to a test. By sitting down next to him, I had evoked this attitude. Although I felt not the slightest inclination to do so, I placed my new headgear bottom-up beside the beggar's hat.

I would have wanted to clarify some passages of Kant for my neighbor, but my language did not suffice. I would also have reconciled myself to his explanation, but I knew that I could not understand such complicated language. For some reason, I wanted expressly to discuss the great philosopher.

Nodding at the book, I said, "I've been to his grave at Königsberg."

"I'm at his grave right now," said my companion, motioning to the open page.

A strange comparison. Doubtless there was nothing like that written there. Kant's thoughts are alive even now. No book written by someone is his grave, I wanted to believe.

Two older ladies went past us.

"That's a Balt," said one, and she put a ten-mark note into my hat.

Directly in their line of vision, I tilted my hat into the beggar's. The ladies contorted their faces contemptuously and waddled on.

How did they know that I was a Balt? The world is full of people with blue eyes and slightly curly blond hair.

"You see," exclaimed the gentleman, who despite his gray hair might have been younger than I. He did not offer to return the money.

What was I supposed to see?

I grabbed my hat and left.

—1992—

THE FISH'S REVENGE

WHEN I WAS YET A SMALL BOY, I LIVED IN A VILLAGE ON THE banks of a small river. At that time, larger fish like perch, roach, and pike were also found in the river, although poaching and the general polluting of nature has probably already destroyed them by now. Yet even now it is still possible to find many kinds of tiny fish in the river, and during my childhood there were an incalculable number of them. I shall not begin to enumerate those diverse species of tiny fish more precisely here because the possibility of observing these fish as fully grown specimens, which they presumably are in fact, does not interest me. But one must never be certain about this, not even when equipped with the most precise determinants. Chance is always possible, let us not forget this. After all, in the final analysis, it is anticipation of chance that keeps us alive. Even the most hardened, systematic person could not endure it were chance not possible. Of course, one can argue a great deal over degree of probability, but that argument is fruitless if we have not yet experienced chance itself. Something that occurs once in a million years can happen any day—we simply don't know when the last time was, exactly a million years ago today perhaps. We don't have the information. An interval of a thousand years emboldens us. But never mind. Now I'll tell you about the chance event I am awaiting.

As a small boy, I gathered those small fish and put them into a jar to live. Sand had been scattered on the bottom of the jar, a few oxygen-producing water plants had been tucked into the sand, as handbooks instruct small boys to do. The tiny fish had lived with me for many weeks already. They were almost three centimeters long, pallid, gray. Then, however, I rode to the city unexpectedly to visit my aunt. Upon my return, I discovered that the water in the jar had half-evaporated. The fish were swimming in the water, their bellies upward, their gills barely moving. I understood that there was nothing to save here anymore. With a cynicism that amazed even me, I poured the contents of the jar into the sewer system. More precisely: I poured it down the john. Twenty years have passed since then. I am already a full-grown man; it is a summer night, windy and dark. I have come to the seashore at about midnight, to swim alone. I take off my clothes and go into the water. Yes, the wind is indeed warm; nevertheless, I begin to shiver because my sensitive nature has imagined what could happen now if chance began to take effect. I have to go out a long way before the water rises to my chest—this is a health resort in southern Estonia with a gently descending seabed. I stand up to my chest in the warm, shallow, but nevertheless large bay, which is located on approximately the fifty-eighth parallel. I am about to begin swimming when my glassy eyes suddenly notice a sharp tail fin, which slices the waves at a distance of some hundred meters. Yes, it is unbelievable, but this time, true. From literature, I know of instances when solitary sharks have swum very far to the north, strayed in cold undercurrents, and ended up the devil knows where. For instance, in 1916, a shark forced its way into a small river that flows into the Raritan Bay, which in turn becomes the Lower Bay, which, as is well known, is the gateway to New York's harbor. That little river is so small that during low tide it is left completely dry. Nevertheless, the shark forced its way up there and slew many boys swimming in the river. Specialists have characterized shark psychology in the following manner: if a shark has chosen a course of action, it clings to it until the end, no matter what obstacles it might encounter in its path. If fate has directed a shark to the Baltic Sea, then the shark will no longer stray from its path. And now it is here. I begin to run through the water, but make no progress forward. I am well aware that it is one of my little fish, which I flushed down the toilet, a little fish that made it through the sewer system into the river, from the river into a larger river, onward into a lake and from there into the sea, from there through straits into the ocean, a fish that, despite all the ordeals, remained alive, grew large, and has now returned to this country. It has searched for me, found me, and it is completely justified in taking revenge. There it comes now. It is a blue shark, about five meters in length, unduly long even for this small though popular health resort. A blue shark can be recognized immediately, for two back fins and a tail stick out of the water. Its stomach fin is sickle-shaped, its body is completely blue, except under its stomach it is blindingly white. Standing in the shallow water, I wait for it. Our glances meet. Its tremendous jaws close around my thigh, flesh comes off the bone as if cooked, blood colors the nocturnal sea red, and my cries for help are heard by no one. Actually, this hasn't happened yet. That is in fact why I am able to write stories. I come out of the night sea, clothe my wet body, and stroll a distance of half a kilometer through the rustling August night to a private apartment in order to philosophize about the fate of art and the tasks that stand before us. There have been a damned lot of problems with art lately, many men are in fact threatened by an early feeling of resignation, here and there intrigues burst forth, the will to work is sublimated, finds expression in shark images even before the shark's arrival.

—1974—

THE FISH'S REVENGE

THE BLACK MOTORCYCLIST

IN 1969, KONGO WENT TO THE SMALL TOWN OF N. FOR THE first time, although he had already long yearned to go there. He didn't even know himself what he was hoping for, but as far as small towns were concerned, he was not yet the least bit satiated; he still seized every opportunity to go to a small town. Whenever he stepped off a bus, he felt his heart pounding and the palms of his hands grow sweaty. A sweet quiver went through his stomach as he read the first shop signs. In his Algerian essays, Albert Camus talks of towns that lack a past, not to mention memories or traditions or renown. "The sadness in those towns is intense and cold, but not melancholy," writes Camus. This could doubtless also be said about the small town of N. where Kongo arrived together with a journalist friend. They arrived in early autumn, during potato-picking season. The central square of the unfamiliar city inspired the desire to buy a keepsake of some sort, anything whatsoever, and the journalist bought balloons. The men had a friend here, an old Catholic priest whom they had not seen for a long time, and with whom it was interesting to discuss issues of transcendentalism, and not only that—the old priest was also fond of discussing the psychological roots of transcendentalism.

"Where to? Right to the priest's?" asked the journalist, and Kongo nodded. They went on foot—there weren't even any buses in this small town. They went through the wet grass, and the journalist blew up balloons. A housekeeper met them at the door and said that the priest was in the sauna, he'd be back in an hour. The men declined to enter, said they'd walk a bit in the forest behind the house. There actually was a forest behind the house. Kongo had remembered correctly—the firs dripped mist, a crow cawed in the fog, grew silent. They walked along the forest path until they came to a deserted firing range. People had been here recently, orange juice cans lay on the ground, but those drinkers were no longer marksmen. The actual marksmen had departed years ago, ceased their training. Kongo and the journalist stood on an old firing line. Kongo said that deserted firing ranges are like mute and gloomy witnesses of something. The journalist replied that his generation didn't know history, didn't understand what the mute witnesses were saying, didn't know anything at all. The journalist said that he didn't know who Hugo de Payns was, didn't know anything about the Knights Templar. I don't even know when the Battle of Ümera was,[1] or whether it actually took place at all. A generation without history. The journalist stopped his groaning, and in passing he burst a balloon with a cigarette. Kongo consoled the journalist, lied that he himself didn't know anything either. Actually he did indeed know, he knew a great deal. Then they sat down on a tree stump and listened to the forest silence. Now and then a droplet fell onto the moss. The journalist opened a beer bottle.

"You know what I dreamt," suddenly the journalist began talking. "It's well known that the ancient Estonian religion forbids responding to an unknown call, right?"

"Who called out?" asked Kongo, flinching.

The journalist, however, continued: "The dream goes like this. On a summer evening before sunset I'm walking along a village road with my wife. Barefoot through soft, fine dust. Beside the road is an alder forest, also dusty, of course. We walk and remain silent. Just as if we're coming from somewhere or going somewhere. Suddenly my wife is being called. Like a man's voice, but very high-pitched. From how far off, from what direction—that I can't discern. The air is still, perhaps that's why. My wife pretends she hasn't even heard that call, and, well, what recourse do I have but to pretend likewise. So this is how we continue walking, two deceitful ones, and we wait for the call to recur, because he who has begun to call out will not desist until he achieves results. And, in fact, a call comes. My wife steps off the road and jumps over a ditch. She doesn't even look back as she directs her steps toward the forest, and the thought occurs to me that this must be the English manner of departure, unobtrusive. Nevertheless, I call out: where are you going? I'll be right back, she lies. Well, all right then, go. I permit her, for my principles are humanistic, I never forbid anything at all. But when I have given her permission, she suddenly begins to vacillate, looks at me scowlingly, until the voice calls again. Then she continues to stare at me as if I were guilty of something, or as if she felt herself to be very guilty. Well, you know my wife, a bit squat: imagine her in melodramatic circumstances. Go, I shout, and in fact she goes across a wet corner of the swamp, so that I still hear the water squishing between her toes and this, in fact, is how she disappears into the thicket. I stand, as if superfluous, in my own spot. Then I walk on, encounter cheerful farmers with sweat on their brows, who earn their daily bread in the fields, and they wave their weathered caps at me in greeting. The sun descends into the horizon, the flock is called home, and everything is as in days of old. Upon the slope of a ridge where the view opens out to manor buildings gleaming below, I comprehend, as if for the first time, that what has just occurred on the road is neither natural nor an everyday occurrence. How will I tell this to my parents, elderly and melancholy people who live far from here, a journey of many days, as paternal homes usually are? By riding there myself? No, I must write a letter, but it will nevertheless be abhorrent to describe all the circumstances, especially that sunset light, that detailed, sickly atmosphere—my parents wouldn't believe me, they'd think I was drunk. Moved by a sudden impulse, I begin to return along the traversed road. It grows increasingly dusky, a wind has risen, the landscape is imbued with a basic anxiety, dust rises and leaves whirl. I run, and I ask myself: where is that spot, where did it happen? There's not a single human soul to ask, however. And what to ask, anyway? Then a distant rumble through the gusts of wind, a point approaching me across the yellow sand. Yes, of course, a three-wheeled motorcycle! On the cycle sits a man wearing black glasses, a leather jacket, black gloves on his hands, a man like night itself. I step onto the road in front of him and ask whether he has seen my wife. He shakes his head and says: I can't hear. I repeat the question and again he says: I can't hear. The third time I begin to think that perhaps the man has been deafened by the long ride, but then I understand that he is simply joking with me. A black motorcyclist, three wheels under him, what are we talking about. Then his face recedes into a demonic mask, and he revs up the motorcycle. Sand is hurled against my eyes, with a roar the somber motorcyclist departs, and only then do I also see my own wife coming across the sand dunes. She is limping, her eyes glisten, upon her hair a wreath of clover blossoms, her dress covered with burrs, and her lips bloody. I take hold of her hand and lead her to the highway. There we find a chance truck, and in its van we ride through the wind and night. A thin trickle of blood flows from the corner of her mouth, and she does not open her eyes. I look intently at my wife's rigid face and say convulsively, with quivering lips: 'I have loved you more, dearest, than you were capable of believing.'"

The journalist finished. Kongo sipped beer and didn't say anything. An hour had passed, certainly the priest was already home from the sauna. They walked back along the forest way. The priest was indeed present and received them cheerfully. Soon coffee was steaming on the table, and the conversation moved along the old, beloved paths of existential philosophy. Kongo mentioned that, in Heidegger's opinion, the Greek term *phenomenon* should be translated into German as *"sichzeigende," "offenbare,"* but most precisely as *"das Sich-an-ihm-selbst-zeigende"* (finding-oneself-within-oneself). But it can also be, specified the priest, that one finds oneself in such a manner that one isn't even within oneself. That would be *Scheinen.* The conversation continued in this manner. The journalist remained bleakly silent and reflected on where indeed Kongo had come to know Heidegger so well and why. He dozed off in the interim; the others went on talking, however. When the journalist opened his eyes, Kongo was vowing to the priest that anarchists and radical youth were actually spiritual soldiers in the service of great senile cabinet members (Marcuse). Finally the old priest grew weary and went to sleep. The men, too, lay down on their beds, between the white sheets prepared by the kindly priest. The journalist fell asleep immediately. Kongo, however, remained awake. He rose to a sitting position and, in the gleam of the night lamp, he studied his friend's childish face, which was in a spasm of sleep, or, expressed more precisely, in the slackness of sleep, his teeth gleaming between his red lips. It was past one. Karin was asleep in a large city many hundred kilometers distant from here. Was the journalist again seeing her in a dream? The sleeper's lips moved. Was he forbidding Karin to go? The journalist's eyelids trembled. Was he seeing his defiled wife? Or, in his dream, was he instead seeing Kongo rise from his bed, sneak quietly out of the room, enter the yard, shiver with cold, and begin to go down the village road? After a few hundred meters he turns into the forest, finds a motorcycle with a side carriage hidden in a bush behind the old firing range, searches for black gloves and a leather jacket, gets dressed, starts the motor, and disappears toward the city. At that moment the journalist opened his eyes and looked at Kongo with a wide-eyed stare. He was, in fact, having that dream, thought Kongo; what else is there for him to see now? He bent over closer to the journalist and took his hand. Calm down, he said hypnotically, sleep. There's really been nothing between me and Karin. A brief, passing flirtation. And even that was already over three months ago. It wasn't really anything, in fact, a strange feeling of fate. She's your wife again. You'll learn to know each other again, you will discover each other anew, anew, within yourself, *sich-an-ihm-selbst-zeigende*.

The journalist didn't have the strength to respond. Kongo let go of his hand, lay down in bed on his back, stretched out his arm, and took from his briefcase Goffman's book *A Presentation of Self in Everyday Life*. Kongo was by nature a generous and good-hearted person. But he who has once become a black motorcyclist finds no road back anymore. He who has the taste of newly slain flesh in his mouth goes on killing.

—1974—

Mati Unt

HE TRANSLATED

I

I KNOW MANY GOOD TRANSLATORS, I COMMUNICATE WITH them readily and gladly avail myself of their services. I don't know any language well enough that I could fully enjoy a work, especially a masterpiece, in the original. From time to time, a dictionary must be used and this tends to be irksome. It's true, the number of nuances increases, but the work seems to vanish in your hands, turn to sand, you understand that it consists only of words and behind it lies emptiness. There are too many variants. I am a nervous person and I prefer therefore to depend upon one fixed variant that a trustworthy person has made for me. Goethe did indeed say that in translating one must plumb the untranslatable, but who has the courage for that? What or who must then be confronted? Whew! And so I prefer a translator's version. They are, for the most part, educated and refined men, often entirely oriented toward their favorite country. This is betrayed by their use of wine, pipe, or women. A real translator is a clean type. Usually a tolerant man, often a good-hearted roly-poly. Seldom have I seen hysterical translators who chew their nails and tear their hair. A dark flame seldom burns in a translator's eyes. He is an altruist, a lover of someone else, he is not so much a sadist as a masochist. That is why it is pleasurable to drink good red wine with translators and to sniff their good tobacco. Translators seldom drink vodka. I repeat, they are not wild. But chance people do also happen among them. In fact, many a person who is more sensitive than average to the texture of the world, and who could express his sense perceptions in the form of an original creation, suddenly becomes a translator. Exactly so, I repeat at your astonished cry, a person suddenly becomes a translator, and it is not easy to tear him away from this work anymore. No one has the courage to tell him outright that he smells differently, that he is strange. The errant glance that so readily betrays him bores into us with the frank question: well, what shall we translate today? And you are helpless before this naïveté. You talk, suggest, mention what has not yet been translated, what is being translated. And that is how the days pass. And nothing changes. He is among us and sows a singular, perverse atmosphere. Many people have such an aura. But in particular those who have chanced to become translators.

II

At night, in a dream, in a trolley, in a foreign country perhaps, a man struck a translator in the chest full force. The man, a young man, was wearing a bright windbreaker. He struck twice, before others could come to help. The translator no longer remembered what had precipitated the quarrel. Those strangers had initially been on our (our own) side against a third party of some sort. That third, whose points of view and face the translator did not remember, was in serious trouble because he had been left in the minority. But he was clever, he turned the tables, so that he began playing along with them (us) against the strangers. He offended the strangers in such a manner that the strangers were left with the impression that actually they (we) were doing the insulting. And that third party offended the strangers more than they (we) would have done. He upset the whole apple cart and then he himself split. At that very moment the trolley stopped, and he succeeded in escaping through the back door. But the translator and his companions now stood eye to eye with their newly created enemies. And then came that man, he the most peaceable among them, if one were to judge from his eyes. But no doubt he had principles at stake, no doubt his patience was full to the brim, selflessly. He attacked the translator like a naturalist who is protecting a white-tailed eagle, like a pacifist who has spied a ditch filled with corpses. He insulted the translator with a brief Portuguese profanity. Someone stepped between them.

Then the translator awoke. He knew, in addition, that the man had come from among the others, low and exceedingly fast, fist extended, head to the ground. He struck twice in the chest. Upon awakening, the translator felt a pain in his back. It was difficult to breathe and to move. The translator tried to relate the blows in his dream to the actual pain. Is this it, then, he thought anxiously. He remained lying motionless. He attempted to explain to himself why he had in fact remembered that dream. Usually, upon awakening, he didn't remember nightmares; he knew only that there had been nightmares, but had no evidence to show. His nightmares weren't surrealistic, they always consisted of commonplace situations and details. Very seldom indeed was there a sprinkling of war, arrest, parachutists, or sadism. He himself smirked when he occasionally dreamed that he was once again unprepared for his Russian lesson. Then he awoke in a cold sweat and understood how great a role school had played in his life. While attending school, he hadn't yet understood this. He also seldom saw symbols. He didn't recall having flown or swum in a dream.

The translator always awoke early. But what was there to do wide awake, especially early? The translator then sometimes took a book about botany, ethnography, or politics from beside his bed and read two or three pages at random. Occasionally he read from the back toward the front. His wife advised him either to get up or to continue sleeping, but in any case not to fidget and sigh. However, the translator sighed because dawn was breaking. Who had the wherewithal to comprehend it? Sometimes he got up and drank absolutely pure water, even though he was bored with its taste. But he drank in anger. Now he had no wife. His wife had ridden off. His wife was an actress, and she was playing Ophelia in the eastern part of the country. The guest performance would take two days, and the translator stared at the ceiling for a long while, motionless. It was eight o'clock, the store was still closed. Suddenly he had a brilliant idea.

After all, I am a translator, he said to himself, what could be more natural in my circumstance than translating? Why do I sometimes forget that? Shame on me! I should translate Dante Gabriel Rossetti's poem "An Old Song Ended" today. That would suit my wife's being away at guest performances. It would be just like hitting the nail on the head. It would be more than precise and it would even have its own subtext, which needn't in fact become evident now. The translator got up and walked naked across the room. He was 175 centimeters tall and weighed 75 kilos. But he had not done a great deal of physical labor. He took a collection of Dante Gabriel Rossetti's poetry from the shelf and brought it to bed, under the blanket.

The poem began with a citation in italics: *How should I your true love know / From another one? / —By his cockle-hat and staff / And his sandal-shoon.*[1] The translator knew this poem, and he knew that it had to do with Ophelia's song.

Ophelia is mad then. Tombach-Kaljuvald[2] had translated it into Estonian in the following manner: *Kuidas ma sinu kallima / Tunnen teiste seas? / Ta kepist ja ta sandaleist. / Kübarast ta peas.* [How shall I know your dearest / Know him among the rest? / His cane and his sandals. / The hat on his head will attest.] Georg Meri's[3] newer translation sounded like this: *Kuidas sinu kallimat / tunda teiste seas? / Sauast ja sandaalidest, / kulunud kaabust peas.* [How to know your dearest / know him among the rest? / The staff and sandals, / the worn slouch hat on his head will attest.] The matter was confused slightly by that "cockle-hat." What kind of a hat, then, is a *cockle-hat?* Webster said that a *cockle* is a mollusk with a heart-shaped shell. What kind of hat could that be, then? The translator picked up the telephone and called a colleague. The colleague thought that *cockle* also meant to pucker, as a noun it is also an oven, *warm the cockles of the heart* means to warm the heart or to console; nevertheless, in his opinion, a *cockle-hat* was simply a wrinkled slouch hat. "I have a strange feeling for some reason," he added then.

The translator waited in vain for his colleague to continue, but he did not continue. "What strange feeling?" asked the translator, and he himself offered: "*Angst?*"

"Oh no," responded the colleague, "I don't even know myself." A long pause followed. Then the colleague said: "Let me look in one more place."

He left. The telephone emitted vague sounds. Someone coughed very close by. Someone lit a cigarette. A *cockle-hat,* said his colleague, is a hat to which a mollusk shell has been attached in order to signify that its wearer has been to Spain, at Santiago de Compostela, to the remains of Saint James. In this way, love and the religious path of prayer are equated. The translator said thank you and quickly hung up the receiver. All this wasn't the least bit important! The devil take it! The first verse was a quotation anyway. Rossetti quoted Shakespeare, and the translator could in turn freely quote a canonical translation of Shakespeare. The translator had once planned to translate the second verse in the following manner: *Kas ta on ju koduteel? / Mis sa temast tead? / Ammu tuli kevadkuu, / kus siis tema jääb.* [Is he already on the homeward road? / What do you know of him? / Long since here the spring month, / where then is he?] The rhyme was not pure, but at that time the translator had not done any further work. Now he decided to continue. He turned over on his side, there was no more pain. He must revise either the second or the fourth line, there was no other alternative. In addition, he also rearranged the lines: *On sul uudist tema käest? / On ta koduteel? / Ammu käes on kevadkuu, / Mis ta ootab veel.* [Have you news of him? / Is he on the homeward road? / Long since here the spring month, / Why then he so slowed?] But the last line was still not right. It seemed as if there was too much anger at the beloved man. The mind pulls homeward? Whose? The one waiting? The one coming? The one there? The one leaving? Pulls, but how actually? Does he come or doesn't he? That remains unresolved . . . The translator got up again. First he looked out the window. All in all, it was quite monochromatic, a particular brownish-silver shade. Some things gleamed a great deal. More distant details remained unclear. *Kas ta on ju koduteel? / Kirja said ta käest?* [Is he already on the homeward road? / You got a letter from him?]—too brief a question, even aggressive almost, but he probably wouldn't think up a better one initially. It should make no difference whether "kirja" [letter] is in the second or third duration.[4] How big a difference is that anyway, although the linguists maintain that it is. The last line should have been: *Küll kevad on ju käes.* [For spring's already at hand.] The rhyme would have been a bit purer. But the third line no longer needed to be rhymed.

The translator still lived in the same place. He no longer had the wherewithal to say where he lived. (He lived on a fifth floor in the seventh district of the new city, turn in to the left, pass before a nine-story building.) He went into the kitchen and considered what he might undertake there. First of all, he opened the door to the trash bin and looked. A mouse hadn't chanced into a trap, had it? What was it they were looking for there on the fifth floor? The translator's wife was afraid of mice. The translator was afraid, too, but he didn't tell anyone that. He thought ecologically, but he feared animals because he had managed to become estranged from nature. He didn't understand what animals wanted. That's why he killed them, in fact. Only the very smallest, of course: a mouse was the largest of the animals he killed, and even that he killed with a trap. Let very large animals, cows for instance, be killed by those created for that purpose, thought the translator. There was no mouse in the trap. The butter in the trap had been eaten. Perhaps the butter had melted? At any rate, things had gone well for the mouse. The translator felt a subconscious sense of relief. He himself didn't know that, for we don't know what transpires in our subconscious. That's why it's the subconscious, in fact. From the kitchen, the translator went into the bathroom. There he looked at the potassium permanganate stains on the bottom of the bathtub. He had had tonsillitis. He had gargled. His throat got better; the bathtub was ruined. The translator brushed his teeth and washed his face too. In doing so, he looked at himself in the mirror. He wanted to know whether he had aged, but there was nothing with which to make a comparison: the former translator no longer existed, the translator was changing with time.

His brain automatically continued the translation work, weighed variants. He's probably sure to come? Surely he's coming right now? He's almost coming? He's coming shortly now? The time for coming is at hand? My dearest will be arriving then, when spring is at hand? My dearest will be arriving now, when spring is at hand? My dearest is arriving, for spring is at hand? The translator was incapable of choosing. He decided that initially he would leave the following variant: *Kas ta on ju koduteel? / Kirja said ta käest? / Küll ta tuleb kindlasti, / kevad on ju käes.* [Is he already on the homeward road? / Had you a letter from him? / Oh, he's sure to come, / spring is already at hand.]

At that, he went out of the bathroom and began to get dressed. He told himself that he'd be sure to eat later. He listened in the corridor, just in case. He had no peephole in the door, and he didn't even want one. And he also didn't know why. But he always listened, just in case. Actually there couldn't be anyone there because the outside door was locked all night. But caution was necessary. Each day could be the first time. Sometimes they drank in the stairwell, and it could happen that one of them might come up, lose his bearings, chance into the dead end. After all, the translator did live on the uppermost floor. No trapdoor led farther up. Of course, one must also understand them, they too are human beings. One mustn't wear blinders, one must maintain a broad point of view. They must not be insulted. They are very sensitive. On the other hand, it is impossible to always maintain peace, even though you know how you should relate to them. The translator smirked: what a psychopath! Of course there was no one in the hall. After all, he had already known that beforehand. It had been quiet in the stairwell all night. Perhaps clouds in front of the moon had merely cast a weak shadow that moved across the wall. And so the translator descended the stairs. He passed closed doors. He looked at the locks as usual. Some had installed large Finnish door locks. The translator thought that he would certainly not dare install such a large and shiny lock for himself. Why it's like an advertisement for a burglar. Any burglar would understand that behind such a door there was something to steal. Actually the burglar would want to steal the lock itself. But then everyone had to judge for themselves what to do. It was quiet in the apartments.

With regard to Dante Gabriel Rossetti, here in Estonia we are more familiar with his paintings than his poetry. The Pre-Raphaelites were very much in vogue throughout the world a few years ago. In all likelihood, they are already beginning to go out of vogue. That is a pity; some things should surely remain in vogue all the time. In Estonia, too, articles appeared about Rossetti and his circle. It's said that Rossetti long wavered between literature and painting. However, in the year 1845, he nevertheless enrolled in the Royal Academy of Art, having already attended its preparatory school since the age of thirteen. It is known that other Rossettis were in the arts as well: brother William Michael was an art theorist; sister Christina Georgina was a poet. Here in Estonia we are even less familiar with Christina's poems than with Dante Gabriel's, thought the translator. That doesn't mean we have no knowledge of them at all. However, our sparse knowledge of them doesn't hinder us from living and working, and sometimes quite productively at that. The older sister, Maria Francesca, also nicely complemented that English family originally from Italy: namely, she wrote a structural analysis of Dante's *Divine Comedy.* The children had evidently inherited their spiritual gifts from their father, who, likewise, was a great authority on Dante, and a professor of Italian at King's College. The translator had seen many portraits of Dante Gabriel Rossetti. It's true these were dim reproductions, but it was nevertheless possible to discern that Rossetti was tall and thin, laconic, carelessly dressed, and had a hypnotic effect upon those around him. An inward-turning expression burned upon his countenance. His nerves were supposedly so shot that he slept during the day and worked at night. This kind of thing also occurs among infants. And also when you've been a hard drinker in the evening. But they say this is a bad sign.

The translator looked into the mailbox. He had not written any letters for a long time now. Actually, there's nothing to write about. Everyone gets to know the same things more or less simultaneously. If someone knows something others don't know, then he keeps it to himself. Or simply forgets it. And even when something does in fact happen somewhere, it's difficult for us to intervene. You could manage with the language, thought the translator, but it's difficult to travel far. Events are over before you get your visa. And even if you could travel, you don't know whose side to favor. A deeper overview is lacking. Thus it can easily happen that you choose the wrong side, make a blunder, compromise yourself before history. Appearance often veils essence. Reactionary forces are masters at enticing with cunning slogans. It's well known that mass psychosis is contagious. You don't know who to ask. After all, you can't tell at first glance which junta is reactionary, which progressive. Tourist brochures do not provide exhaustive explanations about burning political issues. Local collusions were formed long ago, the rosters of secret organizations sealed. Oh, we are where we are, thought the translator, what's the use of being obstinate. He looked up instinctively, it was as if a crime of some sort were coming to light. There was no one at all at the windows. Even the man on the second story, who usually kept watch day and night, had disappeared from his post this time. Perhaps he was in the lavatory? For it's impossible to ceaselessly keep watch, something is bound to intervene. The translator checked to see whether he had his keys. There was asthma in the air. And the laundry was also moving a bit. The translator considered air merely a word (see also airbrush, airy, airglow, airburst, airstrip). He always thought about that when he aired out a room or some friend. He didn't much believe that air is composed of gases. It's true you can't grope at gases, but they should at least have color, odor. Otherwise what do they have anyway? The translator was well aware of the scientific facts, but he didn't believe them anymore.

He looked around and already thought about the next verse. *And what signs have told you now / That he hastens home? / —Lo! the spring is nearly gone, / He is nearly come.* Does he have a sign of some sort? A sign peculiar to him?

The translator was just then standing upon unseen warmth: an underground hot-water pipe that came into his building. During winter the snow on the surface of the ground near it melted. Right now there was nothing to see, and the translator didn't even think about the hot-water pipe. He had other things to do—he was angry that the verse had to be immediately revised. At the same time, he smelled something. When translating, you don't notice having progressed some twenty–thirty meters. He was by the trash bins, in fact. There was something to see in them. They are always overflowing. Sometimes cats that have something to be ashamed of leap out of them. But the translator did not let himself be led astray. He had two verses translated and these remained absolutely unripe. But he could no longer concentrate solely on Rossetti. Before him appeared the commercial center of the microregion. You could say that it was quite large, if you only knew to whom. And large in comparison to what? First he saw the flower store, which opens at ten o'clock; beside it, the lavatory, which is never closed at all. The translator didn't know what took place there, especially at night. He had heard inarticulate utterances inside and had been afraid to enter. It was now five minutes to nine. A line had already formed in front of the store entrance. There weren't a great many people standing there, and the translator went behind them as the last. It had grown warmer and carbonated water dispensers droned, although, unfortunately, indigents had stolen the glasses during the night.[5] One person in front of him already had a newspaper. Holding the newspaper, the person's hands quivered, and the translator wasn't able to read over his shoulder. That is why he took the translation out of his pocket. It was snobbish and masochistic to read Dante Gabriel Rossetti here in the supermarket line. He could have bet a thousand rubles that he was the only one on this line who had read Rossetti. A few had perhaps even heard of Rossetti. The translator did not fear that he would be tarred and feathered, he took a gamble. The store was opened. Together with the others, the translator entered in single file and that irritated him.

The last line of the poem also irritated him. *He is nearly come. Nearly—peaaegu* (= *closely, almost, intimately, stingily*). Then could it be at spring's departure, or maybe not?

Upon entering, the translator took a basket, at the same time aware that almost a thousand of them are stolen yearly. The women stormed over to the meat counter, the men to the beer. The translator didn't want beer. He looked on in disgust at how powerful men's hands grabbed for beer. One of those crazies got in his way. He poked the man in the back painfully with his basket. That one turned around, enraged. The translator put on an expression denoting that he knew nothing. The man believed it. The translator felt a bit relieved. He didn't even try to force his way over to the meat counter.

But the precursor of the Pre-Raphaelites, William Blake, had constantly had visions. His wife had to sit beside him quiet as a mouse, through the nights, while he watched the visions. He saw angels, the hanged, Christ, Milton, and Moses. And the Pre-Raphaelite David Scott had so fragile a nervous system that when, as a child, he had wrapped himself in a white sheet and stood before a mirror, he became so frightened that he had gotten a high fever. How little interest anyone had in eating! The translator had read that it was the custom at that time to come to the most fashionable eateries in London, to sit down at a table, and to request a glass of water. A white lily that had been brought along was then placed in the glass and gazed at. When the waiter came to take orders, the response was that there were no orders, that "I have in fact partaken of this beauty."

And here they stalk fatty pork! Before the feet of those jackals (Tolstoy, too, has spoken of eating carrion!), the translator would have spit: go back where you came from, and live your lives, I love you as humans, but not as meat-eating beings. The translator himself was not a vegetarian, but he simply couldn't do anything else. He looked around the store and sought something more noble. Pickled beets? And how noble is that, in fact, and is it appropriate to purchase canned goods in the autumn? What's summerish, then? Cabbage?

The third verse: *For a token is there nought, / Say, that he should bring? / —He will bear a ring I gave / And another ring.* In any case, the translator considered his first version erroneous. It would be simplest to translate it this way: *On tal monda märki ehk, / mis ta temaks teeb? / Minu sormust kannab ta / ja üht sormust veel.* [Has he some sign perhaps, / which makes him he? / My ring he wears / and one ring more.] But haven't those little filler words—"perhaps," "some," "and"—already long been the mark of a dilettantish translation?

The translator looked at the fish. Actually, he looked because he had decided to buy olives, and the fish were on the same counter with the olives. The translator didn't eat fish, but they sparked his fantasy. Mother, phallus, Christ, death. Very diverse things. Incidentally, the fish had odd names: *poutaussou, nototheniidae, meruu, lufaar.* Obviously brought from the distant Atlantic. Now they would be eaten. They are mute and tongueless. Once they were creatures of the deep, phosphoresced down in the darkness. In all likelihood they are escorted by pilot fish. They are accustomed to high pressure; their skin is the color of water.

Rossetti's bride, Elisabeth Siddal, was also kept in the water for many days, that is to say, Rossetti's friend, John Millais, was just then painting a picture of Ophelia. He requested Elisabeth for a model (we also see Elisabeth in a great many of Rossetti's pictures). In order to make the picture more true to life, Millais kept Elisabeth in a bathtub. After all, we know that Ophelia drowned there where "a willow grows aslant a brook." Ophelia had climbed onto a branch to gather blossoms for a wreath, but the branch deceived her, broke, and Ophelia fell into the water. Further on it was revealed that "her clothes spread wide" bore her upon the water for a little while, during which time she continued to sing her archaic songs, as though not perceiving the danger, as if her home actually were in that element. But then her clothes became saturated with water, grew heavy, and Ophelia drowned. That is how Queen Gertrude describes it. In Millais' painting we do in fact see a river, beside the river a willow, in the water Ophelia, still singing, her mouth and eyes out of the water, one hand as well. Her mouth is open.

The translator bought three hundred grams of olives and two beers—notwithstanding! Then he stood in the checkout line. Out of boredom, he eyed the other people, scrutinized what this one and that had bought. Occasionally things were taken home, the significance of which was not understood. Jars with a foreign-language label, the contents of which were unsuitable for consumption and had to be thrown away. Occasionally, in fact, what had been purchased remained a secret. There was no translator! Yet precious money had been given for it. The translator was standing and thinking this way when a high-pitched shriek suddenly coursed through the store. The droning grew silent. Everyone sought the source of the sound. Many hoped that a thief had been caught. Such a thing always gives everyone great joy. Nearly everyone gets satisfaction. They have the feeling that they themselves have thrashed the thief. Everyone would like to twist a thief's arms, to stick a foot out in front of him. Societal retaliation is noble. But it now became apparent that no one had been apprehended. An elderly gentleman had put his little dachshund into a large trash bin in a corner while he went into the store. The dog sat there quietly the entire time and no one noticed it. When its master completed his purchases and came for the dog, it raised a clamor of joy. Here and there the incident was still discussed even after the participants had already departed. On one hand, the incident was quite comical; on the other hand, it could not go unsaid that the matter had left a disagreeable aftertaste of some sort. An animal in a trash bin! A mute and tongueless animal! However, the translator did not stay to listen to the discussions. He took his beers and olives, and went out of the store. At the door, he ran into the local drunk, who, despite his utter demise, was very tough and healthy; he was begging for beer money and drank on the spot. He had a wide circle of acquaintances, he was treated genially; evidently he had once been a functionary of some kind. The translator watched a bit as the drunk left, and he settled down to Dante Gabriel Rossetti.

Where, then, had the translator left off with his poem? There, of course, he answered himself: *On tal monda märki ehk* . . . [Has he some sign perhaps . . .] Then it would actually be better to say *Mille järgi tuunen ma, / et see tema on?* [How shall I know / that it is he?] There is no rhyme to be found for "on" [is]—of course, that's clear. *Mille järgi tuunen ma, / et on tema see? / Minu sôrmust kannab ta / ja üht sôrmust veel.* [How shall I know, / that he it is? / My ring he wears / and one ring more.]

The translator passed flower vendors; he cast a sidelong glance at the roses, the carnations, the marigolds, the asters, the cornflowers. Then he passed two telephone booths. He had used them when he himself had not yet had a telephone.[6] Then he turned the corner and saw the main road from a bit higher. Is the autumn being reflected from windows a metaphysical experience? The stairs down which the translator descended were strange: the steps were too broad, too long for one step, too short for two. The contours of the buildings, however, were as pure as in Onegin's times.[7] There were Romanian-language magazines at the newspaper stand. However, the translator didn't know Romanian. He wouldn't have said that to the Romanians. He knew many Romanians and had a high regard for them. He left the stand feeling a certain degree of shame. He was, after all, a translator, *interpreter!* He went home.

III

The sequel takes place many years later, elsewhere. In the meantime, quite a bit has changed. The first blow came the evening of the same day he was translating Dante Gabriel Rossetti's poem. In front of the apartment door, waiting for the translator, stood a man who seemed familiar, but where from he couldn't remember. That man handed him a paper and spoke for a long time in Estonian, so there was no need to translate anything. He announced that the translator's wife wished him to say that she was not returning to her husband anymore, and she requested that the items listed be given to the man presenting this letter. Quite some time passed before the translator understood that he was now a lovelorn man. The visitor smiled sadly and reticently. He was wearing sandals, but the translator didn't see a staff anywhere. There was a ring on one of the man's fingers. He wasn't wearing a slouch hat, which was entirely normal in the summertime. The translator never actually recovered his sense of reality that day. He put the requested dresses into a suitcase mechanically and handed it to the stranger. Then, just as mechanically, he finished translating Rossetti's poem. It was published, but where, no one remembers anymore. A lone poem attracts no attention; had it at least been an entire cycle . . . So the poem, upon which so much time and effort had been lavished, concerning the translation of which so many necessary and unnecessary chains of association had formed, is now lost, drowned in the river of time. The following day, the otherwise abstinent translator began to drink. As usual, this despair of a broken man was forgiven him. The drinking bout lasted almost a week. Other measures followed, as if unrelated one to another, but an astute observer could discover in them a hidden method. He sent insulting letters to former mutual family friends. He spoke ill of his wife's lover, who was highly respected by the community. Of course, the translator's own stock also plummeted immediately, if he could be referred to as a translator at all anymore, for he had not translated anything in a long time. He fell back in with the company from whence he had risen by dint of his marriage. There he was received with joy, just like a prodigal son. He had, in fact, been considered uppity in the interim. Now it was as if he had returned home. Once again very erratic facts, difficult to connect, follow. It is rumored that he took part in a fight. Unfortunately we didn't find out whether he was the one to strike or the victim. But he took part, became involved, what of it that this was for one brutal moment. Perhaps that was his final stellar hour, who knows what ideas he was acting against or on behalf of, but he acted. I forgot to say that he was then already living in a small town. His form grew dim. Previously so rich in detail, now only a shadow in the moonlight. We saw him as through a telescope reversed. Specific psychological characteristics were lost, he became a type, which made generalities possible. Had he in fact even been created to be a real translator? Why his interest in the humanities at all? That senselessly accumulated erudition! His face was turgid, and he had sideburns. Nothing about him was reminiscent of Dante Gabriel Rossetti. He could perhaps have translated Whitman, if he had wished to translate anything at all. There he could have dealt with material more freely, wouldn't have caught anyone's attention, the primary objective being a sufficiently dynamic translation. More elegant verse evaded him. Oh, why speak of elegance, all his rhymes were very forced. Of course, we are being too harsh on him. He had nuances. He was no dark figure. Occasionally he surprised the snobs with dream. He had a sense of color. But he thrashed about here and there. Humanism, which had been fashionable, was also dear to him. But when ecology came into vogue, a broader way of thinking, an organic stance toward life, he, too, had participated immediately and supported everything worthwhile. There's no understanding such types, actually. Culture, I mean in the more narrow sense, is attainable by everyone. It is very difficult to distinguish between a true genius and a charlatan. He died of a heart attack a year ago. The news reached the capital after a few weeks had passed. Everyone had forgotten him. There's no harm in that really, quite the opposite in fact. It was better that he disappeared out of the spotlight. In a certain sense he cluttered the spiritual atmosphere. He was individual enough to variegate an already variegated picture. A sergeant in urbanization's great army of counselors, he retired, became one of life's simple foot soldiers. Since he was distant from us, we don't know how he spent his final days. We don't know his days or nights, don't hear the rustlings he heard. Perhaps he suffered, perhaps he felt joy, but fortunately no one learned of this anymore. He played out the final scene of his life alone, before an empty hall. It's more honest that way. During one's youth there is a great desire to stand out. Usually that goal is also attained, but what then? To continue to stand out? Well, and then? To play translator, cultural mediator, customs official for emotions? For whom, for what? Who's even interested in anyone else actually, in a neighbor, let alone some Rossetti from the southern hemisphere.

Thus the translator was variously discussed. From being a typical member of the literati, the man had become a symbol. His fate seemed a human's fate. We could say: we don't know what manner of man he was. We know only that he was born, that he translated, stopped translating, and died.

Paul Valéry has said that translations are just like architectural drawings, splendid in themselves, but an untutored eye does not discern the buildings, palaces, temples behind them. They lack a third dimension.

IV

The translator's wife, actress N, is even now in our midst. Her second marriage did not prove enduring. She went from hand to hand, but not down. Everyone saw how she was becoming seasoned and ripening as an artist. Smut did not adhere to her. It's true that she too had depressions, even rehearsals that were unfocused, but she was forgiven. They knew that she mobilized herself quickly. She had a clear spirit. Of course, she too was a translator of a sort, an *interpreter.* But she did not translate lifeless words into lifeless words. She translated words into human voice and quiverings of the body. In her, word materialized into flesh. How different two interpretations can be! But the beautiful, unknown theme of the translator's wife is a completely new story. Her career as an actress continues still, we know the beginning but not the end. We will come to her later, separately, when the evolution of a theater person begins to cast a spell over us, her path of cognition, her internal fire. Until then we shall wait, and gather patience, as long as her tour lasts.

—1986—

Mati Unt

TANTALUS

WHAT DO WE KNOW ABOUT THE PROGENITOR OF THE HOUSE of Atreus?

Very little.

He is standing up to his neck in water, and of course he wants to drink. Everyone knows that Tantalus loves to drink, has always loved to do so, and this now seems a particularly advantageous situation: water is lapping right beneath his nose. Let's say, in fact, that his nostrils know the scent of water, and yet this tremendous drinker remains forever without water. The gods have decreed that the water recede from his lips. We, however, stand at the shore of Tartarus, we who love water not the slightest bit less than he, stand and say: perfect! In all likelihood this pertains to a malicious delight at Tantalus' misfortune or, more precisely, to our delight that we ourselves have escaped this fate, at least this time; but if, for instance, we were asked right here and now about the significance of this situation, we would barely know how to respond. We would refer to fate or to chance, which is as good as not responding at all. It's easy to say "that passed us by" when we don't know what "that" is. We merely feel we're still free, that's all. Our moral condemnation remains bounded: we think that perhaps Tantalus is as innocent as we are, the gods have sacrificed him on a lark. The fault also lies with the gods: they have not informed us more precisely about all the circumstances. Perhaps we would wish to participate in the punishment process, to add a little droplet, so to speak—so that we might fully respect the harshness of the law, we should have adequate information about the nature of the crime. Perhaps we would want to deepen the punishment: for example, it might occur to us that Tantalus should not stand in water, but rather in urine. On the other hand, it is possible that we might intervene and demand mitigation, that, for example, we might wish every third bout of thirst eased, but not the two in between. Though I repeat: we are ill-informed. We know that punishment is chosen in accordance with the proclivities of the one being punished, it has always been done this way: he who craves freedom is decreed to jail, a bookworm is banished to the steppes, a miser's property is entirely confiscated, he who thirsts is left thirsty. However, there are too many versions of Tantalus' guilt. We do not know how to choose among them. Each day he tells us a new version. When we reach the shore, we sit down on a rusty iron bench and turn our expectant eyes toward Tantalus, standing up to his neck in water; we can be certain that we will hear a version that will topple the one heard the previous day. For instance:

(1)

"The thing is that I wished to become immortal like them. I didn't consider such a wish the least bit arrogant. I've known of enough instances in which a corresponding request has been responded to generously and has not surprised anyone at all. In principle, I am not a proponent of immortality, oh no. In fact, I don't even believe that such a thing actually exists. At least from the standpoint of us humans. We are dealing here with an abstraction that may be valid in certain instances; in other instances, however, it's not even worth discussing over coffee. The most banal solution: perhaps the gods simply live longer than we do; we have not as yet had the opportunity to verify their actual immortality. It may simply be that, in the brief amount of time mankind has existed, not a single god has yet had a chance to die. But, as has been stated, this is too simple a variant. Possibly, for them this word has a different meaning. In Finnish the word *surra* means mourning, although initially it, too, was the equivalent of dying.[1] But dying is a different thing from mourning: different individuals carry out these activities. And in conclusion: perhaps my doubts are superfluous and immortality does exist. In any case, I wanted to verify all this, and I put forth a corresponding request. The result you now see for yourselves. I want to drink, but the water recedes from my lips."

(2)

"The thing is that I'm said to have divulged the gods' secrets. Why should simple matters be referred to so harshly when they themselves are vaguely expressed? Actually, I was at a festive dinner, I heard what they were saying. They weren't speaking in secret, quite the opposite; they were speaking very openly and other people were there as well. It seemed to me that their boasting could be heard even as far as the street. They said: soon it's going to burst forth. And others responded: yes, very soon. I returned home through the nocturnal, springtime city, if that's of any interest to you. I was thinking: what's going to burst forth soon? War? Hardly, for a war had just ended. Peace? Hardly, for there was no war on just then. It was impossible to guess. Who knows about the gods' matters? Perhaps dams will burst forth, but dams between what, and in the literal or the figurative sense? Between states, rivers, people? But remaining silent was impermissible. I was the one who knew. I had tidings. And no one had forbidden me, no one had warned. Here and there in people's company I repeated that it would soon burst forth. What, I was asked in response, and of course I didn't know how to answer. Years passed and nothing burst forth. Or it did, but concealed from the human eye. Or perhaps it didn't burst forth because I had talked? Had I remained silent, would something perhaps have burst forth? Who knows. I am accused of betrayal, although I was merely the messenger. The result you now see. I want to drink, but the water recedes from my lips."

(3)

"The thing is that I'm a common thief. Not that I'm ashamed. After all, I had to live on something. Yourself you can still support somehow, but the children, and they are not few! Of course, the decision wasn't made lightheartedly. The multiplicity of meanings in language came to my aid. Why call my deed thievery? Perhaps I wanted to set justice on its feet? From where did the gods derive their privileges? What right do they have to riches that actually belong to human beings? Thinking this way, I lathed a skeleton key and chose unguarded buildings. One night I began to act. At first, everything went simply. The door opened with unexpected ease, no one was at home. I took only as much as I was able to carry. I forgot only one fact. The gods, of course, see everything. Even through walls and darkness. And this time, too. At eleven in the morning, they came for me. At first, I attempted denial, but they reminded me about every little detail, even the flower vase I had knocked over. Then I gave in. I confessed, which was in fact what they were waiting for in order to designate me a thief and hence also to punish me. They didn't inquire about the fact that I would have divided the booty among all the people. Actually, that might have precipitated additional punishment, even broader in scope. This way, however, they limited it to my individual torture and the result you now see. I want to drink, but the water recedes from my lips."

(4)

"The thing is that I wanted to put the gods to a test. I had grown weary of hearing that they know everything. I considered that story a version fabricated for the gullible. I concurred that they might in fact know something, but a great deal remains secret even from them. I had to provoke them, to embark upon a brutal experiment. Brutal, namely, because there's no sense in playing around with the gods on nickel and dime issues. I had to come up with something that would be worthy of the challenge. I admit that my plan was satanic, but in fact it couldn't have been any other way under the circumstances. I invited the gods to dinner. On the morning of that same day, I got up at dawn and slew my unsuspecting, sleeping son. I spent the entire day transforming the corpse into tasty food. In the evening, the guests arrived and sat down at the bountiful table. The gods gave the impression that I had succeeded in deceiving them. But only the impression—actually, the gods completely deceived me. When the dinner ended, I was told that they had seen through me. Actually, I wasn't even very surprised. Subconsciously I had surmised this the whole time. I was accused of cannibalism, although I had merely organized an *experimentum crucis*. The result you now see. I want to drink, but the water recedes from my lips."

(5)

"The thing is that on the preceding day I went to the field and lay down in the fresh hay. My nostrils filled with the scent of clover in bloom, my ears filled with the murmur of old birch trees. I looked straight up into the summer sky and saw there a wondrously tiny cloud, a white puff of cotton, extremely solitary in the midst of the deceptive blue behind which we know there supposedly lies the black and cold darkness of the cosmos. Without a single companion, that cloud stood directly at the zenith and didn't move even a millimeter, although a strong wind was blowing here on the fields below. The shape of the cloud didn't change either, although I lay in the grass for many hours. It was almost entirely circular, only its edges a bit thinner, scattering against the backdrop of the sky. It reminded me of—yes, but of what? I didn't know how to express it. Toward evening, the wind subsided and I got up. The shadows had grown longer, a flock was being driven home from the fields. At ten o'clock they came for me. The gods are not obliged to explain their deeds. Meekly, I accepted my fate. The result you now see. I want to drink, but the water recedes from my lips."

Yes, we see it. As if forced by invisible atmospheric pressure, the water sinks into a hollow that grows deeper the more Tantalus bends. And it is like this each day we come here to the banks of this river and listen to the sufferer's endless explanations.

One virtue of thirst is that it gives birth to copious mirages.

—1986—

■ □ ■ □ ■

Jaan Kross

HALLELUJAH

AT THAT TIME OF YEAR, IN THE MIDDLE OF DECEMBER, Iljits's small lamp on the ceiling of his felt-drying room burned the whole day long. Your see, the sixty-six-degree latitude manifested itself as darkness. The temperature did not fall that far below zero, but early on a few mornings the frozen thermometer had already registered minus forty. Only to rise, like a curse, to minus thirty-six, immediately canceling the day off that was hoped for by the worker brigades. Of course the temperature had no effect upon the underground brigades, and there had to be a fire blazing in the felt-drying oven anyway.

The drying chamber itself was a room approximately ten by twenty feet in size situated behind the barrack vestibule and between the two sections of the barrack. In each section, on double-decker bunks, lived fifty men, comprising a precise *centuria,* three-quarters of them political prisoners and one-quarter *blatnoi.*[1] The felt-drying oven was the height of a dining table, four layers of brick four and a half feet thick, inside a whitewashed rectangle with a cast-iron hearth at its center. In the air above the ribbed surface of the hearth, two rung gratings, the same size as the hearth itself, upon which items to be dried were placed, i.e., primarily felt and rag foot-wrappings, but frequently padded coats and pants as well, for all too often these got wet in the mine. The drier things dried on the upper, the damper things on the lower rack. In general, the surface of the oven was kept bare, because it was usually so hot that whatever was placed or fell there got scorched with devilish speed.

Of course, we could have had sufficient coal. After all, we were a coal-mining camp. And formally speaking we did have enough coal. The man who dried the felt had to make arrangements to have it transported to the barrack by sleigh from the large heap of coal in the northwest corner zone. The problem was that, although the amount of coal was, for all practical purposes, limitless, the State maintained stringent Socialist economic savings measures with respect to quality: the coal sent to heat the ovens was of fourth-grade quality. In other words, it was half-mixed with nonflammable stone shards, so it became a great ordeal for the felt dryers to incite this mixture to burn and to keep it burning. I only stayed afloat in this process thanks to two helpmates. Those two, Laas and Kônd, were farmers from the Ardu region at the border of Harjumaa and Järvamaa,[2] taciturn, older men who'd been mobilized into a border guard regiment of some sort at the end of the German occupation. After having deserted, they had waited for a white ship, for better days, somewhere in the wilderness and primeval forests of that region; but now they were here serving their ten-year sentences, working as stalwart carpenters, constructing barracks at the western edge of our camp, where quarters were being built for the new miners expected to arrive. The builders had a great many lumber resources available there, and by trading in various ways—from me, a morsel of my stores—in the evenings, upon returning from work, they would bring me a bundle of pine chips and splinters tied together with a string. When these had thawed in the drying room and dried for a week, they crackled and burned with a roar in the oven and slowly set the stone-mixed coal around them aglow. Especially when a few dashes of water were thrown onto the kindling coal. To this day, it is unclear to me what principle of physics caused the water to make fire burn more efficiently.

In any case, I kept the oven constantly burning, and although it was almost minus forty outside, in the room it was eighty-six degrees warm. So that, despite the disagreeable work, I couldn't deny a certain feeling of coziness in that dusky suffocation: a room to myself in any case, and the spark of imagined independence which accompanied all that; not only was there a bunk but also a table for my own use, a personal stool at the table, and on the table a few personal books and notebooks. The only problem was that there was almost no personal time at all to sit at that personal table. The stench from the drying felt and the foot-wrappings was such that, despite the many incentives to get used to it, when I was there, I still didn't dare think about the existence of my uvula. For I imagined that such a thought might trigger the vomiting reflex.

Then came a knock on the door. I threw the last dash of water in the tin cup into the oven and turned to look over my shoulder, to see who the devil that might be. For, after all, knocks were customary here, but *knocking* on the door, not at all, really. It was only the night guards who might perhaps knock if they wished to check the drying rooms; because of bandits and thieves, the doors were hooked shut from inside. A knock on the door by those night guards was a knock in only a rather figurative sense. For usually this was done with a fist and at a volume three times louder than necessary—bam-bam-bam, *"Otkroi, yob tvoyu mat'!"*[3]

I shouted: *"Da—daa—"*[4]

The door opened. Poof—a white puff of frost forced its way into the room and, out of the cloud of vapor, into the dimness illuminated by the electric bulb stepped a large man in a gray twill coat. He closed the door carefully behind him. I got up from in front of the oven. With his left hand, the man took—my God—a gray Hückel-cap off his head, thrust it under his arm, and began tearing a thin gray glove off his right hand. He then managed to uncover his right hand and extended it toward me.

"Guten Abend. Doktor Ulrich."[5]

He had a large head with an ashen cloud of hair and a large, bony, pale face, bluish from the cold, and, despite the absurdity of the moment, dead serious.

I shook the ice-cold, extended hand and said something. He said "Pardon—," and, from beneath his chin and around the top of his head, he tore a narrow strip of fabric attached to which were oval earmuffs cut from felt.

"So. Jetzt höre ich Sie absolut normal."[6]

After a two-week journey in a prison transport railway car, he had arrived yesterday from Moscow. He sat down on the stool I offered him and answered my questions in a strange, hollow, deep voice, which was, however, stifled to almost a whisper. Yes, he was a Berliner. A Ph.D. in history. Oh, his most recent place of employment? Yes, that was the issue, actually. Since 1934 he had been in the service of the Prussian Foreign Ministry. Such a ministry had continued to formally exist even during Prime Minister Göring's time. Dr. Ulrich had been the Ministry's Director of Archives, and when his superiors had finally fled to Berlin in droves, he had stayed there. For he hadn't been a Nazi, but rather a historian, and he was responsible for the treasures entrusted to him. Included among those treasures were—good God—for instance, the thirty years of Bismarck's correspondence. So Dr. Ulrich had considered it his self-evident duty to remain there in the ruins of the capital city. To remain there and hand over to the victors his archive keys to the cellar door of that building, which had been shelled to a rubble heap. But the victors hadn't stopped at the keys; they had also taken along the one who relinquished the keys.

In Butôrka (I think it was there), the doctor had probably spent over two years. Before, somewhere in a corridor, his fifteen-year sentence had been read out to him from a slip of paper, and he'd been sent back to his cell. Other Germans, considered important enough, had also been held there. Including Major Linge, referred to even in our printed word. Regarding the latter, Dr. Ulrich said (on the third or fourth evening, as he was drinking tea at my place in the felt-drying room) that Linge had been the son of a Bavarian bartender who, in his own house, had concealed Hitler from the police of the Weimar Republic. For this, Hitler had pledged to make a great man of the bartender's son, then probably a ten-year-old chubby lad. Hitler had, in fact, later taken the boy into his closest circle, but he hadn't become a great man. Doctor Ulrich said the boy had plenty of gray matter. The boy had nevertheless advanced to the rank of major, and that of the Führer's valet. In his position as valet, over the years Linge had received under his command, in its entirety, the remnants of the Führer's underwear, shirts, handkerchiefs, and socks. The Führer had usually discarded these effects after a single wearing. Suspenders he hadn't cast away quite so readily, perhaps, but from time to time these, too, were among the items discarded for Linge's use. The valet had gathered his master's effects together and sold them; the further the war had progressed, the better the price he received, and he himself wore only the choicest items.

And so, a quarter of an hour later and even paler than he had already been for a long time, with his thoughts even more distant than usual, Doctor Ulrich had returned to his cell with his sentence of fifteen years.

His fellow German inmates, five or six men, five or six gentlemen as we would again say now, had each reacted to Ulrich's fifteen years in his own manner. The Volkswagen director had laughed and said: "Normal." The mining direc- tor from Sudentenland, an old Henleiner,[7] had gloated: "So ultimately what good did it do you to avoid the party for twelve years?!" One of the gentlemen from the *Reichskunst-*

kammer had said: "Of course. Göring's corpse weighed only ninety kilos in Nuremburg. Too little, apparently, to ransom all his underlings." And so forth. No one had said what most of them were actually thinking: What else could you expect from those Russian brutes? Major Linge was probably the most active among them.

"Doctor, experience has shown that after the sentence has been decreed, said prisoner is removed from here in short order. Shouldn't you take this into account?" he asked.

The doctor had muttered impassively, almost cheerfully: "Well, if it's to be away, then it's away. We'll walk then, I guess."

The others, those not initially affected by the sentence, had been more practical. The *Kunstkammer* man had felt boots. And the Volkswagen director, a knife made out of a piece of tin. From the top of each felt boot, at the hollow of the knee, they had cut two ovals the size of porridge spoons to protect the doctor's ears.

"Yes, yes, Doctor. Here in Moscow it's already fourteen degrees. Up north it's bound to be four."

All their belts and suspenders had been removed when they were brought here. And none of their stomachs had expanded, but had shriveled instead. So the doctor's pants, too, were held up only by dint of a forbidden piece of string that served as a substitute for a belt. Up to this point, however, given the restricted space for movement in the cell, lack of garters had been no concern.

Now Linge said, "Doctor, you cannot go like this—taking manners into account as well as the cold— with your socks sliding down to your ankles. Wait. Amazingly enough, I still have my garters. Take them and pull up your socks."

He had sat down in a corner not visible through the peephole and pulled off his brown silk garters.

"Take them. And wear them—with honor."

Actually, to this day I don't know why he sacrificed his garters. It's unlikely that this was out of friendship for the doctor. More likely, perhaps, it was the knowledge that sooner or later, here in jail, he, Linge, would find himself without them, and at the next search most likely. Or perhaps it was a fantasy that, by offering this last relic, he could buy from fate a favor of some sort, his life perhaps.

The doctor extended his hand and muttered: "Oh—I thank—"

And Linge added: "For these belonged to the Führer himself!"

I imagine for an instant—for a significant instant—Doctor Ulrich's hand stopped in midair. But then, rationalist that he was, he accepted the garters. Since he had already thanked the major for the garters when they had been a nondescript item, there had been no need for him to add anything to these thanks due to the additional information.

That same night he'd been ordered out of the chamber with a "s vestsami," that is, with a gray canvas bag containing a change of underwear half-washed in the sauna, and, in a black raven, he'd been conveyed through a Moscow unknown to him, to a railway station unknown to him, on his way to an even greater unknown.

Now he sat here in my drying chamber, raised the cuffs of his pants made of dark gray prison cloth, stuck his finger through the garter, and let it snap against the leg of his long, pale gray underwear.

"Here they are now. The Führer's own."

From the table, he took the teacup which he had sipped empty, placed its edge to his lower lip and—how to express it?—whispered-mumbled-boasted with the aid of the cup's resonant quality, *"Ich sage euch: wenn die Plutokrraten und die Juden mich dazu zwinngn marrschierrn wirr um das deutsch Blut und den deutschen Boden zu schützen—bis ans Ende drr Welt,"*[8] so harmoniously that, at least according to my past impressions from listening to the radio, it was possible to squeeze my eyes shut (keeping my nose shut as well, of course) and imagine myself physically in a certain historic Munich beer hall.

I said, laughing, "What's your problem, Doctor? Someday you'll sell your garters for a hundred thousand dollars. There are certain to be crazy Americans who'll pay that."

The garters were stolen from him within two weeks. He laughed at his one hundred thousand-dollar loss in a manner completely un-Germanlike and told me the following story.

He'd been living in Berlin; his archive was located there, too. He'd had a three-room bachelor apartment one hundred and fifty feet from the northern edge of Tiergarten, three or four girlfriends, as I understood it, just intimate enough and distant enough to preserve the independence he felt he needed from them. And an array of selected friends. Selected, apparently, based upon on the principles that permitted and restricted friendships in Nazi Germany. In other words, first of all, trustworthiness, and, second in importance, areas of mutual interest. Of primary interest to the doctor were German history and, perhaps even more so, music. Nineteenth-century German history and eighteenth-century music. Especially the early eighteenth century. And even more specifically, Handel. On the subject of Handel, his most fruitful contact was a Swede with whom he'd become acquainted a few months before the war while leaving Potsdam's Garnison Cathedral after a Handel concert. Mr. Palmquist had turned out to be the new cultural attaché at the Swedish consulate.

They had begun a familial acquaintanceship. Doctor Ulrich had visited Mr. Palmquist and his wife at their apartment in the Swedish consulate building. The attaché, together with his wife, had repeatedly visited the doctor at Tiergarten. For the Swede and his wife, these visits had posed no danger whatsoever. But Doctor Ulrich had to take into account that for him they might not be so entirely harmless. Because Germans who associated with foreigners, moreover diplomats, and particularly the diplomats of such primarily British-minded countries like Sweden, might be watched by the Gestapo. And the Gestapo was, of course, watching. But the feeling of human fellowship between the two apparently rather isolated individuals had ignored such likelihoods, and perhaps, to a certain extent, acted with bravado against such possibilities. I didn't know Palmquist, of course, but in my opinion a certain amount of bravado on the doctor's part would indeed have been believable. In any case, I refrained from steering our conversation to matters that might have indicated curiosity about whether the doctor had or had not felt a secret affinity for Mrs. Palmquist. All the more so because the attaché had sent his wife back to the security of Stockholm quite soon after the war had broken out and the bombing of Berlin had begun. But the men's concert attendance had not diminished one iota, nor their music-making, sometimes on Palmquist's Steinway, sometimes on the doctor's surprisingly powerful home organ, nor their passion for some of the trumpet parts in Handel's "Water Music," for instance.

The war continued and the problems of wartime Germany deepened. The nights spent cowering in shelters became more and more frequent, and, consequently, so did the nervous days spent with half-somnolent, stinging eyes. The disparity between the food on the tables of the two friends also became more marked. While Mr. Palmquist ate delicacies brought in by means of the consulate's special postal system (with greater and greater frequency, he tucked these into his briefcase for the doctor), the doctor, inept as he was at practical matters, more and more often ate sawdust-filled bread and marmalade made with saccharine as his basic staple. The air raids grew incessantly more frenzied, the number of ruins continually increased, and there were no concerts any longer. Then, in March 1944, came Mr. Palmquist's fiftieth birthday.

The doctor wanted to observe this occasion in a fitting manner. His purpose was not, of course, to prove to the Swede that Great Germany still afforded great opportunities. Right from the start, the doctor eschewed any positive impression that Great Germany might have bestowed upon a foreigner. Not like an overzealous exposé artist, perhaps, but more like an honest citizen, painfully, nervously, from the beginning he'd directed the Swede's attention to the inhumanity of Nazism. So everything between him and the Swede had been made clear in this regard. In both their opinions, this country, with its present government and leaders, was the embodiment of madness and already irrevocably ablaze with the apocalyptic fires of Ragnarök. As for Palmquist's birthday, the doctor had simply wanted to express his personal esteem for his friend on the occasion of his jubilee, and, despite the circumstances, he still wanted to do so in a rather original way. But opportunities for originality no longer existed. Until recently, through friendships in the back rooms and basements of art galleries and antiquarian bookshops, you could still find something degenerate and forbidden, in other words, something valuable. But no more. For stores had now either been evacuated, simply closed down, or, even more simply, bombed into rubble heaps. To tell the truth, even under the best circumstances the items until recently available in stores would not have measured up to the standards of originality sought by the doctor. His gift had to be something personal and unique.

Then, amidst the eternal sleeplessness brought on by nocturnal raids and the continual flagellation of idiotic regulations (Evacuate the archive within twenty-four hours! Stay in place! Await instructions! Mine and detonate, as soon as. . . . Risk your life to safeguard every scrap of paper!)—nevertheless, amidst all these regulations that nullified each other and amidst the ceaseless bomb scares, the doctor had not lost his capacity to turn up the corner of his mouth as he imagined small and quite individual ideas for celebrating Palmquist's birthday. Until it finally seemed that he now had the best of these in hand.

Mr. Palmquist had a car. Apparently, concealed somewhere within his straightforward but measured, rather cool nature, he was also a bit of a snob. And why shouldn't he have been allowed a bit of that in his own discreet manner? Perhaps, against the inconsolable backdrop of Berlin at that time, he'd simply given the doctor that impression once in a while. In any case, Palmquist's car was spanking new, with two uncomfortable backseats, but basically a bright red two-seater, a very sporty Mercedes. For 1944 Berlin, this was a provocatively lustrous item. With his diplomatic plates, Palmquist drove it about the rubble-choked streets of the capital unhindered even by police warnings.

So Mr. Attaché had a car. But the doctor—he wasn't at all a wealthy man, although he did own and still did have in his possession his family's table silver, handed down for many generations: quite a few kilos of dishes, knives, forks, and spoons, originally colorful, but now with monograms growing more and more deplorable upon stolid, helplessly clumsy, absurd stems. . . . In addition to this, the doctor had the old gentleman, Jakob Klemm.

This same Uncle Klemm was either Ulrich's relative or a friend, I don't even know. He was growing continually thinner like everyone else, but more and more immaculately groomed, for there were fewer and fewer of those over seventy like him. In any case, he apparently belonged to the Ulrich family's previous generation of artisan-craftsmen: he was a bit of an organ builder, a bit of a mechanic, a bit of an inventor. He was without doubt a clever fellow, a *Bastler* (which has no fair equivalent in Estonian).[9] Before the war he'd had a tiny one- or two-man workshop which he had liquidated upon retiring, but he hadn't had the heart to throw its wares away. Now all those things were in a basement room beneath his apartment, packed and stacked into a pile with a German's love of order. At a time when the populace lived primarily in their basements, Uncle Klemm had been able to use that room for such a purpose thanks only to the propitious fact that the house, located somewhere in a suburb near Jungfernheide, had been only two stories high and the inserted ceilings were too flimsy to serve as bomb shelters. There in that basement, during February's massive bombing raids and in between them, the doctor and Mr. Klemm brought the doctor's idea to life. That is to say, the doctor actually provided only the idea. Plus the silver, of course. And a rather indistinct sketch depicting what seemed to be a slender goblet with a stem that, for some reason, was twisted.

Before Mr. Klemm had set about cutting strips of sheet copper in his basement, searching for wires, molding porcelain clay, and melting silver, the doctor had invited him over to his place in Tiergarten. While the doctor himself had been improvising on the organ in the salon with Mr. Palmquist, Mr. Palmquist's bright red Mercedes had stood in front of the building's courtyard gate in the moonlight— on one side stood the doctor's still-unscathed house; on the opposite side, behind the leafless park trees, stood a row of crumbled facades like absurd, dark gray theater scenery, blue-pocked with moon rays. At that time, Mr. Klemm had made all the necessary measurements at the left end of the car's dashboard with precision. Within a week, the gadget ordered by the doctor had been completed. It had also been tested in the basement at Jungfernheide.

The doctor sipped tea from a large tin cup, the same one whose overtones he used to mock Hitler's speeches, as he loved to do, and he said:

"But on his birthday, on the sixth of March, Palmquist came over to my place. As we had agreed. He parked his car at the back door of the building as always and came upstairs with two briefcases. Two, on the occasion of his birthday. I went into the kitchen and said to Mr. Klemm: Now. And he went rustling down the back stairs with his tool box. Well,

Palmquist opened his briefcase in the dining room. In one, two bottles of Mumm. In the other—you know, I've forgotten what. We sat, listened, wasn't a siren going to sound? It didn't. We drank our champagne, we ate. We talked—about music, art, women, heaven and earth. As if, behind the cover of darkness, a world still existed. I put on a few records. Then Handel's 'Messiah.' By the way, as for Handel, we enjoyed him doubly at that time. Both of us, I believe, but I without a doubt. First of all, because he is truly unique. Perhaps greater than Bach in his clarity and brightness. All right, this can be argued endlessly. But, secondly, because he really wasn't, well, a Mahler or Chopin, some sort of Frenchman or Pole or Jew, who, if you listened to him, you might be summoned over to the military police the next day. Rather, he was as purely German as Wagner himself. And a much greater German. As a composer, isn't that so? Yet, most diabolically, considered by the English to be the greatest English composer. And a subject of English kings for forty years! And buried in line with those kings in Westminster Abbey! And in England, he is still so very much theirs that—I've seen this in London's Covent Garden with my own eyes: when it came time for the Hallelujah Chorus of this very same 'Messiah,' two thousand people stood up in the hall and listened, standing until the end. In other words, I put on the 'Messiah' recording and we listened to the Hallelujah Chorus standing up. Then I stopped the record player, switched off the lamps, and looked into the yard through the covering of darkness. Mr. Klemm had disappeared from the vicinity of the car, and his work had been completed. To the extent this was discernible in the moonlight.

"I said to Palmquist, 'Come. I want to give you your birthday present.'

"'Ohoo? And what is that?' There was a childish air in Palmquist's gray eyes, slightly bloodshot from alcohol, and it seemed to me that this was not simply due to the cognac we had sipped after the Mumm, but rather from sheer curiosity. We went into the vestibule, I motioned for him to take his coat, and I took my own from the rack. It seemed to me that we might need our coats. We walked down the stairs and stepped into the courtyard. He noticed the horn on the car's shiny red side instantly, of course.

"'Oh! It's fabulous there! You know, it's shaped like a baroque organ pipe. Only, what does it sound like?'

"I understood his apprehension about the horn's sound. It was so great, in fact, that he didn't think to thank me.

"'Go sit down and try it out.'

"He sat down at the steering wheel and I beside him. He immediately caught sight of the silver knob Mr. Klemm had positioned on the dashboard.

"'Give a signal.'

"He pressed the knob.

"HAL-LE-LU-JAH! HAL-LE-LU-JAH! the horn, powered by the car battery, called out amongst the bare trees, the moonlight shadows, the ruins, and the walls of the buildings still standing whole. Silvery. Clear. Victorious. Palmquist squinted his eyes in astonishment and shook my hand enthusiastically.

"'I thank you! This is magnificent! That bar, precisely. That one . . . '

"But to the ears of the building's residents, long since on edge, naturally the sound of the horn was too loud in the stillness of that rare night. So that many windows were thrust open:

"'*Was is da los?!' 'Donnerwetter, schon wieder Fliegeralarm?' 'Wieder die verdammten Tommies?!' 'Oder doch nicht?'*[10]

"'Let's drive away!' said Palmquist. He started the car and we sped out of the yard.

"And we raced through the city. I don't remember exactly how it all went," said the doctor. "You know, in the March night, with the temperature a few degrees below freezing, the car's artificial leather roof was drawn shut. It was one of those cars sometimes open, sometimes closed. But we rolled down the windows. So the wind would howl around our ears. And the more it howled, the more the champagne and the cognac went to our heads. To mine, at any rate. The ruins, the trees, the buildings, the ludicrously straight heaps of rubble beside the highway, the squads of rubble cleaners, the police, all flew past. Some Schupos[11] tried to stop us, but seeing our license plate number, they jumped back. And, every three hundred feet, Palmquist sounded the horn: HAL-LE-LU-JAH! HAL-LE-LU-JAH! That gave us hellish joy. You understand, it was inspirational and hooliganistic—the fact that it was in that rhythm."

The doctor raised the empty teacup to his lips and hallelujahed into it. The cup resonated at three times the volume, so that the foot-wrappings hanging from the wooden racks quivered: HAL-LE-LU-JAH!

"For concealed in that rhythm," continued the doctor, "was glorification of God, but God was persona non grata in Great Germany. To the extent that he was not the God of the State Church, wearing high boots and bearing an iron cross, but rather Handel's omnipresent and omnivisaged Lord. The main thing—inspirational and hooliganistic— was the fact that the word behind our horn's call—hallelujah—praise Jehovah, right?—was elusively and outrageously Hebrew . . . "

The doctor continued: "I scarcely recall how I got home that time. Palmquist helped me up the stairs, covered me with a blanket on the sofa, put the 'Messiah' on quietly, and tiptoed out. Well, I slept soundly—to the extent that this was possible through my dreams, and with an ear listening to the Hallelujah Chorus air-raid siren. As for Palmquist, well, thereafter he drove about Berlin cheerfully with his car horn. As cheerfully as the circumstances permitted. In other words, more feverishly than cheerfully. For the air raids grew more and more ghastly, the terror more and more horrible. Especially after the twentieth of July. But now I've rushed ahead. I wanted to say that the food ration cards now yielded less and less margarine, and the bread contained more and more sawdust. But naturally this didn't affect Palmquist. During the latter half of March he came to visit me again. The building where I lived was still standing, but it had been severely shaken by the most recent air raids. There was a bomb pit where Palmquist usually parked his car. The windows were covered with plywood and the electricity hadn't yet been repaired, so candles burned temporarily in the rooms. It wasn't his birthday this time, so he came up with a single briefcase. But it was noticeably and, I felt, ominously hefty. With two bottles of Mumm, it turned out.

"'Doctor, I came to bid you farewell. Damned sorry, but there's nothing to be done. I've been assigned to our embassy in Moscow. I'm flying to Stockholm tomorrow and leaving from there in about a week.'"

The doctor continued: "Well, that was quite a gloomy evening. The Mumm didn't go to our heads. When the bottles had been emptied, the air raid alert began. So we cowered in the shelter across the street until one o'clock and, amid the jostling crowd, said farewell at the shelter door as the final siren still pierced."

The doctor went on: "I haven't seen him since that night. After his departure everything that happened, happened. The strangulation which we as a nation had earned, the physical one, externally, and the moral one, internally, continued for yet another year. Until the Russian artillery advanced close enough to fire upon our ruins. Those which the British-American bombs further shattered each night. Until the Russian tanks arrived. And I was cashed in together with my keys. But all this is already known to you. Up to my black raven ride."

It was true. The doctor's more recent little adventures, up to the time he arrived at Inta, were known to me. He'd visited me almost every other night during his three weeks here and, sitting beside his tea mug, had also told me his Butôrka tales. I'd followed his swift physical deterioration with concern. He'd chanced into an above-ground, auxiliary brigade working at the mine's sawmill, unloading boards from flat cars that had arrived from forest regions in the south. So these could be sawed into support props for mine shafts.

That was hard work, at times even dangerous work. If it was done in the slipshod, hasty manner characteristic of labor camp work and necessitated by the frequent −40-degree temperatures. Of course the men made great haste to return to the warming hut *bōstro-bōstro-bōstro*,[12] for there, within the shelter of the board walls, among a heap of men reeking of makhorka smoke,[13] there was at least shelter from the wind and a spark of warmth near the iron stove. This work could prove particularly dangerous for someone (like the doctor, it was said) who constantly got in others' way because of his pedantry. The doctor was a bohemian, true enough, but namely a German bohemian. And, in that peculiar work at the camp, his innate pedantry grew irksomely apparent: when taking logs off the train, he attempted to thrust his own and his partner's logs as precisely parallel to those of the other laborers as possible. He would try, sometimes by pulling foolishly and wasting energy, to shift a pile of eighteen-foot-long logs so that their ends would form as smooth a surface as possible. But the flat cars often arrived with the frozen logs in clumps, so it became necessary, on icy, slippery felt soles, to climb up and hew the boards loose with a crowbar. When the support pegs that held the logs together in a load six feet high, two pegs on a side, were torn out of their clamps, sometimes by pounding a turgidly frozen peg with a large hammer, the frozen logs could even roll onto the legs of the men standing there below—and cut off the legs of the very same men who had climbed onto the platform. In order to jump down from above and avoid the logs below, you had to be nimble. A few times, his co-workers in the brigade had seized the absent-minded doctor by the hand or the collar and pulled him from the path of onrolling logs—pulled him aside, *"yoban-nyi fashist,"*[14] from the certainty of a broken leg. *"Yobannyi fashist,"*[15] at least in the vernacular of this third of the brigade, characterized by *blatnois*. In other words, the doctor was constantly getting in the others' way, and he didn't help them fill their damned quota; instead he hindered this. As a consequence, the man who allotted bread threw him the most leathery pieces and the brigadier consistently left him without *zapekanka*.[16] Consequently, given the sparse diet allotted to him in any case, within three weeks he was already quite transparently yellowish-gray, although at first glance he still appeared to be a sizable man because of his sturdy build. It seemed to me that at night, when he stepped in to see me, and, in a high-pitched eunuch's voice rumored to be that of someone named Walter Ulbricht,[17] he would squeak, mocking: *"Habe die Ehre, Genossen Pflizstierfeltrock-ner 'nen guten Arbeitstagsabend zu wüschen!"*[18]—it seemed to me each time that his knees were actually quaking from the weakness that was beginning to overpower him. At the same time, his spiritual energy actually seemed to grow. His anecdotes seemed more polished all the time. There were more and more surprising points in his personal tales. And their manner of presentation—including many different kinds of citations—constantly ranged from the deepest rumble to a more complex stage whisper.

By the way, like many people removed from the issue, I have always been interested in the question of where the boundary between normality and abnormality actually lies. Which kinds of deviations from normal deportment—bolting of the fancy, for example—can still be deemed normal and which cannot, anymore? To what extent and how is this related to the overall psychological context of society? Included among the four majors offered by our law faculty, bookkeeping and whatever else they were, I had unhesitatingly chosen forensic psychiatry. But actually, within the comfort of the relatively superficial, normal circumstances of my youth, I had the opportunity, in those environs, to experience either absolutely normal people or truly mad ones. A small percentage of the latter exist in the world. Only in the depressive, high-pressure cells of prisons and labor camps did the surprising complexity of the intermediate zone between normalcy and madness begin to dawn on me. But the question of the zone between normalcy and madness became all the more complicated. Apparently, in my thoughts, I had already also linked Doctor Ulrich to this question. Because of his absentminded, smiling calm. And because of his unexpectedly intense, almost theatrical story bursts, which erupted from this calm with greater and greater frequency. In any case, his odd sentence or, actually, the odd tone of it caught my attention for some reason: "But all this is already known to you. *Up to my black raven ride . . .* "[19]

So I said, not asking anything directly, "That must have been a singular journey for you."

"Oh, yes," said the doctor in a whisper. "First of all, because it became clear to me how currish human beings actually are. In other words, how currish I myself am. For you know, as I was being escorted across the jail courtyard toward the black raven—around me, four walls of barred windows, up above, a sky with an urban glow, and before me, ten or fifteen thousand kilometers—Novaya Zemlya, Karganda, Magadan, whatever all those places are—then I felt that the same stuffy cell which I had been cast out of, no matter how disgusting it had been, had nevertheless been a protected place. A homey place. Compared to the total unknown into which I was now traveling. It was an absolutely currish feeling. With not the slightest hunger for gnosis, not the slightest twinge of Faust, as I would have wished. And then—that vehicle in which I had to ride: just like a black coffin. A board hut built upon a Jeep or a Willis. In the front, a windshield, of course, and door windows. But halved in the middle by a traverse wall, so the driver and his companion were separated from the passenger in back. Inside the cargo section, a sheet-metal lining without even the smallest slit. And as I said: the entire vehicle, completely black, inside and out. My Germans have told me that here in this camp, as on the outside, prisoners are supposedly transported for interrogations, etc.—from one point in the labor camp to another or to headquarters—in a closed truck. But in a gray one, at least. And they say that on its gray sides, painted in white lettering, is KHLEB.[20] It should be LYUDI,[21] but it is KHLEB. All right, that's erroneous—nevertheless, it's still information. But over there—absolutely no information whatsoever. Not even a lie. Inside and out—a darkroom. All right: when I had climbed inside and the back wall door had been shut—an iron bar fell after it with a clatter—inside, there was total darkness. I stood there, hunched over because of the low ceiling, and I asked just in case: *'Jemand da?'*[22] and then also, as well as I was able: *'Člověk jest?'*[23] But there was no one. Groping, I found a bench alongside the wall; I sat down and held onto the edge of the bench, so that I wouldn't fall when the raven took off. Then we rode. And I listened. With particular acuteness, because of the total darkness.

"Frozen snow on the cobblestones. Brakes. The sound of high military boots. A door window is rolled down. The guard outside checks papers which the person sitting beside the driver has in his hand. Silently, of course. So the mortal enemy whom they are transporting will not find out that which he is not intended to know. The iron gates creak open and clatter against the wall, on both sides. Again, the crunch of frozen snow beneath truck wheels. Once again, brakes. Another document check, probably. On the street in front of the jail now, it seems, based on the motor's drone. Then, motion on the cobblestones and snow again. Then, in the clumps of ice, asphalt. Then, growing denser and denser, urban sounds. Some cars driving in front of the raven, some behind. Some toward it, some past. The procession decelerates, accelerates. Idiotically, I think, as if I weren't fifty, but rather fifteen: if a heavy truck were to drive down an unlit street—and there should be quite of few of those in Moscow—and smash our driver's cab, if it were to crash into us from the side so that the driver and his partner—damn it, let's say didn't get killed, but lost consciousness, and the partition behind them shattered and the sheet-metal lining of my rook tore, and the tear were large enough, and I had a minute, a minute's time, before the people and the militia ran to the spot, a minute's time to step over the two unconscious men and slip through the shattered windshield or out the door, broken at its hinges, a minute's time to step out onto the street and get free—what should I do then? And I understand—even though in the depths of my consciousness I'm fleeing triumphantly through unknown yards and portals and arcades—I understand: if something like that were to happen, in other words if there were such an accident, I should stay beside the black raven and call for help. That would be more than currish, but only right.

"I shake myself free of that depressing vision—if the word 'free' can be used at all in my black coffin—and again I hear, hear the city sounds again with satanic sharpness.

"Apparently my coffin is now riding down a large, more or less direct street. Right there we brake; I don't know whether that's for traffic lights or a traffic cop's signal. I hear other cars braking alongside the raven and behind it, then the cross-street traffic whizzes past us. There isn't the abundance of cars driving here that there doubtless would be in London or Paris two years after the war. Or that there would also be driving around Berlin, if Berlin still existed. Nevertheless, this is a large, and because of its unfamiliarity, a terrifyingly large city—"

The doctor had risen, and he said, "Then we brake at the next intersection. Quite near the sidewalk. I hear crunching footsteps in the snow. A snatch of someone's voice. Someone's coughing. Then the whiz of cross-street traffic begins.

I listen: snow crunches against the wheels; wheels scatter sand against the sides of other cars; some cars honk in warning. Then—believe it or not—then there's a car driving in that flux, but faster, at some distance, crosswise in front of the raven, and it signals

HAL-LE-LU-JAH

HAL-LE-LU-JAH

HAL-LE-LU-JAH

Three times. No more. But no less, either. Well, of course, I don't have to explain to you how I felt.

"Then the raven rode on.

"That's all.

"Now I'm here. And I bid you good night. In order to roll my precious logs with a flourish tomorrow."

He stepped over to the drying-room door, waved to me, and exited. Right then I decided that I would speak to the doctor about him, that same Doctor Kačanauskas who had assisted me and about whose praiseworthy help I've written somewhere.

In the days following, Doctor Ulrich did not come to visit me. Later I met Kačanauskas in the library and spoke with him about the doctor. He recalled the German immediately.

"Yes, I do indeed know. That archive director or whatever. From the eleventh barrack. He was at the clinic a few days ago. A cold. Well, yes, quite exhausted too. But he isn't the only one. He'll rest four to five days and be on his feet again. If he doesn't get pneumonia."

I asked whether Kačanauskas couldn't admit him to the hospital for a while. And he did admit the doctor. I heard that there the doctor had recovered from his cold without getting pneumonia. That he'd taken tranquilizers of some sort and been able to sleep like a human being again. Before that he'd been terribly plagued with insomnia, but he hadn't mentioned that to me. So Doctor Kačanauskas let him revive in the hospital for a few days. And he did even more: when it came time to sign him out (to stay in the hospital for more than two weeks he would either have to be at death's door or the doctor's personal friend), Doctor Kačanauskas had called over the head cook and ordered him to take the German on as a kitchen helper for a while. Recovering patients were sent there from time to time.

"He's a sensible man. Let him slip a morsel or two into his mouth in the kitchen and gain strength for a month or two."

Well, I didn't consider myself a close enough friend of Doctor Ulrich's to go searching for him during the time when, according to Kačanauskas, he had been working in the cafeteria. I was certain that the doctor-gentleman would appear sooner or later. Would knock on the drying-room door, I imagined, and, lest he be taken for someone else, he'd whistle at the door—HAL-LE-LU-JAH!—and walk in. But when he hadn't appeared, and when I met Kačanauskas in the library again, I asked how things were going with our kitchen helper.

Kačanauskas said, "I asked the head cook the same thing the day before yesterday. And he said: 'I threw him out.'"

"Why?!" I asked Kačanauskas in surprise, just as he himself had asked the cook.

And the cook had explained, "I assigned him to cut cheese for the brigades. Those twenty-gram bits that are included with supper for those who've filled the quota."

"Well?"

"I happened to look through the door slit at how he was cutting them—"

"Too slowly?"

"He could have been faster, that's clear. Nevertheless, I tolerated his clumsiness. But you know, I peered for a quarter of an hour. During that time he cut a couple hundred bits. Then I got myself a stool and sat down and peered some more. An hour. He cut over a thousand slices—damn it—"

"What happened then?!"

"Well, can you believe it, over a thousand pieces! But he didn't stick even a single one into his mouth! Then I called him into the kitchen and said: 'Hand over your apron and from tomorrow on I don't want see you here anymore!'"

In front of Doctor Kačanauskas, the head cook, a man from a restaurant in Pyatigorsk or Makhachkala, with a white cap, whiskers, a double chin, a man who'd probably been arrested for stealing butter, had put his hands on his hips and said, "But, Doctor, we can't give a place meant for someone recovering to that *yoban* . . . "[24] But he had looked straight at Doctor Kačanauskas, and at the last moment had altered his words just in case and said sparingly, " . . . to keep it for that idiot when there are hundreds who want to recuperate. If not thousands . . . "

The next morning, Doctor Ulrich had been shoved into the convict transport before Kačanauskas had a chance to do a thing. And I've never heard any more about him, i.e., Doctor Ulrich, or his Palmquist, or their hallelujah-car since.

—1990—

THE DAY HIS EYES
ARE OPENED

AN ORDINARY TARTU TRAIN FROM THE LATE FIFTIES IN Tallinn's Baltic Station on a September morning. In the new, or actually the old Baltic Station, rebuilt from wartime ruins of the original limestone structure.

The train is an ordinary six-car milk train. The kind that halts at every whistle-stop for two minutes, and at every official station for five or ten, taking an hour and a half longer to get to Tartu than the Pihkva, Moscow, or Riga trains do. So it is actually incomprehensible why so many people use it besides those traveling to the whistle-stops. If you don't assume they do so because the ticket is in fact some twenty kopecks cheaper. No doubt, there are those who don't weigh or very strictly calculate the half-hours spent on a train, even among people who wish to arrive at Tartu at a very precise hour.

For a long time now, the cars have not been those niggardly, toy car–like rattletraps, those spoils of war used for a while after its end—with their wheels like duck's feet on lengthened axles to fit the gauge of our Eastern European tracks. From either side of any of those cars, you stepped directly out into the blazing sunlight or the rain or the cold, whatever the weather happened to be just then. No, no, the cars have long been our own old, normal, prewar third-class ones. The brown linoleum floor still smelling of floormop mustiness and freshness; under your bottom, wood-hard, worn, brown oil-colored benches; as a headrest for the scruff of your neck, stalwart old plywood rubbed to a gloss. And, leaning on the bench back supports, foreheads, napes of necks, sports caps, slouch hats, women's hats, head scarves, berets, and many kinds of bare heads. Not that many passengers, actually. Besides me, in the row where I've taken a seat by the window, only one freckled boy who got off at Aruküla, I think, and whom I do not recall, and, at the window directly opposite me, that woman.

About sixty, with ash-blond, gray-peppered hair, high-cheekboned, blue-eyed, every once in a while she looks just like a mixture of an Estonian farm woman and an Indian woman. Her glance childlike: swift in touching yours, yet demanding. As it falls, I get the feeling that I may have met her somewhere before and that I will finally recall and recognize her. So I prefer to open the morning's *People's Voice,* to become absorbed in Nikita Sergeyevich's[1] most recent speech about cultivating corn, and, hidden in the shadow of the newspaper, to remain sheltered from all possible social obligations.

A minute before the train takes off, yet another passenger enters the car. A tall, thin man about forty-five, wearing a suit too light a shade of gray for September. The deeply lined, tanned face beneath his forehead, with its deeply receding hairline, is such that, if you were to divide all of humanity by likeness into two theatrical masks, you would say: tragic rather than comic, but with an undeniable dash of inner humor. The man stops at the aisle between our benches, eyes the woman opposite me, and suddenly makes a small, slightly hesitant, but nevertheless visible bow of recognition and greeting. He even seems to blush a bit beneath his suntan. Then, in the half-articulated mumble characteristic of such circumstances, he asks whether the empty place next to me is empty, and, upon my nod, he takes a seat.

The train has taken off. Lilleküla's roofs of cardboard and tin, moist with the gray morning dampness, slide past windows tearstained with fog. I glance from behind the newspaper and make my next attempt to ascertain the human and social characteristics of my two neighbors. In all likelihood, the woman can be categorized as *housewife*. A housewife not so much from an urban home as from a home in the suburbs or a village, a home with a small garden and an apple orchard somewhere near the village meeting house and the library. The woman's inexpensive but new, clean, gray cloth shoes as well as her inexpensive but barely worn bluish-gray autumn coat, plus her blue silk headscarf, beneath the edge of which grayish hair is visible on her weather-beaten cheekbones, all indicate as much. Yet this conjecture is called into doubt by the unpretentious, matter-of-fact air of authority and presence one intuits from the woman's bearing, a trait or aura that is, it seems, expressed with greater ease and more self-evidently by women involved in public or professional activity than by men.

I'm unable to say anything about the man. Perhaps only that he certainly isn't a bureaucrat. He gives the impression of being an intelligent, nervous person who discerns everything. A person whose nature it is to be uncertain about his vulnerable freedom, and because of this uncertainty, he is inconstant. In fact, I'm unable to describe him more concretely than to say that he must be an artist of some sort. Not professionally, perhaps, but spiritually. And the latter can always be argued if, for example, this enigma should enigmatically prove to be an accountant for, say, "Salvage" in his professional life.[2] And the use of "artistic soul" to explain essence and appearance is all the more relevant at the time our story takes place. For, as far as I can recall, the end of the fifties was a time when there were no artists and poets to be found among salvage workers any longer, and poets employed as night guards and boiler operators had not yet come into vogue.[3]

My neighbor turns to look out the window. To do so he must look directly past my nose. He has very bright gray eyes and his glance, directed toward the window, seems a bit spasmodic. Then the woman opposite me extends her hand, which has been drawn into her coat sleeve until now because of the cold. She has a massive, gold wedding ring on her finger, and her hand, despite the care with which it has been washed, betrays an autumn of garden work. She extends her hand and touches my neighbor's knee, "Pardon me, young man—tell me, where do we know each other from?"

She has a surprisingly pure and resonant, but even more surprisingly loud voice. So deep an alto that her question must be audible across many rows of benches.

My neighbor turns toward the inquirer politely, looks, smiling, and blushes again: "Well I was Comrade—Mr.—your husband's student. At Varbola High School. Mr. Kaasik was my principal. He taught us Estonian. And you were—"

Mrs. Kaasik—for that is who she must be—raises the palm of her hand into the air toward her conversation partner; she smiles and moves her hand from left to right, which apparently means: stop your talk. This is in fact how my neighbor interprets Mrs. Kaasik's motion, and, either blushing anew or continuing to blush, he remains silent. His expression is filled with questions quelled only by his upbringing and the circumstances: But why then are you asking in a public place if your don't want me to mention contacts and names audibly . . . ?!

But right then, in a tone just as audible, Mrs. Kaasik explains the situation, "My dear young man—unfortunately my hearing is poor. But let's try to remedy the situation. Just a moment—"

She opens a large, iron-mouthed, fairly worn leather

handbag, rummages through it a little, and takes out an odd piece of equipment. It consists of a flashlight casing, the type sold twenty years ago: in other words, a blue-green plaid tin hull, and where the reflector and bulb were once situated, a tiny funnel covered with wire mesh has been mounted. Attached to the case, at the end of a thin, yard-long wire, is an old eyeglass temple, that is, the part of the eyeglass frame that rests on the ear. At the center of the temple's curve, fastened to the casing by three wires, is a bright metal lens, apparently surplus Japanese audio-technical equipment, sits on a shaft like a spider in a web.

Mrs. Kaasik pushes the edge of her scarf and her gray hair away from her ear, she places the temple behind her ear so that the lens is positioned in the opening of her ear, and she extends the mesh-covered funnel toward my neighbor's mouth.

"Let's try now. Sometimes this gadget does work. I asked, where do we know each other from?"

In a normal voice, my neighbor says into the funnel, "I went to Varbola High School. I graduated in 1935. Mr. Kaasik was our principal. And you substituted for our earth science and geography teacher a few times."

Mrs. Kaasik shakes her head. "No. It's not working now," she says in a tone audible to half the car. She opens her apparatus at the bottom and pulls out an ordinary flashlight battery. "Let's see if it's got any current in here. That's simple to do, with your tongue. They used to teach this kind of thing in second grade. Isn't that so?"

My neighbor nods patiently and Mrs. Kaasik tests the terminals with the tip of her tongue.

"But it's still sourish. I think so, anyway. You try it too—" She thrusts the battery under my neighbor's nose, and he in turn tries the terminals with the tip of his tongue.

"Yes. There certainly still seems to be a current here—"

"What did you say?"

"Pardon me," says the man. He takes the tin case into his

hands, presses the battery back inside, and says into the funnel that is to serve as a microphone, "Yes. There certainly still seems to be current here."

"So, you see," says Mrs. Kaasik victoriously, startled at the volume of the voice she has heard. "Didn't I say it works from time to time? You see, my hearing worsened gradually. For a long time I more or less got along. It's only been a year that things have gotten worse. Now I'm on some kind of a waiting list. For a hearing aid. But that takes time. And 'til then my nephew Ain, a tinkerer, made me this. So, where is it we know each other from?"

The man explains for the third time.

"And what is your name?"

"Suursepp," says the man, "Edgar Suursepp."

"Listen," calls Mrs. Kaasik. "This is a nuisance—"

"What, what?" puzzles the man.

"Of course! This contraption," Mrs. Kaasik flails her apparatus, "is on strike again! What was your name?"

"Suu . . ."

"No, no. Don't tell me! I can't hear anyway. I know what we'll do, we'll turn to old-fashioned, tried and true methods. Just a second—" She opens her large purse again and takes out a medium-sized writing pad and a pencil. "Now write down your name for me here!" She looks at Suursepp and gets the impression that he's stalling. And maybe that's true, actually. Mrs. Kaasik says: "Write boldly. Oh, there's nothing suspect about this. It's my conversation pad. All the names are jumbled up here. Unimportant ones and important ones. Mostly unimportant, though. Are you afraid? Why? A single conversation in a train car doesn't mean anything anyway. There's something very interesting about you. I remember your face clear as a bell. But not your name—"

The man writes his name down on Mrs. Kaasik's pad.

"Yes!" shouts Mrs. Kaasik, once again at a volume audible throughout half the car. "It's coming back, it's coming back: you're that tall, curly-headed boy—you were probably in the

THE DAY HIS EYES ARE OPENED

ninth grade then. We used to say, his name could also be Titmouse! You were, well, in the same class as Taaver and those . . . "

The man nods, smiling, and Mrs. Kaasik recalls, "Taaver, who's an Academician now, and Maripuu, who was a minister for a while, and also that . . . Randmäe, who was given something by the Germans. What was it he got?"

"I don't remember, actually," mutters the man, but then he remembers after all: "An iron cross, with oak leaves, wasn't it?" (Peering from behind the edge of *The People's Voice*, I can clearly see that he is ashamed about this same Randmäe.) "But then he died shortly afterward—"

Mrs. Kaasik recalls: "Yes, he lost his legs and then he died. Poor boy. And what was he to do, in fact—no legs under him and that cross around his neck. But listen—you yourself—tell me who and what you are now. But speak quickly. My box is working at the moment."

My neighbor turns his thin but broad shoulders slightly to the right, then to the left, as people do when trying to avoid a question.

"I—I began to study agronomy. My father was a gardener, in fact. And nothing appealed to me more. I chanced to study in Denmark. Father had studied there, and he had friends there. When the Germans forced their way in—during the spring of '40—I barely got out. Since that time I've been mussing with soil here. And I've taught about mussing with soil. Tried to write a little about it. For twenty years already. Very quietly, very inconspicuously—"

"Why so very inconspicuously?" asks Mrs. Kaasik. It seems to me she isn't pleased that a former student of hers and her husband's has proved to be so very inconspicuous.

My neighbor responds in a muffled voice, smiling sourly, "You know, as a person who was here during the German period.[4] A person who'd studied abroad. A person who hadn't agreed with everything in the interim. So, the more unobtrusive, the better."

"Oh, I didn't hear the end," calls Mrs. Kaasik. "It's gone silent again!"

"There must simply be a contact loose," says the man, "but now while we're moving, with everything shaking, there's no way to fix it."

"What did you say?" asks Mrs. Kaasik, and she extends her writing pad to the man.

The man writes a few lines on the pad. I myself am unable to stretch over far enough to read what, for I don't want to stare openly.

Mrs. Kaasik glances at what's been written, she nods, looks out the window for a moment, and then turns to my neighbor again.

"Are you married?" She holds out the pad to him again.

He nods and the matter is settled.

"And what's your wife's profession?"

The man takes the pad from Mrs. Kaasik and writes on his knee so that I'm able to read: *She's a soil musser too. I.e., a landscape architect.*

"Oh, that's precious," says Mrs. Kaasik ardently. "You know, I think it's terribly advantageous for marital happiness if the husband and wife have their work in common. Don't you think so?"

Once again, Mrs. Kaasik's enthusiastic point of view resounds across many benches. Her far-reaching speaking voice with its half-telephoned tone has long since caught the attention of fellow travelers in close proximity. Two coeds sitting at the opposite window, each seemingly involved in her own book, have been so absorbed in following the conversation for some time now that it's obvious they're only pretending to read. The flash of their glances and the play of the corners of their mouths constantly betray the true object of their attention. A middle-aged woman is sitting behind Mrs. Kaasik, and I can see no more than the nape of her neck and a freshly curled, brownish frizz of hair. She now gets up for the third time, it seems, and adjusts her suitcase on the luggage rack—although it needs no adjusting—simply to take a sidelong, curious glance at Mrs. Kaasik "with her currant eyes," as they used to write in bygone days. At the window neighboring that of the coeds, two men are plugging away at cards on a small window table. One younger, with badly shorn, light hair and a strapping, ruddy-face, phylum *machine operator of the broad fields;*[5] the other, older, thinner, darker, more smug, more crooked, is, let's say, a small systems supplier of some sort. Ruddy-face says in passing, his eyes with their white eyelashes narrowed, "Hey, Auntie here's got a thing for evaluating marital bliss."

"And why not," says the supplier softly, driveling. "Look at that knockout hairdo of hers. She'll see to that bliss business with her husband lickety-split. If the old guy's up to it, that is—"

From Suursepp's and my glances, and perhaps from the young coeds' blushes as well, Mrs. Kaasik notices that something's been said to her from the card players' direction. She turns their way, smiling—I notice that she still has pretty, dark blue eyes—and she looks at the two faces smiling at her, the red one and the earthen gray one.

"Did you . . . add something interesting . . . to our conversation? Please—" She extends her pad toward the men, and for a moment the dissonance between her smile and theirs simply makes me uncomfortable. As she finishes trawling through her impressions, she puts the men's repartee in its correct context. Even before the machine operator has a chance to wave off her pad and call out to the supplier—"Damn it, I already told you, pass!"—even before that, Mrs. Kaasik turns toward Suursepp for a moment, as if a bit saddened, and she asks, unperturbed: "So—don't you find that a husband and wife's mutual profession . . . "

Suursepp says, "Just a moment, allow me. . . . " From atop Mrs. Kaasik's handbag, which is sitting on her lap, he takes her apparatus into his own hands and tears out the battery. He straightens out and bends the contacts, jerks the wire from the contact points, massages the tiny earphone, puts the battery back into the case, and blows into the funnel with the wire mesh cover. The train stands motionless in Raasik Station for the duration of this activity. Then it takes off again, and the clickety-clack-clickety of its wheels immediately halves the audibility of their conversation for their neighbors. Suursepp extends the temple of the apparatus back to Mrs. Kaasik, and she fastens it to her ear.

"Well, is it working—?" asks Suursepp through the large microphone.

"What do you know—it's working!" Mrs. Kaasik calls out.

"Very good," says Suursepp smiling. "My response is too long to write on the pad, in fact. You see—" His tone changes from the louder, more dashing tone of an instructor to that of reminiscing. His listeners apparently cause him some embarrassment, and as a result he speaks very softly. But it appears that, when she takes the trouble, Mrs. Kaasik's emergency hearing apparatus works exceedingly well. "Yes, yes. It certainly is nice for spouses to have a mutual profession. Not just theoretically. Practically as well. Mutual discussions and advice save you sometimes. But it certainly has no greater significance in a marriage. In my experience. A marriage requires *so many* diverse congruities. And incongruities as well—which are often congruities from the standpoint of a marriage—I'm not in a so-called happy marriage. No, no. Tiiu says that straight out, too. So I've nothing to be ashamed of in this. Yet, actually, the two of us are very much in the same field. Well, we've lived together for fifteen years. That's true. But we've also been close to divorce many times. And we are even now. So happiness requires—I don't know what. Luck, presumably. Having a mutual profession doesn't work any wonder."

"Why, then, a *wonder*, namely . . . ," says Mrs. Kaasik, in what seems like a conciliatory tone. *"But why not a wonder, in fact?!"* she continues, suddenly animated. I'd almost like to say coquettishly, but that wouldn't be quite correct. "What is a wonder, in your opinion? I think it's highly dependent upon the person experiencing the wonder. *Do they see or don't they see—"* And then she asks suddenly: "Do you have children?"

"One son," responds my neighbor, slightly bored.

"Oh, this cowbell—it's gone silent again! Write, please," and Mrs. Kaasik holds the pad out to my neighbor. He writes and Mrs. Kaasik calls out in total candor: "Only one son?! Why only one child?! Where will we end up this way?!"

My neighbor blushes visibly. "Well, you see, it turned out that way. . . . And you?" he asks, apparently in a clever attempt to divert his interlocutor's attention elsewhere. "As I remember, you have more children, don't you?"

"Oh, my cowbell isn't working! I didn't catch that. Write, please—" says Mrs. Kaasik, holding out the pad.

My neighbor writes, and the woman responds immediately.

"Us—yes. We certainly did. If we'd had only one son, we wouldn't have a single one now. We had five children. Four boys and one girl. In order of age, as they were, so they went. Vello was lost at Velikie Luki.[6] On the right side.[7] Meelis was lost at Sinimäed.[8] On the wrong side."

Suursepp's face was a foot and a half away. With detailed clarity, I see his acridly raised upper and repellingly thrust-out lower lip, the barely perceptible toss of his head tending toward the side, the quiver of his half-lowered eyelids and lashes. Yes, I see clearly how Mrs. Kaasik's overly audible and childishly clear utterances are again making my neighbor suffer. Apparently it is nothing more than the politeness instilled in him by those very same Kaasiks that now compels him to remain here and to continue the conversation. Mrs. Kaasik explains:

"Aksel wasn't on either side. He went to Finland in '43,

from there to Sweden, and now he's in Australia. He wanted to become an archaeologist. Already in '39 he went off with those Vassars and Schmiedehelms,[9] and whoever they all were, to digs on Saaremaa and wherever. Well, after he left Estonia, such a thing became inconceivable for him. In Sweden, he worked at a phonograph factory. And now he's manufacturing ties in Brisbane"—Mrs. Kaasik smiles a sad smile—"an industrialist, so to speak. He himself, along with nine workers. Three of the workers are Estonians. But his wife is an Australian woman and his children Australian children. Well, and then we had Jaanus. It was his fate not to be accepted by the physics department at Tartu University in '51. Because his father was under arrest at the time. Jaanus then went to Moscow and there they found him quite suitable for the university. And that's where he stayed. He completed his master's last year and wants to get a Ph.D. as well. But now he has a Russian wife and Russian children—"

"Well, and what of it," says Suursepp, "if she's a nice woman and they're nice children." By the way, I have no idea with what degree of conviction he's saying that. It seems his words are indeed meant to console, but has he really forgotten that her cowbell isn't working? I can't be sure of that. If he does remember, then his words are intended, so to speak, for all listening ears—to indicate that he has, at any rate, disputed Mrs. Kaasik's vicious nationalism. . . .

Mrs. Kaasik extends the pad to him: "Write, please. I didn't understand."

Suursepp writes, and Mrs. Kaasik immediately says, "She's really a nice woman. And they're nice children, too. So, actually speaking, I can't have anything against it. After all, love doesn't ask about such a thing. It's just that I think if there's too much love of that sort, we'll soon disappear from this earth as a people. And love could also be such that it would enable us to live on as a people. What?"

Suddenly she stops and looks at Suursepp a bit provocatively, it seems. "Listen, Suursepp—Suursepp was your name, wasn't it, or am I confusing you with someone? No? I'm looking at the expression on your face and I must ask: am I saying something forbidden? Is such talk still forbidden, then?! That can't be! I don't believe it! Tell me, what's happened in your life to make you—such a frightened Titmouse?! It's true we all used to think that way, only we didn't express it in a public place. But that time is past now! Or do you think it's still going on?"

Mrs. Kaasik extends her pad to Suursepp. In fact she forces it into the man's palm and watches him with a slightly provocative expression. He puts the pad on his knee so that I read his words along with Mrs. Kaasik.

He writes: *I don't know!* And he underlines his words. And then, in order to return the conversation from this questionable aside to an appropriate direction, he also writes: *But your daughter?*

As the train is going clickety-clack-clack, probably already on the other side of Tapa, Mrs. Kaasik explains, "And then we also had, yes, Helvi. The youngest. Twenty-one now. All's well with her. She's studying Estonian at the Pedagogical Institute in her father's footsteps. She was accepted straight from high school without even an interview. For Father was already back then—"

"Oh, is that so?! So Mr. Director is back?!" Suursepp is audibly amazed, and it's unlikely that this is intended to divert the conversation from daughter to father. "It seems to me, I'd heard in the meantime that . . . "

Apparently he wants to conclude: " . . . heard that Director Kaasik died there." But, upon receiving this contrary information, he joyfully cuts off his sentence. Mrs. Kaasik extends the pad to him and he writes: *How have things gone for Mr. Kaasik?*

At this, our entire end of the car, at least, gets a detailed picture of Mr. Kaasik's fate during the interim. And Suursepp, it seems to me, is given a more precise description than he would wish, at least about some of the details.

Mr. Kaasik's tale had its origins long ago. In the summer of 1940, during the Vares government,[10] a county newspaper had published an interview with the principal of its coeducational secondary school. Why had Kaasik, in particular, been interviewed? Probably because his leftist pedagogical views were known locally. And probably also because, shortly before that, he'd had a fundamental disagreement with the Minister of Education, a general during the Päts administration.[11] So, in the eyes of those like-minded, he had become something like the hero of the day. And, as part of the interview, the ambitious new editor of the county paper had printed a sentence by Mr. Kaasik, probably the final sentence of the interview, in fact: *But what kind of flag is more beautiful than the red flag—beneath our blue sky, upon our black soil and in our pure heart?!*

"Suursepp, you do remember," says Mrs. Kaasik, smiling forgivingly, "he *was* a bit of a romantic—"

Suursepp nods and writes on the pad, so that I read along: *Like many Estonian language teachers of his generation.*

And Mrs. Kaasik nods thankfully.

Yes. Because of Mr. Kaasik's well-known general attitude, the educational authorities in power during the occupation had initially removed him from his position as director—and then from his job as teacher to boot. Initially he had been shoved into a job at the local educational society's library. But then, along with lists of books designated for destruction, directives had arrived stating that the library must be purified. Mr. Kaasik had ridden to Tallinn to protest, and in a week he'd been fired. By that time, his sentence praising the red flag had also been brought to the attention of the appropriate bureau. In March '42, they had come for him.

"Well, what's the use of talking about how it was. Those who've been through those things know for themselves. And those who haven't, won't know anyway. So, yes, of course I went to all the old school officials. At least the ones who held forth even the slightest hope of a favorable response. Suursepp, you're probably old enough, you know yourself: such trips bring more sadness than joy. But joy as well, in some instances, in some completely unexpected circumstances, you know . . . "

Mrs. Kaasik had also found a lawyer who had written a splendid petition for her. "And, in addition," says Mrs. Kaasik emphatically, "one that didn't compromise August's dignity in any way. That was also very important, you understand—"And the lawyer had worked for almost no remuneration. "You know, he'd said right out: you yourself have nothing, what could I take from you, then? Just bring me a couple of packs of cigarettes, Maret or Ahto or Caravan . . . "

In any case, five or six of the more courageous men among Mr. Kaasik's colleagues had signed the petition. And Mrs. Kaasik had taken it where necessary.

"At that time the children and I were living with August's sister and her husband at their place in the country. You see, in the city there wouldn't have been anything for the children to eat. Linda and Martin agreeably tolerated our presence there. And about a year later, August was freed. Of course we didn't even consider working at a school, neither he nor I. I tended Martin's pigs and August dug a ditch. And then the Germans were gone, too. And then the new bosses, the Andresens[12] and who all else, reinstated August as principal at Varbola. I had a full-time job teaching natural history. Yes, indeed. And life was what it was. You yourself remember, of course, I've no need to talk about it. We had lost three boys. But at that time the four of us were still together. Again and still. But you remember, of course, Suursepp— my August's tongue was a bit unrestrained. And he was a bit vain. Like men in general. So, of course, from time to time he opened his mouth about one thing or another. As a live human being is wont to do. And then once, in a speech, he explained to the students—this is God's honest truth, I myself was listening—he described the sentence he'd been imprisoned for by the Germans. But when the time came, in '50 wasn't it,[13] the issue was again raised that Principal Kaasik, who had been principal during the bourgeois period, was openly advocating the blue, black, and white colors to the students![14] For he'd mentioned the blue sky and the black soil, hadn't he! What color but white could a pure heart possibly be! And, in addition, there had been that base exhortation to duplicity: for what else could that tale about the beautiful red flag and the pure heart mean? It meant let the children wave red flags openly, but they should keep their hearts white! Once again August was removed from the job of principal with a clatter and—sent to jail. It was simply, you understand, simply that the speed required for relearning was too great for him—"

And I must admit: I didn't even understand whether or how much of Mrs. Kaasik's last sentence was irony. And if there was irony, then what proportion of that irony was directed at the political circumstances and what proportion at human dim-wittedness or overconfidence? Or was it perhaps simply a neutral statement. . . . Suursepp apparently wished to interpret it in the latter spirit. During Mrs. Kaasik's long talk he has been tinkering with her apparatus and now he says into the microphone: "An Estonian is, of course, a type slow to relearn things."

Apparently the apparatus has begun to function again because Mrs. Kaasik says: "Not always, not at all. But August—very much so. I recall as much from 1940 on. How difficult all that relearning was for him. Just imagine going to school one morning and saying to Inspector Kopp, *Comrade* Kopp. When he's been *Mr.* Kopp the entire time. And when he's been your colleague but not your friend in the slightest. August was simply flattened by that. But that same Comrade Kopp—you remember him, don't you? Of course! The inspector, after all—"

"No, he wasn't around yet in my day," notes Suursepp.

"A mobile hustler and organizer like him, with a tuft of hair hanging down his forehead and he himself always a bit sweaty," Mrs. Kaasik recalls. "I remember what he did clear as can be. Two days before the June takeover[15] I was substituting for a geography teacher, and I myself was in the lecture room. Mr. Kopp made a speech to the students in the morning—under a picture of Päts, you remember—and he pointed to the picture and talked about *our dear President* and tears streamed down his cheeks. I saw it with my own eyes. I was three steps away. But in the autumn he again made a speech to the children in that very same spot. Only then Stalin's picture was already hanging there in place of Päts's. And I was three steps away again. And Kopp spoke about the *great leader of the workers of the world.* And tears were again running down his cheeks. Streaming, again. August has been incapable of that. His whole life, he's been so stingy with his tears that . . . "

"Well, what's the use of talking about tears anymore now that Mr. Kaasik is back happily—"

Suursepp says this rushing a bit, and it's a bit cheap on his part. So I conceal my smirk in the shadow of the newspaper. An acid smirk over my neighbor's attempt to slither past the rough spots, as they say, at any price, even at the price of logic. But Mrs. Kaasik's apparatus has gone on strike again in mid-sentence.

"What did you say? Why shouldn't there be any more talk about tears?"

Mrs. Kaasik offers Suursepp the pad, but Suursepp is fiddling with the wire to her hearing box, which makes me think: is this so his response, which argues against tears—and only such a response could be expected, of course—would be, as they say, audible to all possible ears?

"Well, can you hear now?" asks Suursepp.

"Yes," Mrs. Kaasik calls out cheerfully. "Why mustn't I mention tears anymore?!"

"Because," Suursepp says into the microphone and, it

seems to me, in a tone louder than necessary, "because Mr. Kaasik has returned safely, I hear—"

"Yes," says Mrs. Kaasik in a hollow tone, "he certainly is back—the third year, already—" And it seems to me she's also still drawing a deep breath. "But of course it wasn't those tears I was talking about! Oh, there have certainly been tears spilled, too. Hardly any by him, of course. Oh no, not by him. But by me, yes. Oh I don't conceal—"

And now Suursepp gets his punishment. For attempting to sneak past the tears at all just then, because such an attempt deserves punishment. Especially if you yourself haven't even been among those who precipitated them. Those who provoked them might even somehow be forgiven their attempt to weasel past. And of course Suursepp is punished especially because, in attempting to avoid tears of concern, by pretending not to notice, he mixed those tears with tears of stupidity—and affectation. Mrs. Kaasik recalls:

"I clearly recall one great weeping spell. . . . You know, as I stood in the hallway of the tribunal—in February, I think, February '51—on Roosikrantsi Street, or wherever it was, in what was formerly the home of wealthy folk—and I waited and I knew that there somewhere, in one of those rooms, August was being sentenced. . . . The relatives of those being tried probably weren't even permitted to stand there, actually. But no one came to chase me out. And when I had waited a couple of hours and paced along the sawdust scattered on the stone parquetry—then, escorted by two soldiers flanking him on either side, August was brought into that hall and led through the hall, past me—I hadn't seen him for a year. I wanted to absorb him totally in my glance. He was old and gray and transparent somehow—but actually I saw only his mouth. To me his mouth looked strangely red and young. And I was all ears and expectation, and I listened for what his mouth would utter. After all, he had to tell me what the decision had been. Although we were forbidden to speak to each other. And, as he went past me, quietly but clearly he said: 'Ten years. Let's try to make it through. Right?' I nodded enthusiastically and smiled encouragement with all my soul. . . . Then he had passed and was on the other side of the door and gone. And I stood there—and I began to cry. It's embarrassing to admit, but uncontrollably. For in my stupidity I had somehow still hoped that they would set him free. And that ten years—I had also considered it a possibility, of course—but when it suddenly became a reality it seemed to me just like being buried alive—I stood there, my shoulder against the wall, and quaked with tears. Then a young soldier boy passed close by me. I don't believe he was from that building. Or God knows. Apparently he wasn't permitted to speak to me. Or he didn't want to. But in passing he said, half mumbling, and generously, you understand—generously: *'Nu, mamasha! Nu, značit ty plačeš'? Detskii srok že stariku dali.'*[16] And then he was gone. And at first I didn't grasp whether this had been solace or mockery. I squeezed my eyes shut and thought: which was it? And the soldier's sad, pimpled child's face rose before my eyes, and I felt a searing shame that I had doubted him. I wanted to run after him and say: Dear boy—you really don't know what you're saying, but—thank you! Because you said it out of the kindness of your heart! And I understood that ten years was actually only a child's portion—for at that time the majority of sentences were twenty-five plus five. . . . But the boy's frayed military coat and high military boots were already far away and it was embarrassing for me to run after him. . . . So I dried my tears and rode home to Varbola. After all, Jaanus and Helvi were waiting, and they wanted to know what news I'd bring. For their sake, I couldn't be too weepy. And do you know, because of the children, it turned out that I wept relatively little. For I thought: who will they have to lean on if their mother constantly turns on the waterworks . . . "

"Right, of course," Suursepp was in agreement with Mrs. Kaasik, "what's the sense of crying?"

"Well, I don't know," said Mrs. Kaasik. "Perhaps, in the right amount, crying also serves a purpose. It's unlikely that nature has simply given it to people for no purpose. It probably cleanses a person of something. But I didn't even have time for waterworks. There was nothing for me to do in Varbola anymore. I had already been fired from my job at school long ago, and they wanted me to vacate my apartment. Because a new teacher was to come from Tallinn to replace August and myself. And, in fact, I was able to exchange apartments with him. Four rooms in Varbola for a room and a half in Tallinn, but still. And I found a job in Tallinn too, as a salesperson in a bookstore. They didn't keep me in that senior sales job long, it's true. I was still a jail-bird's wife. And perhaps I hadn't kept my mouth shut enough about everything either. So, from being the senior salesperson for new books, I became the newest salesperson for old books. In an antiquarian bookshop, right. For a salary of fifteen rubles above the lowest wage. But were I religious, I'd still say: as if by God's own hand. For we couldn't have managed on my salary anyway: Jaanus was already a sizable young man, and Helvi a sizable girl. And I wanted to send August a package every month, and if possible money as well. So I had to sell something. But all our things had been confiscated. Except for three beds and chairs and a dining table. Only the books were left, by some miracle. They had remained in the country at Martin's when we moved. There were at least a couple thousand volumes, in fact. Carefully selected things. When August's sentence had been decreed and the confiscators came over to our place, according to a moral principle of some sort I should probably have directed them to those books. But I chose another moral principle. I didn't direct them there. And then, bit by bit, I began to bring the books to the city from Martin's and to sell them in the antiquarian bookshop. Do you know, from that time on, when I began working at the antiquarian bookshop, Comrade Wolf-ear decreed—he was our director, an understanding man—I don't know whether you know him—he decreed, yes, a price five or ten rubles higher for each book than he would have paid strangers. So that the children and I managed to live, and Jaanus even got a new coat in which to attend the university. And then those missing ones suddenly began to return, and soon they were coming in droves. All his life, August has never been among the first in anything, and he wasn't among the first to return either. But in the spring of '56 he came home."

Mrs. Kaasik looks at Suursepp and then at me as well with such an animated, cheerful face, as if she weren't telling me that August had returned home in '56, after six years of imprisonment instead of ten, but rather that August had won the silver for the decathlon at Melbourne. . . .

Meanwhile, with a smile of relief, Suursepp draws back his lower lip, which had, in the meantime, been thrust forward worriedly and rejectingly. "Well, you must certainly have wept buckets then?" he says—and it seems to me that's to indicate, ever so slightly, that her harmless tears, tears of joy, had still been noticed.

"Then—yes!" says Mrs. Kaasik victoriously. "But those were tears of a third kind, actually. Those I won't discuss."

"Listen to that, Juss!" The supplier, who has managed to remain entirely silent in the interim, titters at the machine operator over his cards, and he winks at Mrs. Kaasik. "Well, it must certainly have been a hell of a party for you and awful hard on the bedsprings when papa came back home after six parched years! But that Hog-ear or Lop-ear or whatever his name was, didn't his ear sag a bit when papa came home? Heh-heh-heh."

That's uttered quite a distance from Mrs. Kaasik's microphone, and one might suppose that she doesn't hear it. But there's also a kernel of truth in this: I needn't hear everything. And then she says as if in passing, lightly but very clearly, very audibly, and in Suursepp's direction of course:

"By the way, my hearing and this apparatus of mine—it

certainly is a hassle and a problem. But it does also have one good attribute: I needn't hear everything. The abominations of pathetic people who've grown awry—I've no need to hear. And even when I do hear, I don't hear them. I've mastered that art."

"That's an essential art, of course," Suursepp says quickly. Apparently he fears that the supplier might feel he's been apprehended and begin to set matters aright, so that, in the same breath, Suursepp asks: "But now, of course, everything's fine with you? In recent years? What does Mr. Kaasik do now?"

"Yes, in principle everything's fine with us now," Mrs. Kaasik says as a matter of course, and she cheerfully looks Suursepp directly in the eyes, with her eyebrows arched. "We moved from Tallinn to Varbola again. August says the city's always seemed alien to him, and now it has become entirely alien. But we've lived in Varbola for over thirty years. We found a small house there. We get a pension. Eight hundred rubles between the two of us. So we don't starve. And we still have enough books left. To read as well as to sell. It would be good—as good as it could be for us without sons—if it weren't for that misfortune—"

"What misfortune?" asks Suursepp—cautiously, it seems to me, and partly out of curiosity of course, but also in part because it would simply be unseemly not to ask.

"That misfortune with August's eyes," says Mrs. Kaasik.

"What's the matter with Mr. Kaasik's eyes?" asks Suursepp—with a certain sense of relief, it seems to me—perhaps because he knows that eyes can have only medical and not legal accidents?

And that is the situation at present, in fact. For Mrs. Kaasik says, "An eye ailment."

But, my God, how strangely she utters that. Not only without a feeling of tragedy, but even victoriously somehow. Almost as if, in speaking about it, it's difficult for her to quell the smile that forces itself to the corners of her mouth.

THE DAY HIS EYES ARE OPENED

"Welll yess . . . A cataract? Or glaucoma?" asks Suursepp.

"Glaucoma," says Mrs. Kaasik, as before almost struggling with a smile I can't explain.

"And how much vision has Mr. Kaasik lost due to his glaucoma?" asks Suursepp.

"He's become totally blind," says Mrs. Kaasik. No, no, not downright cheerfully, not downright victoriously, it would be impossible to argue that, but with a strange radiance, nevertheless. "Yes, he became completely blind; the doctors said that in fact he had to become completely blind before they could operate on him."

"Well, glaucoma is more easily cured than a cataract, isn't it," says Suursepp, "but I don't know. Perhaps it's the opposite. And why did Mr. Kaasik develop that? After all, he never even used to wear glasses."

"Who knows why," says Mrs. Kaasik, smiling, as if forgivingly. "He already had symptoms over there. An eye doctor we went to said: that comes with surviving, and it's clear what he meant. But I don't believe it. There's so much talk now these days pro and con. Some say half the cases of gangrene were the fault of the camps. Malnutrition and frostbitten feet. Others say all recoveries from tuberculosis were supposedly due to the camps: the crystalline Siberian air and a diet of sauerkraut. And God knows, it wasn't so difficult for August in the camps. He only worked at logging a brief time. Later he was assigned to a ceramics shop. August maintains that there, even without my packages, he wouldn't have—yes, yes: 'Forgive me, but even without your packages I wouldn't have faced serious hunger there.' He says that the experience itself wasn't difficult, in fact. What had been depressing was that it was all accepted as a matter of course. He says that a year would certainly have sufficed for him to have seen, in sufficient detail, what he saw in six years. Supposedly, however, it had been interesting in a horrible way. All those different personalities and strategies for self-preservation jumbled together, like being in a smelting furnace and a freezer simultaneously. August says it certainly is a shame that he isn't a writer."

"Well, you know," Suursepp calls out, "it would be downright lucky in that case. . . . " But he leaves unsaid what he thinks would be downright lucky in this case. So that anyone who wishes to can also think: in that case it would be a downright lucky that Mr. Kaasik went blind and can't, thank heaven, write.

No, no, Suursepp doesn't say anything like that. Suursepp merely asks with particular eagerness—or God knows, perhaps in the shadow of my newspaper I've been doing him an injustice right from the start, an injustice by labeling him with superficial, cheap, generic names, an injustice, an injustice?! Perhaps I'm merely projecting myself, Peter Mirk, upon him; Peter Mirk, a chance traveler in a chance train on a chance autumn morning? In any case, Suursepp asks with what seems to me is a special keenness: "But how are things, then—is Mr. Kaasik going to be operated on?"

"He was already operated on, in fact," says Mrs. Kaasik in the same cheerful-enigmatic, take-it-or-leave-it tone.

"When? And where?" inquires Suursepp, with immediate interest now.

"Two weeks ago. In Tartu. At the eye clinic."

"And the result?" I have the feeling that Suursepp and I are asking this together.

"That I don't know," says Mrs. Kaasik almost in a whisper, and then she explains, returning to her former decibel level: "The Professor said that August's case is complicated. The chances are fifty-fifty. The result should become clear today. Today they're taking the bandage off his eyes."

"Aaaah . . . So this is why you're traveling?" I don't know whether it's Suursepp or me who asks.

"Yes," says Mrs. Kaasik, "I would have gone, of course. But the Professor phoned. We don't have a telephone in Varbola, but I gave him the schoolhouse number. They don't mind there. So the Professor telephoned, had me called to the phone, and told me to come. For he'd asked August what August would like to see when his bandage was removed, if he should see—"

"And August had said?" But we break it off, Suursepp and I, and we forgive each other a great deal—for we break it off and don't deprive Mrs. Kaasik herself of the opportunity to state August's wish.

"August had said," says Mrs. Kaasik, looking at Suursepp, at me, and at the young coeds seated beneath the opposite window, with the eyes of a joyful person. "August had said he'd be grateful . . . if the first thing he could see . . . were his wife . . . "

Mrs. Kaasik looks at us and smiles wordlessly: You all understand, of course.

But then she seems to feel that her joyful eyes may well with tears and get her into trouble in front of us, and that would indeed be too much, despite all her candor. So she quickly opens her large, iron-mouthed handbag and conceals her face behind the handbag's broad flap (inside it, there's a mirror of course) and, to conceal the temple of her hearing aid, she begins to arrange her gray wisps of hair beneath the edge of the scarf. She herself no doubt ceaselessly struggling with a smile. As, ten minutes before Tartu, the milk train rides along the twanging railroad bridge across the September flooded river.

—1982—

Toomas Vint

THE SWAN-STEALING

IN THE LATE SUMMER EVENING, WHEN THE DUSK FOLLOWING sunset had muted the texture of the trees and the pedestrians who filled Kadriorg's[1] white paths and pond area during the daytime had flowed back to their homes, Elmer felt no desire to leave the park yet. He had long been fascinated by the fountain jet that shot skyward, its droplets, illuminated by projector rays, gleaming in crystalline rainbow hues. But the patter of the falling water's restless rhythm had such a peculiar effect that Elmer involuntarily recalled a past image of a whitish-green, frothy waterfall which descended incessantly downward along a precipice bordered with ferns. This memory loomed very clear and colorful, and it possessed him with such force that he forgot all else. Suddenly, an unfamiliar sound intersected the patter of the water. It was like a scream, but with a unnatural nuance. Elmer flinched and stood up.

Initially there seemed to be no one at all on that bank of the pond from which the sound emanated, but when Elmer stepped closer to the water, despite the dusk his eye discerned that, on the opposite shore, someone was stuffing a swan into a sack. The bird was struggling mightily, a man was holding it by the neck and trying to assist from behind with his knee. Elmer wanted to frighten the man with a shout, but he realized that the man had thrust the swan almost completely into the sack and could already run off with his booty. The only possibility was to apprehend the thief unexpectedly, and Elmer began pattering over toward the other side of the pond. The man hoisted the sack onto his shoulder, and, crooked under the weight of the bird, he walked down the path out of the park. Having reached the same path as the thief, Elmer didn't dare run any more—the distance between them was too great for him to start a race. Walking quickly, he could likewise catch the thief before he had a chance to disappear into a courtyard or a building, and, looking back, the thief would certainly take him merely for someone rushing home late.

On the crossroad, where the park path became an asphalt street, Elmer was barely ten meters from the thief. At that very moment the streetlights went on, the thief looked back, and, startled, Elmer came to a halt—he could have sworn that the person he had taken for a man was, in fact, a woman wearing a pantsuit. Seeing Elmer, the woman began to run. Elmer rushed to catch her but the street was suddenly barred by a braking car. Elmer's shoulder glanced against the car. He lost his balance and fell. The car's driver brought him to with a curse. Elmer floundered for an excuse, and when he finally reached the other side of the road, the street was empty of people.

Elmer ran a few more steps, but then he realized the senselessness of rushing on aimlessly. He stopped and began to listen. Were the swan thief's steps echoing somewhere or was the door of a building clicking shut? But he heard only the roar of the receding car and, when that died out, an ear-splitting silence reigned on the street. Elmer beat his clothes free of dust and went home cursing the swan thief and especially the car under his breath.

Thinking calmly about the incident later, Elmer found that he had made a stupid mistake. The swan thief couldn't have disappeared into the earth, for if she had supernatural powers, then she would not have come to steal swans in such a straightforward manner. It followed, therefore, that she must have gone into a nearby building. Or hidden herself behind the corner of a building. The latter variant was more probable, for it was unlikely that any of the residents of Kadriorg would begin to steal swans, and Elmer likewise would only have needed to lie low. Before long the thief would have thought that her pursuer had left and she would have come out of her hiding place. Feeling a nervous thrill, Elmer imagined that he might, by chance, even have hidden behind the corner of the exact same building before which the thief had been standing. But the nervous thrill was only momentary, for he now felt as if he himself were indirectly to blame for the fact that a swan had been stolen from Kadriorg.

A few days after the theft, Elmer decided that the appropriate time had come to take action. He knew that, after a while, thieves usually return to the scene of their crime in order to relive the act once more in their mind's eye, and very likely there was a desire to steal yet another swan. In any case, the thief would come, and Elmer was almost certain that he would recognize her, for a thief is betrayed by the psychological moment when her eyes alight upon the object of temptation: the previous experience reoccurs in her consciousness in the minutest detail and she forgets herself; then she looks around, frightened at the thought that someone may have been shadowing her, and she sees that a camera is directed at her. Initially, she is overcome by a rather vague mental association, which immediately grows into panicked fright, and she hastens from the scene of the crime. In a few moments, the thief realizes that the picture-taking was merely a chance coincidence and she begins to walk with feigned slowness; for her peace of mind, she looks back from time to time to ensure that the photographer hasn't begun to shadow her. But she doesn't notice anything the least bit suspicious.

In the meantime, Elmer has torn off his false beard, hidden the camera under his coat, put on sunglasses, and he is already lurking at the thief's heels as imperceptible as a gust of wind in order to then take her by storm.

Having made the necessary preparations, on a late afternoon just at the end of the workday, Elmer was sitting on a bench beside the swan pond. He was reading a book, and every once in a while he would mutter something into his fake beard, absentmindedly drumming his fingers on the camera case lying beside him. It was a beautiful summery day, and the sun breaking through the tree crowns set the water gleaming in iridescent patterns. The swans were bustling about their usual spot and they were, as always, objects of interest and wonder for a great many of those walking. But the fourth swan was sought in vain. Some of the more knowledgeable folk did in fact try to explain that the fourth had flown away, that it had died of some heretofore unknown swan ailment, that it had temporarily been taken to the nature study center at the Rocca al Mare Pioneer Camp,[2] that one of the swans in the Moscow Circus had fallen ill and the swan from the pond in Kadriorg was the only one in the entire Soviet Union capable of replacing it.

Elmer was certain that most of those rumors had been planted by the park guard, that same gloomy little man with watery eyes sitting on the opposite shore who was no doubt afraid to admit that a swan in the park entrusted to him had simply been stolen. But when Elmer himself later tried to puzzle out what had become of the swan, his heart filled only with an evil premonition. He sighed and watched the passersby with enraged attentiveness.

Two hours had already passed, but there was no thief. Elmer began to weary and he felt slightly dizzy: the whole time, a variegated human throng crowded around the swans. Yet there was something monotonous about all this, and Elmer was becoming tortured by drowsiness. The women walking seemed to float freely in the coursing air, their movements grew chaotic and soft, and to Elmer the park trees looked like enticing green pillows. I will not fall asleep—Elmer prodded himself—it's precisely thanks to the reverie which pervades this park that the cursed thief hasn't any chance of escape: she's the only one who'll make a few abrupt gestures here and those will raise her, like a target, high in the air above the others.

And, in fact, the thief didn't escape: an abrupt head motion to the side, a stray glance at the surrounding people, an encounter with the camera lens, a momentary rigidity, then ten swift steps, then some slow ones, and the thief stopped, slowly began to return, peering at Elmer stealthily. Elmer calmly busied himself with the camera, put it aside, and picked up a book again.

The swan thief calmed down and walked along the road leading to the palace. Apparently she had decided to circle around the pond. And the thief was indeed a woman—on that unfortunate evening, Elmer's eyes had not deceived him. The woman might have been about thirty, with short-cropped ashen hair and a pleasant likable face with an odd, seemingly dreamy expression. She was wearing a greenish-blue, simply cut dress adorned with a white, girlish collar. Elmer had gotten the impression that the thief was a brutal female recidivist with coarse features, but she was entirely the opposite, and, with a feeling of regret and embarrassment, he had to consider the unpleasant encounter that very soon awaited him with this likable woman. But there wasn't a thing to be pitied here, for, despite everything, the woman had stolen a swan.

Having circled around the pond, the thief stopped by the swans once again. Then, pensively looking down before her, she headed toward the tram stop. Trying not to lose sight of the woman's delicate form in the crowd, for the first time Elmer was overcome by doubt that he might be on the wrong trail, a feeling that left him disturbed and restless. In the tram, Elmer sat a few seats behind her, and as he now watched this woman who stared out the window intently and whose face seemed to have a faraway expression, he became almost certain that he was futilely trailing an honest person guilty of absolutely nothing. At the Sadama stop, however, the woman grew restless, rose suddenly, and hurried out. Elmer kept still, briefly hobbled by doubts, then he too rushed out. The doors were already beginning to roll shut; he barely got his hand in between them and, straining desperately, he struggled out of the tram.

The woman headed for a taxi stand where an empty taxi stood. Elmer was overcome with despair but just then, as the woman slammed the taxi door shut with a bang, yet another car, smartly rounding the curve, pulled up at the stand. Elmer almost shouted with unanticipated joy. He ran as fast as his legs could carry him and, having barely had a chance to sit down, shouted to the driver that he follow the car driving up ahead. The driver nodded understandingly.

The swan thief's taxi stopped at Lasnamäe.[3] Elmer asked the driver to go on a bit further, and only when the woman began heading toward a huge nine-story building did he get out of the car. The taxi driver winked his eye conspiratorially, and Elmer was moved by the discretion of this driver who hadn't even attempted to talk with him and drove with such expertise that it seemed he had been doing nothing in life but trailing cars up ahead.

A swarm of children was playing in front of the building which the woman had entered. Hopscotch squares had been drawn on the asphalt in yellow chalk, and there the children now tossed a copper ashtray from one box to another. Elmer walked over to the children and asked whether they would take him into the game. The children evaluated Elmer from head to foot and said that they wouldn't; at this Elmer pouted, took out of his pocket a green frog that hopped when you squeezed a rubber ball at the end of a thin tube, and he asked whether they would take the frog into the game. The children began to laugh and watched the frog climb onto the ashtray instead of thrusting it forward. Eventually, the frog wearied of the hopscotch game and its own ineptitude, and Elmer asked whether it was true that the auntie whom the children had greeted a little while ago didn't actually live in that big building? The children said that she certainly did live there. Elmer said he didn't believe that and threatened them with his finger, upon which they began explaining that she did indeed live in apartment 16, and if Uncle didn't believe it, he should go look. Elmer said that he would go, in fact, but from his tone of voice the children understood that Uncle was joking and they laughed.

When the door closed behind Elmer and he began to go through the sour-smelling vestibule toward the elevator, he felt an oppressive recalcitrance throughout his entire body— he would gladly have played hopscotch or watched the children play. Most happily of all, he would have been a green frog that jumps forward two centimeters, always two centimeters forward. But Elmer was already at the door of apartment 16. He cleared his throat, willed a matter-of-fact expression, and rang.

The same woman opened the door. "Hello," said Elmer, "I'm from Central Heating and I have to check your heating system because a blockage has developed in an apartment somewhere in this building."

"Please," said the woman and let him in.

"Could I take a look at your bathroom?" asked Elmer.

"Please do," said the woman, and she opened the bathroom door.

Elmer squeezed his eyes shut in order not to look right away. He took a step forward and then looked: the bathtub was empty, there was no swan, not even a single swan feather, noticeable anywhere. Was I in fact mistaken, he thought to himself, but then why the devil had that woman behaved so oddly in the park? In order not to make a bad impression, Elmer took a manometer out of his pocket and pressed it against the radiator in many places. The woman watched his activity indifferently, and Elmer's sole recourse was to thank God that women know as much about technology as Indian elephants do about central heating.

Just as he was "measuring" the radiator behind the desk with painstaking care, he heard an odd sound behind the closed door of the next room, as if someone were pouring water from one glass into another. The woman turned up the radio volume and said she liked this song very much, that's why she'd turned the volume up, in fact. When Elmer tried to enter the next room, the woman stepped in front of him at the door and said that entrance there was not permitted, that her roommate who always locked the door lived in there, and at present she had gone to the country for a few days. Elmer sighed deeply, sat down on the chair, and looked at the woman with a penetrating glance.

"Two days ago, a swan was stolen from the pond at Kadriorg," he said softly. "I believe you can provide more details about that."

The woman's face blanched, but that blanching and her surprise lasted only a moment. "What do you want?" asked the woman sharply. "I said that entry into the next room is not permitted, and when you have finished your work, then leave."

Elmer grew silent and drummed his fingers on the table.

"Go away!" said the woman belligerently, and she stepped over to the vestibule door. Elmer got up, turned off the radio, and sat back down in his previous spot. Silence reigned in the room. Elmer waited for a telltale sound from the next room but there, too, silence reigned, only the clatter of a tram could be heard in the distance through the open window.

"What liberty you are taking!" shouted the woman angrily, but she didn't move from her spot, and Elmer had the feeling that she was in fact nailed fast there.

"There's nothing left for me to do then but to refresh your memory," Elmer began to say, emphasizing each word.

"Two days ago, at about 11:30, you drove a swan from the pond at Kadriorg. It's possible you've already forgotten that moment when the streetlights went on and a man was almost hit by a car. It's very possible you've forgotten, but fortunately I did not forget you."

The woman took a few steps forward: "Listen, I will not allow myself to be mocked this way, do you know with whom you are dealing? I am Director of Programming for Television and such wretched accusations call into question the honor of Estonian Television in its entirety!"

"I know the Director of Programming for Television, he is a tall man, and he is certainly not about to begin stealing swans. However, in order to prove your guilt, I need only step into your so-called roommate's room," Elmer said harshly and rose.

The woman jumped in his way and screamed: "You are crazy! I'm going to call the police!"

Elmer pushed her aside lightly and opened the door. The woman hid her head against the doorjamb and began to cry. Elmer stepped into the room.

He was immediately struck by warm moisture and that distinct scent frequently encountered in greenhouses. Across the floor rolled a green lawn covered with multicolored flowers. The ponderous green of palms and gum trees intermingled with the bright color of the vines covering the walls. In the middle of the lawn, between a few dwarf bushes, a pond gleamed green. Some butterflies and dragonflies were flying over the water, white down feathers lay scattered about the grass, but there was no swan.

At the wall to the right, there was an actual park bench. Elmer sat down on it and let his glance slide across the room once more, then his eyes stopped in amazement on the ceiling depicting the sky—it was a taut, blue cloth behind which lights burned, creating a blue glow. From the doorway came the sound of a woman crying. A dragonfly flew past, close to Elmer's face, grazing his nose with the tip of its wing. This left a trace of a tickle. Depressed, Elmer got up, he was no longer angry, instead he was sad. He went past the woman, intending to leave, but suddenly he envisioned that the woman could now go swim in the pond at Kadriorg in place of the dead swan, that would be very fairy-talelike, it's true, but the only fitting punishment for this woman.

"I trust," groped Elmer, "that by this evening there will be four swans swimming at Kadriorg and, if not, then you yourself can surmise what the consequences will be."

The woman turned her tearstained face toward him and she was so unhappy that, despite everything, Elmer began to feel sorry for her. "I promise you," said the woman. It was as if, with her entire being, she were beseeching Elmer and all the world to have mercy on her.

"You understand," said the woman through her sobs, "I have so terribly much work to do that it's impossible to find time to go to the park every day and then, a long time ago already, it occurred to me to create this room . . . but without a swan it was lifeless here . . . I understand that I erred, that I had no right to do it . . . but I promise you that by this evening I will take the swan back to the pond . . . ," and she sank down on the couch sobbing so profusely that the entire couch shook.

"And where is the swan now?" asked Elmer, suppressing his agitation with great difficulty.

"I lent it to a girlfriend for today . . . ," answered the woman through her sobs. "She too created a room like this for herself . . . and implored. . . . " The tears smothered her words.

Elmer hardened his heart, he repeated his demand in a resolute tone, he went out the door and down the stairs, he even went past the children who invited him to play hopscotch, but at the tram stop he turned back, went over to the children, and left them the green frog to play with.

—1974—

THIS SO UNEXPECTED AND EMBARRASSING A DEATH

AUTHOR RAGNAR PRANTS WAS MARRIED FOR THE THIRD TIME, and it appeared that the marriage, which had lasted quite a long while, was in its final stages. It was at a point when nothing definite had yet been said, even the idea of separating had not resonated in words, but Prants felt, more precisely, he knew, all that had preceded the previous endings, and it appeared this was a natural calamity that was entirely impossible to ward off. The earlier marriages had ended quite painlessly—they had simply stopped living together, created new families, later they had met on the street or socially, smiled without any ulterior motive, asked about each other's lives, occasionally complained about their concerns as to an old friend. This time, however, separating was complicated by the children—ten-year-old Merle and eight-year-old Livia, who would have to live through it all. Prants had no desire to ruin his children's spiritual lives, especially at this sensitive age, or later either, of course. Likewise, he had no particular desire to build a family for the fourth time, and he made every effort to mitigate sharpnesses or to avoid them altogether.

When, at the beginning of August, his wife had traveled

to a creative center for applied artists on the Riga coast, he had been content—he had hoped that a longer period of separation would be helpful for forgetting many things and that the longing, the joy of reunion, would again right that which the days spent together had managed to tear asunder. His wife was supposed to return in a few days, but now Prants had found a postcard in his mailbox informing him that his wife intended to remain at the creative center and that she had no idea precisely when she would return home. Prants eyed those few lines written with a crayon for a long while and he grew somber. The school year was about to begin and school supplies, uniforms, all kinds of other necessary odds and ends must be bought for the girls, and after all, the Riga coast was not somewhere at the other end of the earth, which would make it impossible for his wife to return home for a few days and see to these matters. It was all too likely these lines she had written indicated that their being apart had had an entirely different effect upon his wife than that which Prants himself had hoped.

He put out his cigarette and lit a new one. The girls were carousing in the next room, a friend had come to visit them and now they were in a good mood, frolicking, carefree, laughing, shrieking. Prants felt himself suddenly grow sweaty, in his heart or beneath it a pain jabbed sharply. A few days ago, in the city, he had gotten together with colleagues who had escaped back to town from their summer homes, escaped from their wives' watchful gazes, and now, enjoying the freedom of the city, they had been on a drinking spree. Since the girls had still been in the country, he had joined the revelers, and when his brother had brought the children home the previous day, the two of them, with considerable lack of restraint, had drunk to restore themselves. Now all this was making itself felt. He wanted peace and quiet, but the children were creating an uproar in the next room, and, on top of everything else, he couldn't rid himself of the thought that, there on the Riga coast, his wife had acquired a male friend who seemed better, more noble-minded, more fun than her own husband, and that those moments of joy had to be extended at her family's expense.

Prants was not jealous; he was sad and thought with fright about the impending divorce which had so unexpectedly—it now seemed to him—become a fact. Suddenly there was a clatter in the next room, and it seemed as if the children's voices had suddenly been cut off. They've probably broken something, thought Prants sluggishly. He tried to imagine what could have fallen and broken with such an intense, ringing clatter; instead there rose before his eyes an image of the girls gathering the shards together right then, hiding them under the closets, the bed, or the floor covering, and acting as if nothing had happened while they continued to play, feigning their previous enthusiasm.

He could no longer continue sitting at the desk: his body felt heavy, his shoulder ached as if he had bruised it, something grated or smarted inside his head. A little cognac would have helped right now, eased the situation, made it more bearable, but for that he would have to leave home. The trivial consolation that women weep their life's sorrows into a pillow while men drown them in the bottom of a glass droned on in his head with maddening persistence. All his years seemed to be a repetition of this, and all those years had now converged around him in a tight circle, pressing their grinning faces up to his face, attempting to kiss him with drunken, slobbering lips, mumbling, sometimes in desperation, sometimes with pleasure. . . . He took the newspaper, let his eyes slide over the movie ads, found a Japanese animated cartoon there, and decided to send the children to the movies. However, he himself would go to the bank—the girls' school dresses, hats, knapsacks, and other necessities would cost a tidy sum. In the afternoon he would have to call his mother-in-law, and the next day send her to the school bazaar with the children—he didn't think he could manage this himself. Then . . . probably then he could have a bit of cognac in a café somewhere and ponder what was to become of his life. After all, something must become of it.

Following a week of rain, the weather had turned clear and warm the previous day; now a late summer sun shone, intensely white clouds seemed pasted on the sky, and bright summer clothing immediately transformed the atmosphere of the streets to a carefree, happy-go-lucky one. Prants stood at the bus stop and felt a mortal weariness: he would have liked to sit down right here on the edge of the sidewalk, but there were a lot of people at the bus stop and he didn't dare: in his mind's eye suddenly flashed a vivid image of a similar situation some twenty years earlier, when it hadn't even occurred to him to worry about what others might think— he had simply sat down, watched the wind whirl fine sand and dust up from the asphalt; the weather, too, had been like this, late summerish. The image expanded: he recalled that one of his past friends had been sitting beside him; they had ridden to the bus station, and from there on to Otepää, where they had stayed until the trees had turned colors and the autumn wind had snatched away their leaves. He thought that, just as he was now embarrassed to sit down, he could never again allow himself such a strange, beautiful episode. A bus pulled up and he didn't look at its number; he climbed on and found an empty seat. There was a pain in his heart: it was like a toothache that intermittently grew stronger. He closed his eyes, let himself go limp, and suddenly he was rowing on the Pirita River as a little boy. From the stern of the boat, his father was watching him with a commanding, slightly smug expression. With each pull of the oars, more strength seemed to enter his frail arms. He was proud and happy, but under the silver birches a drowning victim was being pulled from the water. Row faster, Father had said; the drowned was wearing a bright dress, long dark hair clung about her neck and to her dress.

Prants opened his eyes just as the bus was passing the

birthing clinic, and he felt as if he himself were the drowned: his neck was wet with perspiration, his shirt thoroughly soaked. He could no longer bear sitting in this stuffy, hot bus; he got off at the following stop, and the fresh air greatly revived his spirits. Prants had taken the wrong bus and chanced to a spot where he had not been for many years. During the interim, industrious people had managed to construct many huge buildings here, to construct a vast parking lot surrounded by a mesh fence almost directly beneath the windows of the maternity hospital; the abandoned gardens had been mowed smooth and park grass had been planted there. Prants eyed that cityscape, and it occurred to him that these details could be utilized nicely in a story. One could be ironic about the location of the parking lot—like this, for instance: it was then decided to build a parking lot beside the birthing clinic so that, from their first moment on, infants could become accustomed to exhaust fumes. . . . He improvised a sentence, lit a cigarette, and, along a worn path beside a wire fence, he walked toward a grove of pines visible in the distance.

A few years ago, when he had still been living in the center of the city, he very often went walking in this area—he had been captivated by the former gardens, their beds overgrown with weeds, and the fruit trees gone wild. No one had come here to mow, and lush grass grew chest-high everywhere. The fact that vital nature had luxuriated almost in the center of the city had created in him the odd feeling that this was actually a country locale, and the daily cares that had only recently made his head ache had been replaced by the peace and carefree solace of being away. Now, however, there was a cultural park here, sterile roads strewn with gray gravel and a recently sown lawn that reminded Prants of the high-rise district he had become accustomed to in recent years, and he thought: at no period in history have such ugly boxes been built for habitation, they provoke only alienation; even as they age, these buildings will not become more interesting—they're an absolutely impersonal, mass product like this newly created, senseless green space.

Fortunately, the park was still merely imaginary—the lawn ceased behind the parking lot and the old luxuriance began. Prants felt a pleasant sensation of being outside the city: well-trodden paths led through the tall grass, around clusters of dark yellow flowers flew butterflies and dragon-flies, children walked dogs and dogs children, and a weak gust of wind carried moist warmth as far as Prants. In the midst of the bushes, a man held a woman in his embrace—they were motionless and melted into one; Prants smirked, assumed that these were adulterers who had found a refuge in nature grown wild. The man was his age, the woman considerably younger. A forty-year-old and a thirty-year-old. They had fled from work in order to deceive the others and themselves, and suddenly Prants was amazed at how he had been able to forget, for such a long while, the postcard sent by his wife.

But now it had come to mind again. He longed for his wife: perhaps it wasn't a deep, romantic feeling, merely a habitual fondness, but he was unable to imagine his exis-tence very well without her. He would prefer, a thousand times over, to endure a cool, almost indifferent cohabitation side by side than a conclusive parting of the ways. But her postcard indicated that a third party had suddenly emerged. His own volition meant nothing any longer, his wife was standing, melted in someone's embrace . . . Suddenly it seemed to Prants that everything occurring around him was merely a strange spectacle which had been staged for his benefit so that, as an observer, he would be able to realize himself and write yet one more book.

He crossed the planks covering the ditch and came to an area beneath the firs where mothers rocked carriages and read, grandmothers sat in the sunshine, and little children toddled. Peace and a sunshine-filled idyll reigned here. Prants walked onward—he knew that further on there still existed a deserted parcel of land with gardens that extended to the railroad, bounded on one side by the insane asylum fence. He wanted to go there yet; then he could be content with his walk, ride back to the city, and sit in the company of his colleagues, swear, whine, gossip about someone—this, too, is a fragment of the play taking place around me, thought Prants, and he sensed that, somewhere within the convolutions of his mind, a powerful idea had ignited. His head was extremely clear and alert, only the pain near his heart did not want to abate. Parallel to the railroad, a deep ditch, bounded by a sand rampart, had been dug. At the bottom of it lay pipeworks poured over with asphalt. Probably a heat line, mused Prants; this area will probably also be filled with high-rise buildings, he thought sadly. He wanted to avoid the area between the roadside brush and the ditch, but he hadn't noticed a bridge or a plank anywhere. He continued on, then his strength gave out, his body grew sweaty again, and, severely short of breath, he sat down to rest. There was a great deal more shade under the bush. He leaned his back against the resilient alder trunks and looked at the fragile green leaves, the blades of grass absolutely resplendent in the sunshine. It must be a brilliant idea for a novel haunting my mind, he thought, lighting his cigarette. For quite some time already he had sensed himself to be very close to something; it was as if he had something powerful within his grasp and he believed that he would soon be able to formulate it, to clarify it for himself, to make it visible. The cigarette had a disgusting taste—he crushed it into the soil and glowered at the white mound that rose in the distance, some thirty feet away. He could not see behind it, but he knew that a broad expanse covered with solitary birches lay there. The expanse existed apart from him; somewhere people were sitting at desks, workbenches reverberated, a soccer team was pounding a gate accompanied by jubilation, someone was stalking a seal among ice floes, someone was giving detailed instructions for a coup d'état, someone was running toward a fighter plane, someone was giving birth, someone was being born . . . too much was occurring outside of him, without him, and, in sum, this was a terribly actual world that hadn't the slightest to do with him. The pain grew unbearable: he lay down on his side on the ground, and suddenly it seemed as if there wasn't air enough for him in this world anymore. He tried to breathe calmly and deeply, but suddenly he knew exactly what would happen to him in the next moments, and it filled him with desperate fear.

Dispatching clerk Allan Mägi had not gone to work that morning, either. When awakened by his father, he had let fly a few curse words, and if the old man hadn't begun harping he might even have roused himself, but after his father's harping, it would have been bad form to budge. He slept until noon, then he went into the kitchen and looked at the inside of the refrigerator for a long while before realizing that he could get nothing down. He drank a mugful of water and began thinking about where to get money. Money meant freedom, and freedom meant that he could do anything that came into his head. He reasoned that he'd need a ten—he had some copper kopecks left in his pocket from the previous evening, but those wouldn't suffice. He walked from room to room. There were hundreds and thousands of rubles around him, but all that paper money had taken on strange forms: been transformed into a rug, a color television, a sofa, a vase, or a chandelier; he could not take these, it would be difficult indeed to convert them into money—something more simple and salable had to be found, a record from abroad or a silver spoon. Allan went over to the buffet cabinet, opened a silver box—it's true he'd decided last time that it would be the final one, but he needed money again, and at the beer hall there was always someone to be found who wanted to trade a ten-ruble bill for silver. He now had to find basic capital, and that was hidden in his father's raincoat pocket; Allan took only enough for two beers, he turned the door lock shut and rode over to the beer hall at the hippodrome.

A few hours had now elapsed, and Allan felt lousy indeed. No one was interested in his silver—either the men had no money or they thought him a crook of some sort and wanted no part of him. For a long while there wasn't a single familiar face to be seen. Finally his old friend Viktor came in, they had some beers, but then Viktor had to go off somewhere; said he had an idea for getting some money, and if it succeeded he'd bring back a couple of bottles of wine they could drink in the woods behind the hippodrome. Until then, however, Allan had nothing to do: he paced back and forth in front of the beer hall and cursed his friends, all of whom seemed to have sunk into the earth, ridden off, gotten sick, or simply gone to work.

Suddenly Allan's attention was captivated by a dark-haired woman in a flowered dress who was entering the summer café next to the beer hall. In contrast to the beer hall, the café was nearly empty, and, through the glass wall, he could see how a blond waitress in a white smock poured cognac for the woman, how the woman went through the hall with the glass of cognac and coffee and sat down at a table. There was something attractive about that woman, Allan couldn't say what exactly, but he was already groping through his pockets, hoping to find at least enough there for a glass of juice. Then he could sit down near her and . . . but there was only a two-kopeck piece in his pocket. He entered the café and requested a book of matches. The woman was no longer young, she might have been about thirty, her eyeliner had run as if she had been crying—otherwise she was nice-looking. Allan passed quite near her, his eyes arrested by the low-cut neckline of her dress. He asked the woman what time it might be. The woman looked at him with a glance either indifferent or unseeing and said she didn't wear a watch. Feeling a powerful sense of excitement, Allan went

THIS SO UNEXPECTED AND EMBARRASSING A DEATH

159

out into the sunshine—peering down into her low-cut neckline, he had caught sight of a braless tit with a brownish nipple and he had sensed that the woman was very drunk.

Viktor hadn't come yet—just in case, Allan looked through the beer hall door, but there wasn't a single familiar face, then he ambled back in front of the café. The woman was staring at a light blue tabletop, every once in a while she took a small gulp from the glass. Finally Viktor got off the trolley, a duffel bag in hand, and Allan beckoned to him cheerfully. The woman had emptied the glass and opened her pocketbook. Rummaging through it as if in search of something, she had sorted various rubbish onto the table, then stuffed it back. She wants more cognac, but even a lady as fine as that sometimes runs out of money, thought Allan maliciously. The woman rose and came staggering toward the door.

"Why're you still hangin' around here?" Viktor asked, amazed.

"How much did you take?" asked Allan, and, smirking, Viktor held up three fingers.

"Listen, I've got a feeling we'll have some fun yet with that dame today," said Allan, and he went over to her. "My friend and I are planning to head into nature's bosom and drink some wine. Wouldn't you like to come along?"

"What?" asked the woman as she stopped and glowered at him.

"My friend and I are planning to head into nature's bosom and drink some wine," repeated Allan spasmodically.

The woman didn't say anything. Allan glanced aside quickly and saw that Viktor was watching them, smirking condescendingly—suddenly he felt shame, anger, fear; it wasn't fitting for him simply to leave and so, surprising even himself, he grasped the woman's arm. But she didn't resist— she didn't seem to care at all what she did or where she went. They continued along the asphalt road between the hippo-drome and the insane asylum fence. Allan took hold of the woman's hand and tried to make conversation, but she didn't respond. She walked, staggering a bit, and seemed to be asleep as she walked.

They chose a spot along some brush near a rusty truck cab surrounded by trampled grass. "A very nice spot," said Viktor, snickering, and he winked at Allan. There was lush, tall grass all around and no one would notice what they did there. Allan spread his windbreaker alongside the cab so that the woman's dress wouldn't get soiled, and she sank down to a sitting position. She was quite drunk, sitting there, the neckline of her dress opened still further and her bare breasts were very visible; as a warning, Allan poked Viktor who was staring too keenly, but that was unnecessary because the woman comprehended nothing of what was happening around her. She merely took the proffered wine bottle, held it to her mouth, and drank. But the wine made her nauseous; it erupted from her mouth and flowed onto her dress as pale red trickles.

"What's happened now?" asked Allan, concerned, and as he began wiping the wine off her dress, he slid his hand down into her neckline, felt the softness of a breast beneath his fingers, but then the woman shoved his hand away abruptly. Allan was afraid to try a second time. "My name is Rein and my friend's Enno," said Allan. The woman said nothing. They let the bottle go around, this time the wine didn't make the woman nauseous, and, behind her back, Viktor made a very licentious motion. Allan smirked. They drank in silence. When the second bottle began to empty, Allan noticed that the woman's lips were quivering and tears flowed from her eyes, leaving sooty traces of eyeliner on her cheeks.

"Why're you crying," said Allan and, as if to console her, he edged closer, put his hand on the woman's leg, and then quickly thrust it under her dress. The woman held her legs together tightly; Allan tried to force his hand between them. The woman wanted to shove him away, but Viktor had already grabbed her from behind and forced her prone onto the ground. Allan began to tug off her panties, the woman tossed and resisted, but they finally succeeded and, as if she had used up all her strength, the woman grew limp.

"Well, what're you waiting for, haven't you seen one before or what," Viktor said to Allan hoarsely.

Allan wavered, and when, gasping heavily, the woman said, "You guys, where's my purse, I don't want to get pregnant," he felt an odd sense of relief. Viktor handed over the purse, the woman sat up, glanced around once, and suddenly said in almost a cheerful tone, "Wait, I'll be right back."

"She's gone to put in a diaphragm," explained Viktor, knowingly.

"I said we'd have a good time," tittered Allan, and he picked open a third bottle with quivering fingers, but the woman didn't return.

"Maybe she fell asleep, she was totally soused," Viktor conjectured. After some time had passed, they began searching, but the woman had disappeared. "Faked us out like little boys," said Viktor and he spit. On the ground lay pale-blue lace panties. Allan thrust them into his pocket and, seeing Viktor's strange expression, said he was sure these were foreign goods and he'd probably be able to trade them off somewhere.

The two of them ambled toward the sand mound visible in the distance, vaguely hoping that the woman had headed in that direction too. A young fellow and a girl emerged from among the bushes. They had their arms around each other and they were laughing. "Damn!" swore Allan. He still saw the woman's naked body before his eyes, felt her warm, resilient flesh beneath his fingers, and, once again, he swore.

In front of the sand mound there was a deep ditch, at the bottom of it, a pipe poured over with asphalt was visible, further off stood a bulldozer. The ditch there had been filled in and they crossed it without much difficulty. "I don't think she's here, either," said Viktor wearily, but they went back along the edge of the ditch anyway and there, between the bushes, Allan noticed a sleeping man.

"Listen, I'll just take a look and see what's in his pockets," he said, feigning a carefree tone. "You keep an eye out and see that no one bothers me," he added then, imperiously. The drunk was lying on his side, his face against the ground, Allan reached the man's inside jacket pocket easily but at the very moment he was about to pull the wallet out, it seemed to him that the man moved. Allan straightened himself up and whacked the sleeper in the stomach with his foot, then again, again, . . . He himself couldn't even comprehend the fury that had overcome him. Suddenly he froze—borne by the force of the kick, the man had rolled over onto his back, and with motionless eyes, a face transformed either by fear or pain stared up at Allan.

Immediately, Allan wanted to run away but his feet were transfixed and the dead man stared at him. Then his mind began working feverishly, he forced himself to act: he turned the man over as he had been, thrust the wallet into his own pocket and then, after hesitating a moment, took from the man's side pocket the kopecks he had heard jingling there. As he was about to leave, Viktor was suddenly beside him. Viktor thrust the bottle into Allan's palm and commanded: "Sit down and drink, somebody's comin' right past here." Allan tipped the bottle to his mouth mechanically, and simultaneously a man, a woman, and a little boy with a butterfly net came into view from among the bushes. The family stared at the two men with unconcealed disdain. The man muttered something about drunks and they continued on.

"The guy's dead," snickered Viktor, motioning with his head toward the man lying there.

"Only had kopecks," said Allan, and he stood up hastily.

"You sure were scared, your face turned white," laughed Viktor. "Nothin' to get shook about—they thought we were boozin' it up together."

But Allan didn't hear him—he wanted to get away from this place as fast as possible.

The fact that they'd been seen here was now pounding in his head. The whole thing had suddenly become complicated. Allan was incapable of thinking about a thing except that he mustn't say anything to Viktor. He had to find a way out of this by himself—most likely the corpse would be found sooner or later and then . . . Everything might work out all right, but if there was an investigation . . . suddenly a great number of people appeared in the forest and they saw the two of them coming from this direction—Allan's insides went cold with fear. He didn't know how much time they gave for murder, but he knew it was a lot . . .

At the first high-rises, he and Viktor went separate ways and Allan was alone. Having made a small circle, he began to go back. Most likely, few people went over to the brush beside the ditch; most likely, that family had chanced there. Some couples seeking a secluded spot went there, perhaps, but it was unlikely they'd concern themselves with a man simply lying down. Soon it would grow dusky and then he could shove the corpse into the ditch, throw sand on top of it, and the next day the bulldozers would complete the job. It seemed to him that this was the only way to come out clean.

Time crawled. Allan crouched in the grass for a long time, only when it grew dusky did he set out. The evening had grown cloudy and a misty rain drizzled. There were neither walkers nor couples to be seen—he considered himself lucky that it was raining. The man lay where he had been. In addition to the wallet, Allan found a passport in another pocket as well as a bank book showing a large amount of money. Written in the passport was the name Ragnar Prants, a name that seemed familiar to him for some reason; he thrust the documents and the wallet into his pocket, shoved the man into the ditch, and began to push sand on top of him with a piece of board taken along from the forest—there were other similar, small mounds in spots where children had been playing; this mustn't arouse suspicion of any kind—then he threw the piece of board deeper into the bushes, removed the money from the wallet, and hid the documents in the sand tens of feet from the man. When he reached the buildings, the dusk had turned to darkness. Now everything was in order, but the gnawing fear did not want to subside—it bothered him that the name Ragnar Prants seemed so familiar, the man's grimace of pain rose as a specter before his eyes, and he was almost certain that he had already seen it somewhere before. He hailed a taxi and asked to be taken to the nearest café. Only in the lobby of the café did Allan notice that his hands and the ends of his sleeves were muddy.

The cognac didn't go to his head. He tried desperately to recall where he had seen that man with the familiar name and finally, from the recesses of his memory, he recalled a literary event at school. Author Ragnar Prants . . . The circumstances of an author's death would no doubt be investigated with particular care. It was possible that someone had seen Prants there and recognized him . . . Allan ordered more cognac, he could no longer rid himself of panicky fear. For a moment he thought that he should give himself up, maybe he'd get off more lightly, but then he decided to leave. On first impulse he decided to take his father's car, but suddenly there loomed before his eyes the dark blue Žiguli which one of the neighbors on their street usually drove home at night. Many times, Allan had watched the man park the car on the street in front of his garage; the man had even left the motor running when he'd gone inside to open the garage door. He, Allan, needed only to catch that moment. He even knew that the man usually drove up to the garage at about 11:30. Allan felt that he'd been saved at last.

The stolen, dark-blue Žiguli was found a few hours later that night. It had been smashed up on the other side of Rakvere.[1] The car thief, a young man named Allan Mägi, was dead.

Author Ragnar Prants's children, Merle and Livia, returned from watching the Japanese cartoon. The film had been in color and funny; the children felt excited and thoroughly satisfied. They had bought a tremendous amount of ice cream and now they hurried home before it could melt. Father hadn't come yet. The rooms were in quite a disarray, the shelves were covered with a thick layer of dust on which you could write your name and draw faces. Livia dragged out the toy box to begin furnishing the dollhouse. In order to find the necessary blocks and other things, she simply emptied its contents on the floor. Merle huddled on the couch in the other room and licked ice cream. Suddenly it seemed to her that the ice cream tasted like soap. She put it in a saucer and watched as it slowly melted and flowed down to the bottom of white plate as a pinkish liquid.

Merle was in a strange mood. She felt completely different than she had after the movie. They had only wanted to giggle then, when coming toward them there had appeared an oddly dressed woman wearing a hat with a tremendously wide brim, a pink fabric hanging over the hat like a veil, and pale green, baggy breeches visible beneath her dress. They had stared after the woman and doubled over with laughter. Livia had imitated the woman's slightly staggering gait; she had held a half-extended hand at the height of her chest and thrashed about with the other. Then a man carrying a suitcase had come toward them, and although there had been nothing unusual or funny about him, they had still laughed. But now Merle felt restless, as if she were a bird in a cage thrashing to get free, or a squirrel in a wheel running and running . . . Father had walked around all morning wearing a gloomy expression—it was amazing that he hadn't yelled about the broken vase. He'd probably been angry that Mother wasn't coming home yet, that she had to stay and work there at her creative center. Along the bus route they usually took to the city, there was a wholesale center or whatever it was—long structures of tin that gleamed silvery in the sun, but Mother's center was probably different.

It occurred to Merle that she might straighten out the rooms; when Father returned, his eyes would widen with surprise and, chuckling, he'd say: Oh, what wonderful girls I have, everything's absolutely sparkling . . . and then he'd get into a good mood, he'd joke and laugh. There was a pile of unwashed dishes in the kitchen sink—being alone, Father didn't have the energy to clean up anything. Likewise, Livia certainly wouldn't have the energy. But if she didn't muster up the energy either, finally there wouldn't be any dishes from which to eat, the floor would be cluttered, there wouldn't even be a place to step anymore. She called out to Livia, said now we're going to surprise Father, and, faltering a bit, she added that Father would then bring them a cake on the way home.

It was nearly seven, even later, by the time they had put everything in order. Merle fried bits of sausage and poured eggs on top of them, then she sliced tomatoes and mixed them with sour cream. Suddenly Livia began crying violently—she wanted Mother to come home. Merle explained that Mother had work to do far away and Father had something to do in the city just now, but Livia's crying didn't want to abate in the slightest. Usually when Father stayed in town longer, he called, said that one thing or another needed to be taken care of, that he had to meet with an editor, that he must speak with a visitor. At such times, Mother always became agitated, yelled for the slightest reason, and if Livia asked when Father was coming, she would lash out that Father was sitting in the club, nipping away. Sitting at his own club with a dish before him, nipping like a dog or a cat? Or had his dish been placed somewhere in a corner? But even that thought hadn't seemed funny to Merle. Sometimes Father didn't come home for days, or he'd ridden off somewhere, returned home only the next day. Then Mother wouldn't speak to him. Merle, she'd say, tell your father that he has to go to the store; tell your father that he's been asked to call Mr. Aasmaa; tell your father that he should pay the bills . . . Sometimes Father began explaining something to Mother. They shut the door between the rooms, and for hours Father did nothing but talk and talk in a low voice. Or else Father sat in his study, slept there, and hardly came out at all for days. Merle couldn't bear those days, those disgusting days—no one joked, no one laughed, everyone was somber, everyone was disgusting.

It appeared that Father had indeed gone to his club now, but Merle couldn't understand why he didn't call—she thought the telephone might be broken. She went over to it, dialed zero-zero-five and listened: "The time is ten o'clock," and after a brief pause: "precisely." The sky was clouded, rain drizzled, the room had grown dark. Livia was asleep in an armchair in front of the television. Merle tried to wake her, but her sister only mumbled a sleepy response; later Merle practically carried Livia to bed, took off her dress, and covered her with a blanket. Merle remembered how she herself used to pretend to be asleep and Mother had tugged off her dress in exactly the same way, but Merle had let her limbs go limp, constantly slid out of Mother's arms, and when Mother had finally put her to bed, she had burst out laughing. But Livia didn't even open her eyes.

It was strange how the rooms had suddenly grown tremendously large; Merle went into the kitchen and listened to the silence all around. Outside, lamps burned with a bluish light, their gleam radiated into the dark kitchen. She had no idea why she didn't turn on the light. She stood at the window and looked downward. They lived on the uppermost story of a tall building; the other buildings were considerably lower. Behind many of the illuminated windows, people sat, stood, walked. She thought that, in all likelihood, Father had called while they were at the movies and he'd had to go away urgently. Perhaps he'd gone to

Mother—he'd probably reasoned that the girls were already so big that they would manage by themselves.

She remembered how once, in the springtime, Father had had a long talk with her. She'd gone to ask him about something. Mother had been away just then celebrating someone's birthday. Father had been sitting at the typewriter and he'd had a bottle of liquor on the table. Merle had looked at the bottle and it had occurred to her that all these problems had to do with liquor in one way or another. She became very sad, but then she saw that Father was sad too, and she asked why people drank if liquor always created problems. Father had looked at her for a long time. Finally he'd said: "Listen, you're such a big girl already that I can talk to you." She didn't remember anymore what their conversation had been about; actually, there was a great deal she didn't understand. She remembered that she had felt for Father from the bottom of her heart, she'd wanted to help him, but she herself had begun to cry and Father had comforted her instead.

Father had told her that she was already a big girl, and he thought they'd manage nicely now; Merle decided that she would go to bed but, once there, she simply couldn't fall asleep. In the countryside, where she and Livia had just been, a fir tree was growing right next to the window. The moon sometimes gleamed into the room through the fir tree branches, but here in the city nothing gleamed in through their windows. Suddenly Merle remembered how, one morning, two cars had crashed into each other in front of a store. The asphalt had been red then and covered with glass shards. The storekeeper had swept the pieces together with a broom. The red had been blood. They said that three people had been killed instantly and that a drunken driver had been at fault. The dead people's blood had stayed on the asphalt for a long while.

Merle simply could not rid herself of that image. She had wanted to think about something completely different, but she was weighed down by the fear that Father had had an accident. But Father was always extremely careful in crossing the street: you felt bold when crossing with him, he took your hand firmly and nothing bad ever happened . . .

It had already grown light inside, but the sky was gray with rain clouds. Merle lay motionless for a long while and wished with all her soul that Father were home. Finally she got up, and feeling an angst mixed with fear, she went to look. Rain splattered against the window.

"Listen, girl, get up and let's start eating," she shook Livia. Her sister rubbed her eyes. Suddenly she looked at Merle with an expression not the least bit sleepy and asked whether Father was home. "He had to leave very, very early," said Merle, and she began searching the closet for Livia's warmer clothes, because it was storming outside and inside it was cold enough to make you shiver.

At lunchtime the telephone rang. Merle was just about to go to the store—she was stacking two bags full of jars and bottles—when she heard the ringing. That must be Father. In her rush, she almost knocked the telephone off the table. "How did things go for you in the country?" asked Grandmother. In order to conceal her disappointment, Merle hurriedly began describing how she'd gotten to ride a horse, how she'd gone out to sea in a boat, how she'd gotten a tan . . . But then Grandmother wanted to speak to Father.

"Father went to the city in the morning," Merle lied, wishing this telephone conversation were over.

"I think I'll drop by your place today and see how brown you are," said Grandmother.

The rain was coming down in sheets, the asphalt and the people glistened. Father wasn't even wearing a raincoat, thought Merle, now he's going to get soaked or maybe he's waiting somewhere until the rain is over. Dark, low clouds were racing through the gray sky. Merle returned the bottles and received two rubles thirty kopecks. When she picked up a shopping basket in the store, she suddenly felt strangely awkward, as if she had been called upon to respond and she didn't know how; suddenly all the merchandise on sale at the store had a price—she had to buy something to eat and she had no more money than what she had received for the bottles. Usually Father or Mother determined what must be bought, they drew up the entire list, and the wallet had contained multicolored bills. Merle looked at the prices and calculated. She wanted to get meat dumplings, but there rose before her eyes an image of Livia plucking the dumplings of their dough and leaving the meat uneaten. Livia wouldn't fill her stomach that way, thought Merle. She walked around the store and finally decided that if her sister were hungry, she'd probably eat it all. Livia put a package of dumplings in the shopping basket and, after managing nicely at the cash register, she felt a special pride.

"Listen, Livia, Grandma's probably coming to visit us," said Merle as they cleaned up the table after eating. "I think it's best not to tell her that Daddy came home late yesterday—she's sure to start worrying and . . . " Merle didn't know how to explain any further, but she had a feeling that Grandma mustn't know anything about Father because she'd tell Mother and then those horrid days would return again.

"All right, I won't tell," Livia drawled and looked at her sister oddly.

"Now the good children will get candy," said Merle in the same tone Mother sometimes used, and she took out a bag of candy that she had hidden from Livia before the meal.

Time had dragged the whole day; it seemed that morning had been last week. It was raining and there were no children on the playground in front of the house, not even dogs were walking about, the cats had crawled into hiding, and then, at last, Grandmother arrived with gorgeous dresses and a box full of cakes. They tried on the dresses, told story after story. Merle made fruit juice, then they ate the cakes, and finally Grandmother began to put on her coat. She pulled on her boots, buttoned her coat, tied her scarf around her head, and asked where her umbrella was. Livia ran to get it, but she didn't know how to close it, and she couldn't fit through the door with the open umbrella. Grandma closed it, saying, "Look how nicely it's dried." She took the umbrella to shield herself from the rain, smiled a good-bye. "Well, girls, be good and tell your father that he should call me," she said, turning her back at the door, already about to close it behind her when, to her own surprise, Merle called out "Grandma!"

Grandmother stopped, took a step, and was back in the room again. "Grandma," said Merle quietly, "you know . . . Father went out yesterday about lunchtime and he hasn't come home yet . . . " She pressed her face against Grandmother's coat and began to cry despairingly.

Applied artist Nella Prants was just about to go out when she received a telegram: Come home. Ragnar lost. Children alone. Mother. Nella read the telegram, crumpled it up as if wishing it into oblivion, and she sat down on the chair, enervated. She was mute with anger, incapable of motion, incapable of action. "So things have gone that far," she muttered. After a long while, she got up, went over to the window and, dazed, she stared at the drowsy sea vanishing into the fog.

Nella walked along the seashore. All around, the world was gray, even the sand seemed gray. Sea gulls rose from the fog as dark, nameless birds. The buildings were gray and the trees. That telegram had been a bit too unexpected. Nella hadn't anticipated that Ragnar would go on a drinking binge at so unsuitable a time, and the most depressing thing was that he had left the children alone. She simply could not comprehend such a lack of a sense of responsibility. It was good, at least, that Mother was with them now. That drunk would probably show up the next day, his eyes turgid from liquor. Mother had a habit of creating unnecessary panic, but she herself must go home, if only to have her say and to clarify this relationship once and for all.

Suddenly it all became clear to Nella, the long-festering hatred and the pain from insults erupted. She felt as if everything had already been decided long ago. For a moment, her sorrow for the children nearly brought her to tears, but then she reasoned calmly that it would no doubt be easier for the children too without that drunk, that whole crew of drunks. Of course, for a few years, one could endure a writer's working toward completion of a project and his feeling completely justified in rewarding himself afterward. Unrestrained drinking bouts, friends of some ilk, women, had been his reward. A splendid way to create, which consumed half his income in bar tabs. For him, the only thing that counted was sitting in his room for weeks and pounding at the typewriter, seeing only his own ego. Enough. This, now, has been his last drinking bout, with me at his side at any rate. Let him live as he pleases.

The sunlight cast shadows in front of the retreat, multi-colored shades of striped fabric bleached from the summer, shadows like monstrous mushrooms upright in the sand. Summer was over, you could feel it everywhere, but the striped cloth would remain for the autumn winds to tear, until the first snow, and, that entire time, the beach would remain as if it were anticipating the next day of sunshine, when early in the morning hundreds of vacationers would pour out from among the buildings to the water's edge, lines would form at the dressing stalls, the parallel bars and ladders for climbing would begin swarming with children. But the sun would no longer yield its warmth—only solitary walkers, restless flocks of seagulls, and withered lime grass would remain until the onset of winter. Nella stood on the sand beside the gently lapping waves for a long time. She eyed the sea which imperceptibly became sky, then she walked over to the boats which had been drawn ashore; she turned up toward the main building, passed the tall resort, stepped into a canteen the color of dried grass, and ordered a glass of champagne. She didn't bother sitting down at a table. She raised the glass to her lips right there at the bar, muttered "To your health, Ragnar," and drank. Then she glanced to the side and saw that the aging barmaid was watching her with silent contempt, even hate, in her glance. Nella asked for a pack of cigarettes and the woman practically threw a pack on the counter.

"We're not still angry over that, are we?" Nella said to the barmaid in Estonian. The defiance in her own voice startled her, and she quickly proceeded down the tree-shaded street, opened the green-painted fence gate, ran her hand over the damp, cool phlox blossoms, tapped on a window with its curtain drawn aside, and a man with a dark mustache peered out. Nella beckoned to him with her hand, and the curtain slid across the window again.

In the man's embrace, it was possible to forget everything, to simply enjoy the strength of the hands caressing her. The man was large, tall, and he filled the entire world. "Take me in your lap," Nella pleaded. And the man did so. She was now like a straw, a down feather, a snowflake. "But I'm your *Snegurotska*," said Nella,[2] and, hearing the silliness she had uttered, she began to titter.

"You're my angel [*Tō moi angel*],"[3] laughed the man and put her on the bed. The bedspring creaked woefully.

"I was afraid you wouldn't even come [*Ya dumal, sto tō ne pridjos*]," said the man.[4] "I grew sad and began to drink."

Nella cast a glance at the table and saw a half-empty bottle of cognac. "Oh you, naughty [*ekh tō, moi nekhorosi*]," laughed Nella.[5] She kissed the man on the cheek and said that she too would gladly drink a little cognac. "I had a horrible afternoon today. I got a telegram that things are out of control at home. My husband's drinking and the children are alone."

"What a snake [*nu i gad*]," said the man.

The bed creaked, howled, whined, wept, finally grew

peaceful, groaned or creaked softly only once in a while. Nella stroked the man's hairy chest and then her tears began to flow. "Yura honey, it's so good with you, I feel so secure," she said, sobbing, and looked into the man's eyes. But the man became diffused through her tears, grew foggy, gleamed as a vague splotch. Nella put her head on the man's chest, heard a heart beating very near, and she said: "It's as if I've been existing in virtual death for almost twelve years. You can't imagine what that writer of mine is like. He has no idea how to care about me or the children, he doesn't care about anything at all, he just writes his stories; I think he only even needs me so that he can observe a long-suffering woman to use as material in a few stories. And he cares about nothing else. Oh how I hate him sometimes! I've been thrown aside, leveled to the ground, squeezed empty. Like a lemon, just imagine a lemon that's been squeezed dry. That's me . . . I may be a fool, actually, but alongside him I'm forced to feel that I'm stupid. He scorns everything that's important to me. I've said to him sometimes, take your damned typewriter and go. But he pays no mind whatsoever, he smirks, probably sneers to himself. I feel like ranting for days on end, you understand, I'm a creative person too. I have my own thoughts and desires. But he doesn't take me into consideration. He always does what's important to him. What's important for his work. But that's no life . . . "

"You should drink a little cognac [*tebe nado vópiat*]," said the man,[6] stroking her reassuringly. He got up and poured cognac into tea glasses. The veranda had white painted walls; in front of the windows hung curtains of upholstery fabric; on the ceiling burned a bare electric bulb that emitted bleak, sparse light; in the middle of the room stood a round table, its center turgid from the dampness, a chair with an artificial leather seat; beneath the window stood an electric heater, its orange signal light too bright for the eyes in that colorless room; and into the wall beside the door, large nails had been pounded and from them dangled hangers bearing the man's clothes. Most of the room was taken up by a wide bed with nickel knobs and a spring mattress.

"You know, Yura," Nella whispered into the man's ear, "you're the best of all of them [*tõ samõi, samõi khorosi*].[7] With you, I feel secure and courageous. I feel strong, like you are, and I could cope with anything. When you go off to sea, I could wait for you months, years, honest, I'd never even look at another man . . . You know, when I was still a little girl, I dreamt I'd surely marry a sailor someday, and then I'd sit beside the sea every evening and wait for my dear husband [*svojevo muzitska*],[8] he'd come at last . . . And then I'd eat him up . . . You see, like this . . . no, I'd leave a little too . . . Oh, what fun it is to be an old sea wolf's woman [*žena morskovo volka*]. Just think, you come home, I kiss you on the cheek and it's salty . . . Yura dear, you know, today I decided that I'm not going back to that writer anymore. Living with him, I'll die. Besides I haven't existed for him anymore in ages, there's no forgiving the swinish things he does anymore. But it's you I love and now, Yura, I'm free . . . For you, darling."

The man sat up in bed and muttered glumly to himself. Nella put her head in his lap: "Just imagine, now we can be together all the time, nothing will stop us, we can be happy."

"Listen, little Nella dear . . . ," began the man, wavering.

Suddenly an image from the beach café loomed before Nella: an older-looking woman in a white uniform, at her back a shelf filled with wine and cognac bottles, the hate in the woman's eyes, a pack of cigarettes thrown on the counter, the look of accusation or condemnation that followed. Nella felt a vague anxiety. She raised her head from the man's lap and said, "Do you understand, there isn't a single thing in the way now. My husband himself has made the decision. Our life together is no longer possible. You and I can get married and be happy, without being unfair to anyone."

"What're you talking about [*Tö sto*]," stammered the man.[9]

"You . . . but you said that . . . if I weren't married . . . ," Nella looked at the man uncomprehendingly. He averted his glance.

"You know I have a wife in Leningrad and three children, and I don't want to be unfair to them [*ne mogu ikh obizat'*]," said the man abruptly.[10] He got up, went over to the table, poured a glass of cognac, downed it; the bottle was empty, he no longer had anything to pour, and he poured the empty bottle on the table. "You misunderstood me [*tö menja nepravilno ponjala*] . . . ," he said,[11] not looking at the woman.

"No, I understood you very well [*ja tebja prekrasno ponjala*]," said Nella,[12] and she began to get dressed. The man stood naked in the middle of the room and watched as the woman dressed, closed the door behind her.

"*Nu i bl . . . ,*" he muttered after a long while,[13] turned off the light, and crawled under the flannel blanket.

Nella arrived home late the following night. Ragnar had still not returned; the children were sleeping, and her mother looked despairing. Nella went over to the children, then she went to her husband's study. On the desk was the postcard she had sent; nothing else there caught her eye. "I've called all the hospitals, so it isn't an accident in any case," Mother said tearfully. Nella pulled open the desk drawer, rummaged about, and gathered a stack of documents onto the desk, but neither the passport nor the bank book was there. "Those times when he, . . . did he . . . ," Mother fell silent awkwardly.

"You mean when he's on a drinking binge," Nella completed her thought callously. "But he's always called then or sent a telegram. I think he simply didn't want to do that this time," said Nella, suppressing her anger.

The next morning, Nella telephoned Ragnar's best friend. "Listen, Olav, tell me very honestly now, does Ragnar have a lover?" Olav squirmed and twisted. Finally Nella explained the situation to him and Olav said that, at least as far as he knew, Ragnar had never had a lover.

Interesting, so my husband's never had a lover, in fact, thought Nella, and she found to her surprise that not even a grain of anger or feeling of resentment remained, that she longed for the moment when her husband would walk through the door. And then she sensed that Ragnar had gone somewhere very far away, possibly to his friends in Novosibirsk, or Jerevan, or Sakhalin Island, or . . . and that he would return only after a long time. But she knew that her husband would return because he couldn't live without his typewriter, his piles of manuscripts, his colleagues.

A week passed. One evening Nella sat down at her husband's desk, smoked a few cigarettes, wiped the dust off the typewriter with her palm, and inserted a sheet of paper into the shaft. She wrote: Dear Ragnar. There has been a great deal incomprehensible and contradictory about our life. But in order to live together happily, we must understand each other better, understand each other's characteristics. Over the years, we've memorized each other's faults, and perhaps the secret of living together is concealed precisely in our accepting these faults as natural, in respecting them, and not trying, for all we're worth, to retrain each other. You understand, we must be good to each other specifically with regard to the bad which exists within us. We could . . . She wanted to go on typing, but suddenly it seemed so hopelessly impossible to write Ragnar a letter that, sobbing, she pulled the paper out of the typewriter, tore it up, and threw it into the wastepaper basket.

–1983–

■ □ ■ □ ■

Mari Saat

ELSA HERMANN

IN HER YOUTH, ELSA HERMANN HAD BEEN A GOOD RUNNER. So good, in fact, that when she had to choose between studying and athletics, she decided in favor of the latter. Besides, she never considered herself a top athlete—she had too little vanity for that. But her sense of duty, long legs, and stamina made her a valued team member from whom there was always a hope of garnering points. And she also ran for her father's sake: Elsa's victories brought her father joy—he, too, had participated in sports when he was young.

Elsa's mother had died long ago. Father worked, and Elsa studied accounting at the Institute of Technology. Between the two of them, they kept their home in order and raised Elsa's little sister—Mother's legacy. Elsa had just entered her third year at the Institute and her sister was in second grade when their father died. Elsa went to work and continued her studies at night school. She spent her days off, and afternoons when there were no lectures, at the stadium. But she soon concluded that this could not continue any longer: things had begun to go awry for her sister at school, and on the nights Elsa attended lectures, her sister had a tendency to roam the streets. She did not like the solitude of their three-room apartment.

Like Elsa, her sister lacked egotism, and in addition even the slightest sense of duty. That frightened Elsa. Her sister was so fragile, so open to good and evil, simultaneously so trusting and so curious, that she simply could not be left without supervision. It wasn't that she was bad on purpose; she simply longed for Elsa's company, and when she was with her older sister she was diligent. As her sister lay in bed nights, still awake, and studied in the gleam of Elsa's desk lamp, she pleaded softly: "Don't read a book, you're so far from me then!" This hurt Elsa.

Elsa could take her sister along to the stadium; she didn't feel deserted there. And it was also possible, sometimes, to take her sister along for the infrequent track meets. Or to leave her in an aunt's care for that brief time. . . . And that is why Elsa gave up her studies. Not solely because of her sister—but because it became too tiresome for her to combine work, home, studies, and sports. Sports provided her with stamina for work, but sitting nights at lectures with her head weary from the day's work, with concerns about her sister, about the messy apartment—all those things frayed Elsa's nerves. And it also diminished her effectiveness in sports.

Her sister liked the stadium. But she was restive. Within a summer or two she managed to tire of the bleachers, and, having become a bit more independent, she proceeded to try out every possible type of sport on her own. By the end of high school she had managed to play volleyball, basketball, tennis, do gymnastics, fence, and swim. In addition to sports, she took up the flute at the school music club, and painting in the art club. She was told that she had talent in every field. She was quick, clever, pliant, with a sensitive eye and ear. But she was never content with what she was doing at the moment. It very quickly bored her. Sometimes she said she really didn't want to do anything at all. At other times, however, she declared that she did indeed want something, something she herself couldn't yet name. She finished school with average grades and didn't know how to continue with her studies. It's true she had once tried to get into acting school, but she didn't make it through the competition.

Elsa arranged a job for her sister in one of the departments at her office. In the meantime, however, her sister had acquired young friends interested in acting and other arts. That frightened Elsa: her sister's new friends were long-haired and restless. Often her sister stayed at parties of some sort until late at night, returning only toward morning, excited, agitated. . . . Elsa had to go visit their aunt alone, and even those few times her sister did happen to come along, she sat there estranged and smiled as if she were somewhere far away. Elsa was unable to express what it was exactly about her sister that frightened her. . . . That she would come to ruin? No, not that she might have a concrete accident of some sort from which one could, after all, recover, but that her sister might float away from her like a leaf from a tree. . . . That is why Elsa was overjoyed when her sister began to socialize with a reserved young man from their own office.

That young man, Arvo Laul, worked as a technician in the same department as Elsa's sister. Actually he was a student in the daytime program at the Technical Institute, but due to difficult economic circumstances—he came from a family of many children—and because of his exceptional success at his studies, he took advantage of a special arrangement with the rector: to work and to attend lectures at his own discretion. . . . He was only twenty-one and Elsa's sister was nineteen when they married, and Elsa rejoiced—the young man inspired trust. He was plump, gentle, and very serious. He was a country boy from a very distant collective farm village in the midst of forests and swamps. His mother tended a herd; his father was a smith at the collective farm. They both loved to sing, and his father played the accordion well. Arvo had three brothers, all considerably younger than he. The oldest of them, a crafty, impatient boy, was completing high school at that time; the others, fat, sickly, but good-natured twins, were only in grade school. Elsa's sister and in part Elsa herself were about to find themselves in a harmonious, open, and friendly family.

Before the wedding, Elsa went to the country to visit Arvo's parents. She was received as the mother of the bride. Elsa wondered whether or not it was still too soon for the children to marry, but Arvo's mother was adamantly opposed to such talk: it's not the least bit too soon—they both already work, earn their own keep; if a boy takes a wife, he doesn't go to ruin in the capital; Arvo has tended his own brothers since he was little, oh, he'll manage to take care of a wife, too . . . and they themselves didn't have a daughter—to her and Father, their daughter-in-law would be a daughter. In her heart Elsa agreed with Arvo's mother: when Arvo moved into Elsa and her sister's apartment from the dormitory, he brought with him a feeling of warmth and coziness. . . . The three of them visited Elsa's aunt. And on weekends they drove to Arvo's parents' home. . . . At haying time Arvo went to the country with his wife for two full weeks—as long as their vacation allowed. Elsa, whose vacation wasn't until August, went to visit them on weekends.

It had been a marshy place in the country some years before, but now, since the collective farm had been established there, it had been drained. The tilled land began beyond the yard, then came the forest pasture with tall spruce and alder scrub, further on were narrow strips of hay fields, separated from each other by ditches and strips of brush, then an endless bog.

A lake sparkled within the bog. For skin perspiring beneath the blazing sun, it was a very inviting place to bathe. But it had no bottom. So the courage instilled by the lake's sparkling surface was very deceptive. Suspended peat dust made the water seem opaque, and when you looked directly into it, that black-hued deep was more terrifying than the sea's expanse. Neither Arvo himself nor his brothers knew how to swim. Mother had always used the lake to frighten them. Elsa, too, was frightened of deep water: it's true she could swim the breast stroke a bit, but only once, and at her sister's insistence, had she dared dip into that bog lake while holding onto the edge of the bank convulsively. For Elsa's sister, on the other hand, the lake was a destination for excursions. She said that she would gladly live in the lake. When, in an ill temper, she went roaming about the forest alone, her hair would still be damp when she returned. And that is in fact how it came about that one night, after haying, Elsa's sister was lost. That dusky June night her clothes were found beside the vaporous lake. The corpse was not found—it may have drifted somewhere beneath the protruding edge of the bank.

After his wife's disappearance, Arvo quit his studies and was conscripted into the army. Elsa was left alone. She had given up athletics once and for all the previous summer, and she gladly agreed when they proposed to her at work that she resume the studies she had once cut short. Evenings, studying by the gleam of the desk lamp, it seemed as if past times had returned, as if her little sister lay behind her in bed again, pleading that Elsa stop studying and come over to her.

In two years Arvo was released from the army. Apologizing awkwardly, and with Elsa's generous permission, he once again took a room in Elsa's apartment—after all this had been his official address. . . . He had changed. His gaze was even clearer and more penetrating than before, and his conversation even more scant. In the army he had been a watchman at a textile warehouse, and he had begun to take an interest in art again. Now, after returning from his day job, he created graphic art of some sort at night; he socialized with long-haired bohemians—similar to, although younger, more restless, and probably stupider than the ones Elsa remembered from her sister's time—and he explained that, by means of art, he was attempting to humanize technical thought. All this did not frighten Elsa. After all, Arvo seemed discerning enough. But Arvo's mother worried. In letters to Elsa she always asked what her son was doing: was he drinking a lot, was he keeping bad company; couldn't Elsa get him involved in something more serious than drawing those lines . . .

In the summertime, Elsa traveled to Arvo's parents' home for a few weeks to help with the haying. There she was received like a member of the family, and Mother said to Arvo many times: look what a fine woman that Elsa is. And the day before Elsa's departure Mother spoke out forthrightly: Arvo has changed since he returned from the army . . . grown morose and solitary; he creates pictures not a single person can comprehend; here at home he's oblivious to his father and brothers, and whenever he gets the slightest chance, he goes roaming in the woods alone. And where does he go—probably still to the bog beside the lake. The only person Arvo is friendly with is Elsa. Elsa, he reveres! He says that Elsa is different from other women. . . . So why couldn't they get married?

Appalled, Elsa stammered that after all she was old, over ten years older than Arvo. But Mother said that Arvo in fact needed a wife older and wiser than himself, one who would be a mainstay for the boy with her levelheadedness—and there was in fact no need for Elsa to be a substitute for her sister. Having said this, Mother burst out crying. In contrast to her usually compassionate manner, Elsa fled, leaving Mother sobbing in the back room.

Arvo was crafting something in the threshing room.

"Come over and try out the new billy goat whistle!" he called to Elsa.

As they walked down the cowpath, Arvo asked, "What were you and Mother talking about?"

Elsa shrugged her shoulders. She was embarrassed.

They walked for quite some time in silence. Then Arvo smiled faintly and said, "I know Mother wants me to get married again. What for? I have my pictures. I was happy with your sister. Now—I don't know . . . Probably not . . . Yet maybe there is something more now . . . "

They reached the edge of the hay field. Elsa left Arvo there to lure a billy goat and said that she was walking on into the bog, to see whether there would be a lot of black-berries this year.

"Don't you go into the lake!" cautioned Arvo.

"No," said Elsa, "I really don't have the courage for that!"

She simply wanted to be alone with her thoughts. . . . Happy? Anymore? Had she ever been happy? That she really didn't know. But she had always been content with her life. She was incapable of accepting the path her sister's life had taken: it seemed to her unjust that her sister had to grow up as an impoverished child and lose her life at such a tender age, just when her joy was beginning. . . . But Elsa could indeed be content with her own life. She had fine achieve-ments in sports; she had just received a diploma for com-pleting college. . . . Why hadn't she married? Because it hadn't seemed right for her to respond to any overtures while, at the same time, she had been responsible for her younger sister. In retrospect she didn't regret that: a natural duty and obligation had bound her to her sister. In her opinion, it would have been superfluous to create a family for herself.

Bit by bit, she approached the edge of the lake. She sat down on the bank in the heather, her hands around her knees. She looked, saw that the lake wasn't so terrible after all. This was a home for many creatures. Look, a water spi-der darting over the waves and, quite near the surface, a carp's back flashing; the dark, brownish water lapping slug-gishly. And, in the middle of the lake, something was gleam-ing warmly, invitingly, as if a desk lamp's soft light were ris-ing to the surface. It filled Elsa's heart with longing.

—1986—

Toomas Raudam

DROOPING WINGS

FOR K. S.

"GOING TO CHURCH ON SUNDAY MORNING, IN THE FOREST A woman found a little boy who might have been about two years old. The child was weeping bitterly for his stomach was empty, and he hadn't the slightest idea how he had come to be there in the forest. The fine clothes he was wearing seemed to indicate that the little boy might well be descended from the upper classes."

Jaan and I were sitting on a blanket spread out on the grass beneath a plum tree. The sun glanced on Jaan's back a bit, shadows of branches swayed back and forth across his light skin. Each time I raised my eyes from the book, my glance stopped involuntarily on those shadows. We had been here before: I reading, Jaan listening, the sun high overhead. Silence reigned inside: mother had given us the bedspread from a large, square bed, some pillows as well. It was as if we were on a solitary island or on a raft, which, following a shipwreck, had remained floating about the ocean, gradually wending its way to that island. A hundred-year-old cactus that would sprout new, sharp-spined, fleshy branches every year—against which Jaan once fell while

playing tag or hide-and-seek, and I had to pick the fine needles out of his bare buttocks one by one, that cactus, age-old
but ever young—until, with a creak, it had snapped in half
on the night of Mamma's death and had been taken to the
trash heap, on its final journey, embedding in Father's biceps
hundreds of spines, which later rotted out of his arms on
their own—for us that cactus, with its soft gray beard and
new green shoots, was a palm, and from behind tall phlox
that extended high over our heads, we went to peer at the
natives and sniffed the scent of human flesh being fried.
Behind the stone walls of the building, Mother did household chores: she sewed or stitched (for me there was no particular difference between these two, and there isn't to this
day), she washed clothes, ironed, or prepared food for the
evening meal. She could do so in peace: we were in the yard,
there was no need to fear that we would run off, throw sod
at the cow, or tease the smaller children: stuff nettle into
neighbor Anu's pants, entice Ülari-From-Upstairs to eat
pretty red poison berries and then remain there waiting for
him to die. Ülari was often ill, but that was only a fever, for
he frequently had a fever; he could grow hot instantaneously
and begin to quiver. We felt sorry for him, but we would not
refrain from badgering. We thought up nastier and nastier
tricks—we, Jaan and I, or more precisely, I and Jaan, for
Jaan was my student, I his teacher. We two were the
smartest, strongest, and most handsome boys in the courtyard. Jaan was not my brother. That was unfortunate, but it
may also have been better—I had noticed that brothers
often didn't get along very well, even denied being each other's
brothers, pretended they didn't even know one another.

Actually, I was the smartest and Jaan consented. This was
best evidenced by the very fact that I knew how to read. I
had a lot of books at home. In addition to Mother, I also
had a father, a grandmother and even a great-grandmother—a whole army of caretakers. In order to distinguish
among them, I called them Memme and Mamma. There

wasn't a name left over for Mother, she was simply Mother. Memme looked exactly like a memme, Mamma like a mamma. They were a bit similar too, had to be, in fact, for Memme was Mamma's daughter. Mamma was already very old, it was feared she might fall when she came into the garden to till soil beneath the flowers and . . . I didn't want to think about what might happen then, I knew that old people mustn't fall. Mamma fell once. It happened in the lavatory, and Mamma couldn't get up anymore. Through the door, we had shouted instructions to her, but it was of no use: Mamma was fat, the lavatory small, even for an ordinary person getting up from the floor in there wouldn't have been so simple. We hoped that she would strike open the latch with her cane, but she didn't do that, although the clattering of her cane was audible. It had probably caught beneath her as she fell. Father went to get an ax from the shed in order to break down the door. Through a crack in the door, I whispered to her, "Mamma dear, try to straighten up, the latch is right above your head." I wanted to demonstrate how clever I was at saving people. It would indeed have made me proud if, upon Father's return, I could have said, as if in passing: "Look, here's Mamma, I set her free, she listened to me." I got along well with Mamma, better than with Memme and Mother, that's why I thought I'd be able to influence her, but, through the crack, there came only the bitter, cold smell of chlorine, which made my eyes water. There was silence all around; you could hear Mamma sniffling. It occurred to me that she might be extremely embarrassed—at being so helpless, old, and feeble. Then Father returned with an ax, he thrust the blade into the crack, the latch flew clattering against the john, the door sprang open, and we hauled Mamma to bed. After this, Mamma herself also understood that she was old, and she no longer strove to get outside so much, or, if she did come out, she simply sat and, from the porch (which is what we called that shelter, probably actually a veranda: whenever I must deal with these words, I patter off to look in reference books, but I'm never able to clarify the matter and certainly not because the reference books are deficient), she eyed the moving clouds and multicolored flowers.

Jaan, too, had a grandmother and a grandfather. They lived at the other end of town and didn't chance into our neighborhood very often. I don't even know whether Jaan had nicknames for them or not. If you're not in contact with people, then there's no sense in giving them names either. Jaan and I had never discussed his grandfather and grandmother. From Mother's father I had heard that Jaan's grandfather was gravely ill. Thus Jaan was in a significantly better situation than I: he had only a mother and father, they were at work all the time and let Jaan play with me.

I really did read well: in sorrowful passages, my voice grew sorrowful. I peeked in Jaan's direction—was it having an effect? Jaan didn't let on, but it was indeed having an effect. He was quite a sensitive boy: I had once teased him about his family name and he had begun to cry. His family name certainly was odd: Apothecary. "Listen, is your father an apothecary too?" I had teased Jaan, preparing to make faces. "And your mother too? Are all of you apothecaries, in fact? Apothecary, apothecary, give me some medicine, or I'll die-eee." At first Jaan thought I'd soon let up, but I didn't. I grimaced and jumped around him, pressed against him with my body, poked and shoved him as if he were a plaything. Jaan's mouth soon puckered, and he began to sob. He wept quietly as if fearing that, were he to bawl at the top of his lungs, someone would come see what we were doing and find out that he was being teased because of his name. A grown-up would, of course, chuckle at this, and, though I'd get my punishment, it wasn't a serious matter for nothing had happened actually: there was no blood and no welts visible, the little boy had simply begun to whimper because of "apothecary." Still, I didn't use it against him anymore, no doubt sensing that I'd gone too far—he was so defenseless and pathetic sniveling there beneath the apple tree, large bubbles of snot dripping from his nose and mouth as if he had eaten soap.

Jaan listened to the stories carefully, leaning his body with its angular shoulders on one arm; with the other he picked absentmindedly at the blanket fringe or the rubber waistband of his pants. Once in a while, he asked me the meaning of words.

"With drooping wings, the men returned and told of their accident. Sepasell told how. . . . "

"What does that mean?" Jaan interrupted the reading.

"What?" I asked, hoping that he might be thinking of something else. But no—

"With drooping wings, what's that?" asked Jaan.

"Oh, you mean with drooping wings?" I won some time. For until this passage the men in the story hadn't had any wings at all. One of the men was the very child found under that tree, and he had, in the meantime, grown up and now gone off into the wide world to repay his foster parents for their care; the other, a smith he had found in castle ruins, was his fellow traveler. Together they had tried to force their way into a cave filled with riches, but they hadn't succeeded for, despite the blows of the smith's hammer, the boulder wall hadn't even budged. I didn't know what to think. The "wings" and, in addition, their "drooping" bothered me immensely. Previously, when I hadn't known something, I'd simply lied, added fibs of my own, but now suddenly I was afraid to do that. I don't know what overcame me then, for in fact I did know—from the content of the story, the tone of the narrative, it was extremely clear what those drooping wings were meant to express. Even Jaan knew, no doubt— with similar, even worse, frayed-frazzled wing folds, he had stood under the apple tree and blubbered. I think he wanted to confuse me on purpose, to pay me back this way for "apothecary," by simply asking, inquiring about a perfectly obvious passage.

"With drooping wings, that means disappointment, sadness, grief. Anything can have drooping wings—nature, an animal, a person."

Jaan's glance congealed upon my lips, then he scowled at my cheeks and earlobes as if the voice could have come from there. I hadn't uttered even a peep, but for quite a while neither of us dared look up to the source of the voice. Not that we were afraid. When we feared something, that very thing happened. Our dual power and existence had been severed by the arrival of a third, a stranger. The branches above our heads shifted, something broke, bark debris crumbled onto our bare skin—and there stood the Explainer! All-Knowing-Three-Golden-Hairs[1] (in my thoughts, I immediately referred to him this way) was short in stature; he was wearing knickers with suspenders. A long-sleeved, striped shirt, buttoned up to the neck, covered his narrowish upper torso. I got the impression that, listening to us up in the tree, he had begun to feel cold. Perhaps he was ill? Something about his appearance also prompted this thought. From his dress, one could conclude that he came from a poor family. At that age, none of us wore knickers with suspenders anymore. These were a sign of babyhood—we preferred total nakedness, preferred to stay inside, bawl behind a closet, but we wouldn't put on those knickers. Finally the grown-ups wearied of us and our bawling, they let us be as we ourselves wished. Amazingly enough, our new friend didn't seem the least bit ashamed of his dress. The resinous branches from which he had hung hadn't left a single blemish on his shirt and pants—further proof of his origins and the skills they entailed. Despite instructions and reminders to the contrary, we tossed our own clothes wherever they chanced. "Come-From-Heaven" needn't even have opened his mouth—I understood at once that I had been cast from the throne. Despite this, I immediately began showing off.

"I'm reading to him. He doesn't know how yet," I introduced myself and my kingdom.

"*Ancient Tales of the Estonian People,*" said the boy in knickers knowingly.[2]

A quiver of fear ran down my spine, but I paid it no mind. Instead I asked daringly, "Want to listen, too?"

It was difficult to imagine anything more idiotic. The boy didn't respond. He took the book from the pillow, looked at it, and put it back. That was the judicial verdict.

"I've read it," said he. I had been well aware of that, he needn't even have looked at the book, but I asked anyway. It was as if I wished to taunt myself, although the desire had disappeared—I did the stupidest things imaginable, smiling stupidly all the while.

"What's it about?" (A watery mouth's harelipped smile.)

Once again our new friend did not hasten to respond. Actually, he had forced his way here. From the neighboring yard, where I had thought there lived only an ill-tempered old crone who would not permit us children to take plums from her tree, although the branches extended into our yard. I was prepared to be a knee-high infant simply to obtain my right to taste the bursting, sun-sweet plums. And not the plums in the grass or on the soil (there was no need to return the plums fallen there, although the old crone may have wished it), but plums right from the tree, cold and sweet as ice cream. Only you had to be careful not to stick a bee in your mouth along with a plum. Bees circled about the tree and concealed themselves in the cracks of its flesh, which were like open wounds on an operating table. We'd seen an image like this in the documentary "Soviet Estonia."[3] Some girls had even fainted, but the bigger children had been taken to the film by the classful anyhow. They hadn't been seated in the very first row, but there had been shrieks and groans anyway. We all needed to get smarter quickly. I wasn't attending school yet, but I got to the movies anyway (and always took Jaan along)—Mother had a friend who checked tickets. I'm discussing movies and plums at such length because I'm ashamed, even now, when

I think of how I behaved then: I shrug my shoulders nervously and restlessly blow through my nose.

At this question—the one mentioned in the story—the Writer (for he was that, as soon became evident) again maintained a silence that instilled restlessness.

"Who's that?" he asked instead about Jaan, who was still huddled on the blanket corner as if he wanted someone to finish reading the story to him. In the meantime the sun had moved forward, Jaan's back was out of the shade.

"That's Jaan," I said, and, with a wicked ulterior motive, I added: "Apothecary."

"Nice name," said he. Their glances met, and without even a word it became clear that I was about to lose my last underling, the last friend I could trust. I gritted my teeth and tried to look elsewhere, but wherever my glance turned—to the gooseberry bush, to the rusty tin bathtub hanging on the shed, to the red roof tiles and the dilapidated chimney, the wood pile, the chicken fence—I saw the newcomer and Jaan everywhere, and I felt unseen forces warding me off.

From that time on I was always the third. Although my presence was tolerated, it wouldn't have mattered much either if I had left. Those two, Jaan and he, were now the navel of the world. How they divided power between them, I don't know. It seemed there was a beneficent spirit of some sort reigning in their kingdom, which, by its very beneficence—this can't be can it?—provoked irritation in onlookers. I didn't give up that easily, however. I gradually continued the struggle, clandestinely wove a net, invented games in which my skills, powers, and knowledge became very salient.

Unfortunately they—he—had their own games; initially they didn't want to know a thing about mine. Angrily, I kept track of Jaan: his face had grown haughty, it seemed he knew that I was suffering and watched to see whether it was having an effect. It was having an effect, of course it was having an effect. I would gladly have wanted to run over to him, to put my arms around his neck and to ask forgiveness, but something held me back.

Already on the evening of that same day, he took us (for it was not seemly to leave me behind) over to his place, and he showed us his drawings, his puppets of plastic and carved wood, his airplanes and ships, his books with old-fashioned lettering, and, finally, as if in afterthought, his diaries as well. Those diaries, numbered and in notebooks with plaid covers, confirmed his supremacy conclusively. It also became evident now that he was a great deal, about five or six years, older than we were, that he was in the last year of elementary school. So that we were about even—for what was so extraordinary about a schoolboy's knowing how to read?—if it hadn't been for the *diaries*. As far as I knew (and Jaan also sensed it), this was a pastime of the chosen ones, the writers. Gradually it was revealed that this was what he wanted to become. It may also have been that we, with our jealous thoughts, instilled the profession in his mind, a dream to weigh on his neck. He himself never expressly stated this. It wasn't jealousy, however; it was simply that our train of thought was logical. What else were we to make of ten completely filled notebooks? For they would have to metamorphose into something, it seemed contrary to reason to cast so many words emptily into the wind. The notebooks were of two kinds—some were filled with the contents of books read and evaluations of what had been read. Those he showed us. I didn't dare even lay a finger on them; we looked from afar. The others contained something else. I knew what was in them—clandestine thoughts, wishes, confessions. Later, after his death, those diaries would be discovered and the entire country, all the world, would know the truth. That truth cannot be explained in any way, it is invisible, but it nevertheless exists. The bristling spines of the notebooks, with their wires and seams visible, appeared to know the truth. Will I perhaps be the one to transmit this valuable information to the people? I was gladly willing to step in as mediator, although it seemed that that would be Jaan instead. It's true that I knew how to read well and expressively, but I didn't know how to write and didn't wish to, although I did know the alphabet. I was unable to cope even with letters, a recalcitrance always emerged. Once when Jaan was taken to a Tallinn hospital with a middle-ear infection, and I grew bored, I decided to send my friend a letter, but got no further than the salutation. "DEAR JAAN," I painted on the paper, but then I fell into thought—suddenly too much (is one little boy allowed to be dear to another little boy? isn't there a better word for that?) and too little (for he really was dear to me, I missed him a great deal more than the word "dear" could express) was written on the paper. Now, when I begin to write something, I have a similar feeling or one very closely approximating it. What to say? After all, everything has already been said, hasn't it?

With this, the day we first met came to an end. The Writer's aunt, the plum crone, came home and ordered him to study. To study—how demeaning that must have been for him! "You're carousing with them, you with C's and D's on your report card!" she scolded. "Quick, quick!" It wasn't even clear who that "quick" was meant for, her relative wearing the suspenders or us. We said good-bye politely, but our new acquaintance sank submissively into a chair at the table.

That same night, in a dream, I saw Mother, Father, Memme, and Mamma. They all had large wings on their backs like Chaplin did in one of his films, only theirs weren't clean and white, but worn, frayed-frazzled—in a word, drooping. Yet they were waving them desperately, as if, after rising up into the air, they would have wanted to say something to me. It was as if they were warning me of something, forbidding, and commanding. Eighty-two-year-old Mamma waved with exceptional vigor, almost cheerfully. Looking at her, I burst out laughing and woke up.

Beside me, on the edge of the nightstand, lay a gray notebook, the same as his, in fact. The moon gleamed down on it through the curtain invitingly. I had set the notebook there, ready for morning, in order to begin jotting in it the content of books read. Who knows, starting this way, I, too, might eventually amount to something. I didn't want to become a writer; I simply liked the idea of amounting to something. Holding my breath, I switched off the table lamp (it was as if I were encircled; to my left, behind the closet, slept Mother and Father; to the right, in the large room, slept Memme with her mother, my great-grandmother, Mamma; fortunately no one woke up), and I wrote my dream down on the purple notebook hatchings as simply and quickly as possible. I shall never do so again.

The next day, I showed my dream to the Writer. This sounds like the movies—I showed. Actually, I offered him a look at the first page of the notebook, on which a synopsis of the dream had been jotted down in helter-skelter lettering disoriented with sleepiness. And do you know what?! I got praised for the dream! "You might amount to something," said the Writer. It was as if I had grown wings, and although I wasn't yet able to fly as high with them as my adviser could, I was happy to the point of delirium. Writing this, I'm not sitting on a chair but some twenty centimeters higher instead—an older person's bones are hollow, their body lighter, exhilaration lifts them more easily and higher. Grasping the corner of the table with one hand, I pull myself back to the chair. I must account for what has taken place. The moral, as they say, is contained within things themselves; actually, that's frivolously stated, just try prying it out—the result can very easily be naught.

Nevertheless, my "good" dream was incapable of winning the Writer over to my side. He was more interested in Jaan.

They went everywhere together, whispered about something, but upon seeing me they fell silent. All of a sudden, I had been brutally thrust aside. Only during reading hours was I included in the band. The Writer had with him De Coster's *D'Ulenspiegel et de Lamme Goedzak*.[4] He lay the book down beside him and recounted tales from it as if he himself had written them. We hadn't even an inkling about such adventures. I especially liked, and like even now, the tale about the scratching powder, which we read many times over, laughing until tears came to our eyes when the priest, upon being required to stand motionless in place of a broken saint statue during a ceremony, suddenly felt an itch under his collar. The book also contained passages about which I was not supposed to know. To tell the truth, these didn't even interest me a great deal. They were boring, nothing happened in them, reading them was reminiscent of a hot summer day when the air is motionless and you haven't the energy to do a thing. Those two may have had other books as well, I don't know. They sat together in a haystack and cooed. I myself watched once: the corner of a book remained visible from beneath the blanket edge; they hadn't been able to hide it that quickly. Reading-together-as-three always took place on that same grassy spot in our yard beneath the plum tree; behind the cold stone wall Mamma mended sock heels, Memme peeled potatoes, Mother prepared flour gravy on the stove. No one was interested in what we were doing because we were reading, and compared to the catapult and the popgun, reading was a harmless activity.

Once we organized a play. I say "we organized," but actually he was the organizer. On the lawn reading-ship, too, he was the captain. I was already growing accustomed to that, the only thing I could not get used to was that I had lost Jaan. Those two were also bound together by the fact that the Writer's aunt and Jaan's mother were similar people; they spoke a similar language. When Jaan got scolded by his mother, it was the same as if the Writer's aunt had reprimanded the Writer for poor grades. In their families, they used words condemned in our family: the "devils" and "dirty swine" flew, the "louts" lumbered, and the "deuces" danced. Jaan's mother was constantly saying, "I'll kill him, I'll kill him." That was horrible indeed and sent shivers of fear down my spine; only later did I understand that she was actually a good person and meant no harm by it, least of all killing. Killing we had seen when the Postiljon's Leenu chopped off her calf's head. In fact, the calf had been placed on a chopping block similar to the kind used for wood, Leenu had stood on one side of the chopping block, an unknown man who had been called upon to help was on the other side. Jaan and I had peered through a crack between the planks. There was a vast hoof and mouth epidemic then, and all the cows, calves, and other barnyard animals had to be liquidated. Had that, in fact, taken place as we saw (or now believe we had seen)? One mustn't feel absolutely certain, the picture may have been distorted by fear, although as far as such things are concerned, it's never worth wanting to know the truth. I remember the pig slaughter more clearly, and I'm also certain that it did happen this way. I myself placed the bowl to catch the blood underneath, I was surprisingly cold-blooded, and I didn't understand Memme, who closed the doors and crawled under a blanket. For two days, she wouldn't take even a bite of the fresh pork roast; on the third she already tried it, yet she ate headcheese as if it had nothing whatsoever to do with a pig. Mamma, she was on my side, against her own daughter. "Atta boy," she praised me. The pig slaughterer, a man with a sinewy back and a fire-red face, accepted the money (it was primarily for show, a handful of warm blood was his due; he lived to a very great age, is alive still, perhaps—as in a fairy tale), and he tossed me the pig's bladder. "Take it, boy, to play with," he said.[5] As far as I could see there was nothing to be done with the bladder. I kicked it a few times with my foot—it didn't bounce; I threw it into the air—it didn't fly. I had much better playthings, rubber balls and real balloons. The swine slaughterer was still living in a time when he himself had been a boy and played with bladders.

I am discussing calf and swine slaughter at such great length because I don't want to discuss the play, which, next in turn, demonstrated that he and Jaan could set all the world's matters aright if necessary: I was merely a hindrance to their works and transactions.

We performed *Little Red Riding Hood* and *Puss in Boots*. We staged them two weekends in a row—on Saturday *Little Red Riding Hood*, on Sunday *Puss in Boots*. All the people in the courtyard came to see us. When there was no one left, when everyone, old and young, had seen the performance, most of them twice, we closed down the theater. Again I say "we staged," "we performed," and "we closed down"—it feels more comfortable that way, but actually all the decisions were made by the Writer. We were—gladly!—the underlings. I wanted a better role for myself—the Wolf, the Giant, the Cat—but I had already failed miserably in the first rehearsal. I must say that I'd been given the opportunity to prove myself, the Writer presumably recalled my good skill at reading and in fact he entrusted me with the role of Wolf in *Little Red Riding Hood*.

I was very agitated that day, completely beside myself, it seemed. I climbed under the table and tickled the onlookers' toes, thrust my hand into Mamma's woolen sock. That must in fact be stage fright. I haven't experienced any more of it, all kinds of other maladies, yes, and still. When the curtain opened (everything from the dolls to the theater stage had been made by our own—by his hands) and Gray Wolf was about to appear onstage, the people immediately began to whisper. "This is a deceit," Ülari-From-Upstairs, bundled in a sweater, said in a loud voice. "Look for yourselves, the wolf has been fixed on the pole with plasticine." That was the very worst thing possible—for Ülari to betray the secrets of my drama kitchen. It's true the deception hadn't been particularly great—only babies could believe that puppets crept across the stage on their own, but if we wished the performance to go well, it was necessary that our art be judged worthy. It's true I pulled Wolf (for this purpose, there was a play-wolf made of light, crackling material and worn smooth at the sides, its ears limp, and the wolf was not gray, as one would expect, but light brown instead, even red) downward immediately, but it was already too late. Angrily, the Writer, who felt a trapdoor opening beneath his feet, seized the puppet stick in his hands and acted two roles simultaneously. I don't recall what that other role was. Though—what's there to remember here, to feign a poor memory about?—he himself was probably Little Red Riding Hood; initially Jaan played the mother, later the grandmother. It was exciting to watch how the two of them coped, signaled to each other with their eyes, and dexterously moved their fingers so that, viewed from the other side, it appeared the characters were moving. But there was also regret! Above all, regret!! And jealousy!!!

In the second act, Wolf (the former I) had to whirl around Little Red Riding Hood, to entice her with a honeyed tongue into revealing where her grandmother lived. In the meantime, the Writer had passed on the role of Wolf to Jaan. For, after all, the Writer couldn't act all the roles himself—that talented he wasn't, no one is that talented. Although Jaan hadn't rehearsed (there was in general little time left for rehearsing, otherwise things might have gone better for me, too), it was as if everything came out of him of its own accord. They were very close to each other, they had to be, in fact, for the stage was an upside-down plywood box, approximately a meter in size. At the bottom of it was a space for the actors to move about, but attached to one demolished side of the crate and hung from a fine wire was a curtain consisting of two handkerchiefs, which could be drawn open and shut. Their bodies touched, as if wishing to embrace-cuddle, their arms intertwined in a seemingly inextricable knot, but then, in harmony with the movements of the puppets above, they fluidly unraveled again. Then again! And yet one more time! This was the climax of the entire performance. Compared to it, eating the grandmother was nothing, although that evoked ahs and ohs. So clever, so impuniously clever was Wolf, so simpleminded Little Red Riding Hood! I noticed that their dialogue wasn't even the same as in the book. The fairy tale lay open on my knees, I checked there. And it was true, in fact—I didn't find those words there, although they certainly felt as if they were correct, as if they'd been written that way. Captivated, I watched the actors; the "hall," too, was mouse-quiet. No one shouted that it wasn't so. They could even have raised the poles, upon which all the puppets' "lives" depended, higher above the stage floor; I wager that no one would have noticed. This also made it easier to forget my recent jolt, and I didn't have to look directly at the others with shame-filled eyes, to run headlong past Memme and Mamma, who had read and retold *Little Red Riding Hood* to me hundreds of times.

There is also another reason I didn't feel shame—namely, a more suitable role was found for me the next time. I was completely satisfied with it. I probably wouldn't have succeeded as Wolf (just as I hadn't succeeded as a letter writer). Steadily and calmly, Narrator's voice sounded from the wings. I read (as we performed *Little Red Riding Hood*): "There once lived a little village girl who was so beautiful that no one had seen anyone like her before. Her mother loved her passionately, and her grandmother, even more so."

Slowly and lovingly, I tugged the fine string. Mother's silk handkerchiefs quaked like wings ready for flight and the curtain opened. In the book, at that spot, there was a red vertical line: familiar with my ineptitude, the Writer had marked it there just in case. Going beyond that line was not permitted. One had to know how to orient oneself in these circumstances: some segments had been crossed out, sentences that stood apart had been joined together. I did everything as the lines indicated; at the red bars I stopped for longer and followed the progress of the play with one eye. Although the scene had been readied for it and the puppets on the poles grew clumsy, I uttered no sound before the Writer stretched his head and ear toward me expectantly. Only then (and an instant later than promised, nevertheless) did I utter the necessary words. I felt that I was needed, and I was glad about this. Sometimes (at the final performance) I read from memory, squinted my eyes, made my glance (which faded into the bedspread hung on the ceiling) bleary, and recited like blind Homer: "As his sole inheritance, a miller had bequeathed to his three children a mill, a donkey, and a cat . . . "

Puss in Boots was, likewise, a successful piece. How could it have failed to be successful when the spectators were friends and relatives, my own father and mother, not to mention my grandmothers. It was nice to hear praise. Many weeks afterward I still hung around Mamma, offered to knead her neck, in order to have the pleasure of hearing "I certainly did like it," "that was fun"; then the skin on my back immediately began to tingle. Sometimes, my voraciousness for honor and praise having been noted, I received praise without even asking. "You're going to be an actor," said Mother, who had a ticket-taker acquaintance at the movies, a former prima donna at the Vanemuine Theater,[6] who after a stellar rise had descended even more quickly and come to live in this provincial town where no one knew her. This, of course, lessened the possibility of error. I was happy about that ("You'll amount to something," I thought), happier about this than about "writer." And this prediction has, in fact, come true—in a much deeper and more human sense than Mother could have imagined at that time.

During the performances of *Puss in Boots,* there was no incident. Everyone fulfilled the roles assigned to them. Due to the paucity of actors, the Writer played many roles simul-taneously, made diverse sounds, stumbled like Man-Eater, squeaked like Mouse. Eventually I noticed that he didn't actually trust others very much: he had even given Jaan a role only out of friendship, not taking his actual abilities into account. What abilities could that Jaan have had any-way? Who knows what he wrote about us in the diary? Or anything at all? For that which is important is often omit-ted, only later is it discovered that those omitted things specifically are the start of everything.

The summer lasted a long while. At least it felt so to me. It was bound to feel that way, for I suffered a great deal over the loss of my friend. Not the entire time, it's true, but that "sometimes," which struck painfully and made itself sharply felt at certain instances, and all that had actually happened was particularly hard to bear. I believe that I secretly went behind the porch corner to cry, although I don't remember, but I don't remember because, even now, that bygone feeling evokes shame. Was that really me? I ask myself and a long shadow—probably the plum tree's—nods at great length.

I didn't know how to do anything else when I invited the Writer over to my place for dinner. I still remembered the Jaan-times: Jaan had readily participated in the communal repasts that Mother loved to organize on Saturdays. He'd arranged to be nearby as if by chance, he had whistled out-side the kitchen window or scratched at the stone wall with his nails like a cat until Mother invited him inside. The food hadn't been the important thing for me or for Jaan either. He was fed more than enough at home, but he was still—we were both—thin as whipstocks. We were together, we were eating and drinking beside one another at the same table, we were like brothers—that was what counted and made the role of younger brother acceptable to Jaan. He himself had wanted to be subordinate, I hadn't even forced him much, in fact. And that was apparent now, too—if it wasn't me, it was him, for there had to be someone who'd oblige Jaan by being master-teacher. Ülari never accepted the poison berry voluntarily, he always had to be tricked and enticed, but Jaan fluttered his long lashes trustingly and smirked his soft elk lips at the morsel being offered. This is just talk of course, I didn't do anything bad to him on purpose, if being friends as we'd been up to that point isn't counted as bad.

With the Writer, this wasn't possible: he didn't come to scratch at the wall with his nails, to entice beneath the window with his whistle—he had to be invited. And in fact I did get him over to my place somehow. As if in passing, with my heart leaping out of my chest, I asked if he wouldn't honor us by participating in a modest meal. Holding my breath, I watched him. My eyes glinted at Mother—look, he's immediately turning into a glutton because, surely, his aunt doesn't prepare so much or such good food for him at home. On the other hand, I passionately wished that he would satiate himself and later remember me as his benefactor, a more brotherly brother than Jaan. He could even write a few words about in it his diary. In that other one, the one in which truth is discussed. I offered him headcheese and cabbage pirogi so eagerly that those foods even began to appeal to me. In fact, I ate more than he; in other words, I gorged myself without restraint, as if eating would help in winning his favor. The Writer behaved like an aristocrat— the one I'd thought myself to be. He took a little piece of headcheese, asked calmly, in accordance with all customs and doltish rules of etiquette, for mustard, and he requested that the bottle of vinegar standing in the middle of the table be passed to him. He made a favorable impression on all the others, Mother, Father, Memme, and Mamma, who observed his deportment from the corners of their eyes. I could see that, actually, for him being here and participating in the fellowship was unpleasant if not disgusting. He would have preferred something else, something that could not be found in this house even with the most intense searching, exactly as he had chosen Jaan rather than me for his play-mate. That made me sad.

During the summer, our family took a car trip. We rode to a tiny little village in central Estonia behind which flowed a spring. Beside the spring, on a knoll, stood a dairy. Here, near the source of the spring, was where our family had orig-inated, and this was our dairy, although unfamiliar people now bustled about here. Memme walked around the dairy building, and with the tips of her fingers she touched its crumbled, moss-warm walls. Mamma didn't come out of the car. From the backseat, she looked out the window as far as her glance extended. At the place where the spring flowed out of the ground, right above the ice-cold water, a wooden chamber had been constructed. In that chamber, milk was kept cool, the stream of water flowing beneath it cooled the milk and kept it fresh. Father, who was a stranger to this place, and Mother (she had already been born in the city) did not participate in the homestead scrutiny; they simply walked about and gathered flowers from the banks of the stream.

I decided to invite the Writer along on a trip. This time we did not intend to travel far. Mamma felt poorly, but she forced us to go anyway. "Afterward you'll tell me about it, too," she had said repellingly, when Mother let it be known that the rest of us could also stay at home. Otherwise I prob-ably wouldn't have invited him; in fact, there wouldn't have been enough room in the little Moskvič. Now there was an extra seat, why not make use of it? (I didn't think of Jaan—just as he hadn't thought of me.) I was afraid that it wouldn't be permitted. There was a feeling that next I might invite my friends to sleep over at our place. I asked Father. He looked at me with an odd expression and shrugged his shoulders. "Go speak to Mother." Even Mother found this surprising, but as my new friend had made a good impres-sion at the dinner table, she too finally agreed. Mother was dear to me; by permitting this she became even more dear. I leapt and jumped about and helped to get things together. I was certain that he would come. I was not mistaken. He was a bit late but he didn't overstep the permissible boundary. We were already seated in the car when he walked down from the upper courtyard, carrying a small bag of food between his fingers. "Good morning," he said, opening the door. "I'm grateful to you and (at this point he said my name) for the invitation. My aunt sends you her regards." We sat side by side, Memme alongside the food basket, which she did not want to be parted from, although she herself said that the basket could in fact be placed in the trunk. The basket together with Memme took up half the seat. That's why we were squeezed against each other like Siamese twins. At first this was strange and uncomfortable, then we grew accustomed to it and moved our hands and feet dexterously. Every once in a while, I asked Memme for a handkerchief with which to blow my nose, although I didn't have a cold, and I demanded food when my stomach grew empty (it was true, my stomach always quickly grew empty): inside the basket, covered with a white sheet, cabbage pirogi, juice, and cut meats were concealed. I was like a plant, a pea stalk, which makes its first tentative attempts to bind a helpmate by winding around a wooden stick thrust into the ground. Initially we had nothing to talk about, we merely watched— the peaceful landscapes that slipped past us and the cloud rolls like wash that had been wrung. Usually I wasn't one to look around very much. Once in a while, on a trip, I even read a book that had been brought along, but now looking inspired me. I thought that the next time, next summer, I'd wheedle an airplane trip (I had already dropped preparatory hints), and all those places we were now riding past would look completely different then. I had no way of knowing exactly what that "different" was, but I certainly sensed that our reading blanket with two pillows on the green patch of lawn would seem even more like an island, a raft, or a boat then.

We also went to the spring, but since everyone had Mamma, who had been left at home, on their minds, we stopped there for only a moment. No one got out of the car, we looked at the spring, the dairy, and the cooling room through the car window, upon which fell—we hadn't had luck with the weather—the first raindrops. I held the Writer's hand tightly in mine and doubtless he understood, even without asking, what this place meant to us.

It now seemed as if my wishes were almost fulfilled. Giving my hand a squeeze in return, he signaled that he had understood me, that in the future, too, I could count on him. Only one thing made me doubtful. His hands weren't good—they were soft and cold like the spring beneath the cooling chamber. I had encountered hands that were large, hard as crust, and cool; my father had such hands. The simultaneous softness and coldness of the Writer's hands provoked disbelief, estrangement. After all, how often did I greet people by the hand? Nevertheless: I remembered birthdays and New Years well. But his gentle wince in the dusky car was more convincing, I trusted it more than warmth, which might be accidental, caused by something else like fever or weariness, which sitting in a car and looking around would eventually precipitate.

Now one thing still bothered me, gave me no peace: the confession, the dream, for which he had praised me. It was my final objective, my eternal temptation: to find out who I am and whether I am. Nothing changes with age. Others ask, say, wave their hand contemptuously—oh, those romantics! Then a hunched man, with a thick rim of hair around his bald head, springs up from a chair and begins flailing his arms, asserting his rights, although he could calmly hear out what others think about the matter. He simply has a heartfelt, a heartfelt and spiritual need, as does his liver, to make clear that wanting those things which can never be had, and thinking about those things which are never thought about otherwise, isn't the least bit bad, because all—take note: all!—people are like that. In response to the question, like what?, he no longer knows how to respond; instead he simply falls back into the armchair feebly.

Not a single bit of advice or instruction would have helped me. Rather, I hoped for a negative response, an explicit refusal—that which he hadn't wanted to express the first time. "You're not going to amount to anything, of course you're not"—these were the hoped-for sentences, because, as already stated, I feared writing; to look on and wonder from afar was, in any case, preferable.

In fact, I was as insistent as a gypsy. Perhaps I believed that this—negation or confirmation, whichever—would bind us together conclusively and show Jaan, who had been revealed by his actions, his place among the base and worthless. That is why—in the name of becoming "relatives"—I thought up all kinds of tales. One of the most terrible went like this. "Lightly he came"—as if it weren't even me speaking, but rather someone else who was exploiting me for his own interests.

"Do you want me to tell you something? I've already long wanted to, otherwise we can't be friends. You must know everything about me."

At this "everything," a gulp sounded in my throat, I probably gave the impression that I was about to start crying right then—right then, although I hadn't intended to in the slightest. But had Jaan (in bed with the measles, out of the way for a time, out of the game) intended to when I had teased him, called him "apothecary"?

"Just let it out," he emboldened me. We were standing between rows of peas, and we snapped dry peas from inside yellow pods—autumn was coming.

"I haven't told anyone this," I dragged it out even more. The Writer was beginning to take an interest in the matter, that was apparent from his eyes, in which there flared a small flame indicating that he would remember.

"I'm sick," I said. My fingers froze on the pod, the peas fell down, into my sandal.

He measured me for a moment, a moment longer than would have been natural, and then he asked, "Just like Juhan Liiv?"[7]

I nodded eagerly. I knew about Juhan Liiv. Mamma had read me his poems and stories, that same Mamma who now languished in the sickbed behind the screen and no longer wanted to live. It was as if they'd carried the screen there for my sake, so that I wouldn't see, but when I went into the kitchen to eat, I heard anyway. "Give me something," sounded the feeble voice. "Why don't you give me something?" She wanted to be given poison, instead she got tablets, powders, painkillers, and shots. I decided to leave a red poison berry on her plate, if I were allowed near her. Sometimes I was allowed. She stroked my head and gave me caramel candies from a green tin box. That drove the idea of placing a berry before her out of my head. To tell the truth, that had been more a thought than a serious intent. I was much more serious now, as I said to my friend between the garden rows: "I get shots. Twice a day. Right into my blood."

It was really so. Twice a day, in the morning before going to work and at night upon returning from work, Father gave Mamma a shot in her arm. In a few weeks our house had become an apothecary, there were cotton balls lying about everywhere, for no one had the strength to clean them up anymore. Mamma was old, she had no other relatives, that's why we had to make due with our own resources. Mamma was a good patient. Each time, after a shot, she said thank you to Father and added other praise as well. That was so like her, like her life, like life, about which it would now soon be necessary, in all seriousness, to say—"lived." Father deserved thanks. With admiration, I watched him boil the hypodermic needles, draw in the medicine, cleanse her skin with alcohol, and painlessly jab the needle into her flesh. My feeling of apprehension about life henceforth, already so great (not everyone would have had the courage to think such "dangerous" thoughts), became greater still—I knew quite certainly that if something should happen to me, Father would act in exactly the same manner. Likewise, I could trust in Mother and Memme—they, too, helped Mamma as much as they knew how and were able: they fed her, gave her drink, changed linens and washed linens, told her stories, discussed what was happening outside, how the peonies were blooming, how many eggs there were today, etc., etc. No doubt this—as well as the desire to mitigate Mamma's sufferings with personal (what of it that it was imaginary?) participation—prodded me on to lie-to-tell-the-truth.

"Well then, if things go right, you could amount to something," the Writer, who was again wearing knickers as he had at our first encounter, said to me. As then, there were no spots on his pants now either, not even tangled burrs adhered there. It just seemed to be a quality of his—to come out clean.

I felt no joy, but I didn't know how to be sad either. Not before Father came toward me at the door with a strange expression, placed his hand on my shoulder and squeezed it forcefully, as if he wished to lift the flesh there to give a shot.

I rushed inside: Memme was sobbing, Mother was looking out the window, her back toward me.

When I took hold of Mamma's hand, I felt a motion in her palm. I looked, saw, and understood that those were her fingernails, which were stretching out toward the soil—in order to continue hoeing, to remove dried crust from bulbs.

Spring, summer, and autumn, these are like radiant white doors, similar to each other, which open imperceptibly and never close. We carry them with us in our own souls; we cannot forget, even if we wished it.

Mamma was buried a few days later. She was sent to her grave with care; the final moment and breath are not always one and the same.

As I stepped toward the grave beside Mother and Father, I saw—see—the Apothecary boy. He had recovered in the interim; his grandfather, however, had died the same day as Mamma. Angrily, we glowered at one another: he because I had taken the Writer from him, I mostly from habit. The next moment we acted as if it didn't matter to us, as if we didn't even know each other. We were like brothers who had gotten into a fight over an inheritance. The cemetery was small: even though his grandfather was being buried at the other end, the sound of shovels clanging, coughs, words of wisdom, finally even song, were audible to us, and birds that tired of one spectacle could fly from the branches of the willows growing beside the Apothecary plot to the birch that adorned Mamma's gravesite on the other side of the path.

When Jaan and I met a few days later, all had been forgotten. The Writer had been forced to leave the city: vigilant Arus, half-cop, half-schoolteacher, had caught him at a local canteen. Jaan had explained that he had wanted to buy candy for the boys (there were a couple of fifth-grade boys with him, which made the matter even more dubious) from Aliine, but it was apparent from everything—not even the buffet-keeper, Aliine, was able to suppress a smile—that this was untrue. The boys were wrong to be defending the Writer. They should have feigned ignorance. They had no doubt been taken in by him, he was a hero to them. Perhaps they played puppet theater together, although that's difficult to believe: theater requires room, time, and interested parties. What of it that we, Jaan and I, weren't the best of actors? Those boys had other interests. When I looked Jaan in the eye, I understood that he knew what kind of games those were and how Aliine helped in playing them.

"Do you know what?" Jaan was the first to speak. That was astounding; usually he remained silent. The Writer, too, had grown silent. It was in fact with silence, with precisely measured pauses, that he put an end to my reign.

"I want to say something to you."

"What?" The situation grew strange: only a few days ago, the Writer and I had been standing in about the same place, even our tracks were still visible, and we had repeated the same questions. We were like tiny apes, macaques yelping like dogs, squirrels in a wheel, or parrots with many-colored feathers and curved beaks, or all of these combined—if it is possible to imagine such an animal-bird at all.

"Otherwise we can't . . . otherwise we can't be friends."

I was already beginning to grow angry: who was he making a fool of actually, me or himself?

"I had a strange dream . . . " And he told me a dream he had had several months ago, at the beginning of summer. In general terms, it was the same dream I, too, had written down in my notebook.

Did he want, in this manner, to befriend me again? I didn't begin to inquire whether he too had thought up that dream himself, whether he too had written it in a gray-covered notebook and shown it to the Writer, and whether he too had felt so impossibly, downright suffocatingly bad?

With the first autumn rains, we began playing this game (it was my idea, sharing it with Jaan posed no difficulties for me): we climbed to the top of the old plum tree hanging by the fence, and with a thud leapt down onto ground that had previously been a lawn. He who landed deeper was the winner. Both of us wanted to become world champion at super heavyweight lifting, although we had not decided precisely who would start winning, Jaan Apothecary or I. Indeed, it wasn't possible to arrange this for both of us simultaneously—one was always lighter, the other heavier (this was also apparent from the holes we made), and in lifting, in contrast to jumping, it was precisely the lighter one who was the victor. Turn by turn, that was the only possibility. Turn by turn—and continuing that way until the end of life.

Thud and thunk, splish and splash, our jumps to the ground resounded. Mud whirled, dirt flew. No one came to forbid us, although it would have been erroneous to think that they—the commanders, forbidders, saviors—were fewer now. At our house, yes, but Jaan's grandmother, a spry and belligerent old crone had, after her husband's death, come to live with the Apothecarys, her son and her grandson, permanently.

–1988–

■ □ ■ □ ■

Ülo Mattheus

OUR MOTHER

"THIS PHOTO HAS STARED AT US LONG ENOUGH," SAYS
Rasmus during spring cleaning a year after the death of
Mae's mother.

Mae unplugs the vacuum cleaner for a moment. "What
bothers you about it?" she asks, uncomprehending.

Rasmus is unable to explain precisely; it's just a feeling he
has that the picture shouldn't be there on top of the clothes-
press any longer. "That expression—she's scowling at us so
strangely. When your mother was still alive, it always
seemed to me I was in this house thanks only to her charity.
Even when I was with you, it was as if I'd asked her for
permission. After all, she was cognizant of and could hear
our slightest movement. It's interesting, what do you suppose a mother feels when her daughter's with her own husband?"

Mae wonders where Rasmus gets ideas like this. Rasmus
says it's as if he's been living under pressure of some sort the
entire time. Mae looks at him wide-eyed, and Rasmus hastens over to mitigate what he has said. "It wasn't that I dis-
liked her. I even loved her in my own way. If you and I had
been living elsewhere, it would have even been fun to visit
her once in a while." Mae shrugs her shoulders: all right, let

him put that photo away. Then she plugs in the vacuum cleaner again.

The sound of the vacuum cleaner has always set Rasmus's nerves on edge. He sticks the picture of Mae's mother in a photo album and goes down to the basement. That place is pleasing to him in every way: it's fun to rummage through old stuff and to rediscover things he had forgotten existed. Now he sets out to clean the basement systematically, because new stuff, cast helter-skelter, here and there, has collected over the winter.

Dust from the old things penetrates his nose, makes him sneeze just like snuff. Sneezing stimulates and cleans out the lungs. Perhaps it's a desire to sneeze that induces him to browse here, for who could accurately describe that feeling of release.

There really are a great many things in the basement. Mae's mother's loom makes Rasmus feel helpless, for it takes up a lot of space; likewise the clothes chest containing all manner of useless effects. The chest itself is beautiful, but filled with that moist heap, it's in great danger of cracking.

Rasmus shakes his head regretfully. He begins to pick up things scattered in the middle of the floor; to create even a semblance of order, he stacks them in piles beside the wall. Next he sees to the shelves full of apples and clears them of rotted cores, then all the shelves on the workshop side, until, from one crevice, a plaster of paris bust of Mae's mother emerges, scowling at him, and he sits down on a chopping block to think things over. The bust is sooty and has suffered some damage from having been moved from place to place. It is chipped in many spots. Most recently, it stood on the veranda where variable weather conditions also damaged it. The veranda windowpanes are broken, and winters the temperature there is bone-chilling.

Rasmus gets up and scatters the dust on Mae's mother's face. Life itself has congealed upon the bust; even the vacant eyes seem to see. The bust had been created by the sculptor

Pilzman, an old friend of the family. In Pilzman's opinion, there was something australopithecine about Mae's mother; that, in fact, is what had enticed him to model her. But Rasmus never comprehended Pilzman's vision, for the bust of Mae's mother in her youth, before it suffered damage, had been solely the embodiment of everything beautiful. Had Pilzman perhaps observed the power in her features? For Mae's mother did have a large bone structure—her chin also jutted out a bit, and her cheekbones were angular. In Pilzman's words, she was reminiscent of all our mothers—he maintained that a similar image exists in every child's fantasy. However, the bust is really dilapidated now, and why keep it any longer.

Rasmus takes the dust-covered figure in his arms and carries it beneath the cherry tree in the yard. After all, trees badly need lime.

Mae's full figure has given birth to four children: Viia, Valdar, Eesek, and Tae. The curiosity in the yard immediately draws their attention. They patter around the figure and play "Who's in the yard?" But Rasmus still isn't quite sure whether he has acted correctly, and he goes inside to ask Mae.

They stand at the window. Mae says that the windows are soiled; only then does she respond to Rasmus's question. "It's nice indeed to see them playing over there, but. . . . " Mae thinks that, in any case, perhaps he shouldn't have taken the bust out into the yard, there it will be lost forever.

But Rasmus responds, "After all, the bust has also been cast in bronze. It's simply lying there in Pilzman's studio, and it's unlikely he'd even want a great deal for it."

Mae is silent, and now from the yard comes the sound of Eesek's song: "Who's in the yard? Who's in the yard? Grandma's in the yard." Valdar tells Eesek he's singing wrong, which seems to make him pout. But Viia stands up for him: let him sing wrong, he's still little. Then they all continue in unison: "Who's in the yard? Who's in the yard? A bee's in the yard . . . "

ÜLO MATTHEUS

"Now, at least even the cherry trees will get some fertilizer," says Rasmus. Mae does not respond.

"That's really nice to watch," she says after quite a while. Meaning the children, probably. And she doesn't even attempt to change Rasmus's mind: he might start thinking that he's really not allowed to decide anything here.

When the sun shines, the snow melts quickly. Even the last soiled little islands disappear. Then dense, early spring rain falls. With a slight feeling of regret, Rasmus watches Mae's mother gradually disintegrate in the yard. Every time he returns from work, he casts a glance outside. First the face melted and flowed down the chest, following this a wire framework grew visible from within the head and gradually the chest also began to grow thinner. The melt and rainwater have hollowed a channel in the yard and now little plaster-filled streams flow directly toward the house and trickle down the cellar stairs into a well. During large downpours, it seems filled with milk and effervescent.

Rain is melancholy. Like pinecones, the four children sit beneath a fir-green awning where, in summer, firewood is dried, and they stare mournfully into the gray wall of water that holds them prisoner. It occurs to Rasmus that he should call the children inside, but at the same time he thinks they probably like to squat there that way. Rain can also be beautiful, even if you don't see it as such at times. Those children aren't the least bit sad.

"Maybe we should move the furniture around," says Rasmus.

Mae remains standing at the door, her washbasin filled with wash. "What for?" she responds, uncomprehending.

Rasmus says, "To change things in some way."

And Mae, "I have to wash a week's worth of the children's clothes and take it to dry."

Now Rasmus is amazed: "Why are you taking that wash out there in the rain?"

They stand. Mae says that the rain's bound to let up sometime. And then in fact she goes out into the yard. Rasmus sees her bustling about in the rain. The water splashes against her cape and trickles down into the white streams. The children, too, are there immediately: if mother can be out there in the rain, then they can, too, can't they? With sticks, they poke open the puddles that have formed between the garden rows and set the waters free. Some of the trickles are already quite like streams.

Rasmus patters down into the basement: of course, the water has trickled down beneath the doorsill and now the basement floor is also full of that white stuff. He thrusts open the door. "Kids, you nuts! What are you doing there!" he shouts into the wall of rain. But the children do not hear. They grab Mae's cape by the tail, and when she has hung the wash out to dry, they play train together. Mother is taller than they are, that's why mother is the smokestack. Too bad, though, that there's no smoke. But then Mae rides inside and pulls the children-cars along with her. Tae is shivering with cold. "Look, you've frozen Tae," Rasmus chastises Viia and Valdar, because they are older than the others and should know what they're doing. But of course he doesn't scold angrily; he does so only for appearance sake.

Later they watch a children's program on television. The gray television screen is just like a hole through which they all go wandering out together. Today they are at the zoo. Eesek likes an anteater that is defecating on a hutch roof. They rest their gaze on it, only a bit embarrassed, for they are immediately at the monkey cage and guffaw along with the chimpanzees. From there, they go on to wonder at the buffalo and the bison, one of which is also defecating. They've chanced to the zoo at a very bad time today. In any case, the studio seems more interesting to Valdar. He says that a man was half-tottering over the light bridge railing and almost fell down—who knows what was going on in his head.

Rasmus soon wearies and returns to the room from the tele-world. But he finds that room, with its green wallpaper, disagreeable, which is why he goes to see whether Mae has finished with the wash. Mae can't get over her surprise at his arrival, for if someone is already there ahead of him, Rasmus doesn't insist upon entering the bathroom without a reason. Rasmus himself is also at a loss: he embraces Mae from behind, puts his hands into the sudsy washbasin together with hers, and departs again.

He goes up the stairs to the attic and eyes the junk that has been carted up there. The attic also badly needs a cleaning, but it's unlikely he'll have the energy for that today. Maybe it's spring lethargy. He trudges back down and digs some vitamin C out of a jar on the kitchen windowsill.

"The house seems to need some repairs," Rasmus says to Mae at cherry blossom time. "That green wallpaper feels so cold, it downright makes you shiver sometimes."

It's a moment when they happen to be discussing such things. Mae says that the cherries are blooming madly. They've opened the window and the room is filled with scent.

Rasmus says, "And the vestibule is stained."

And Mae, "That is really amazing."

They're alone in their thoughts. In Rasmus's opinion, the bathroom also needs serious work. With dread, he ponders that there's more work than he'd care to do. And Mae: "In the autumn there'll be a rush to can cherries. I should probably get the jar lids early, 'cause when you need them, there'll be none to buy."

They go into the yard and sit on the lawn chairs. Birds are twittering all around. Some species don't find it burdensome to also twitter in the afternoon. The ravens as well. From time to time, they fly over the house in cawing flocks. Rasmus likes ravens: there's something sinisterly exotic about their cawing. "What do ravens eat?" asks Eesek, who is just at the age to be interested in everything. Valdar has brought the swing into the yard and he is swinging; Viia is waiting her turn. Eesek doesn't know how to swing well yet, and Tae is also too small for that.

"Ravens mostly eat all kinds of carrion and leavings," explains Rasmus. Eesek doesn't understand what carrion is, and Rasmus says, "Carrion is . . . " He falls into thought, for how do you explain that to a child?

Rasmus brings a shovel and loosens the soil beneath some unhoed cherry trees. He presses together the wire framework remains of Mae's mother and throws it into an ashcan. Mae, however, takes a rake, for she likes to rake, although the old leaves have all been raked up already and put into the compost. There's still a bit of trash left here and there. Now seems to be more the time for weeds—which are attacking from every open patch of soil. The lawn alone keeps the parasites in line; only buttercups and tea leaves grow there, and these they use for compresses.

"Yard work never ends," says Rasmus, and he leans on the shovel handle. He once had neuritis; now it's making itself felt in the small of his back.

And Mae, "I'm feeling dizzy again. The scent of those flowers is horrific, it makes your head spin." She puts down the rake and sits back on the chair. Tae crawls onto Mae's lap and plays with her hair. She says something only she understands. And perhaps Mae, a little bit.

Come summer, Rasmus has a serious yen to renovate. Only for a few weeks, actually. By the time he succeeds in getting the paints and the wallpaper, the urge has passed and the materials are left in the basement. He has removed all the pictures from the walls in order to change things a bit, and now the rectangles unfaded beneath them scowl at him vacantly. He thought that he would buy new pictures. He had even been to art show sales, but the cost of original work seemed overbearing. And, of course, he didn't want kitsch either. Household expenses consumed all his beautiful wishes. In their stead, he'd procure coal and wood; he'd haul away ashes and have the john cleaned.

Mae comes over and says that the furrows in the strawberry patches have become clogged and that Rasmus should open them again. Rasmus explains that this won't have a very good effect on the garden at all, actually: moisture will seep from within the raised furrows of soil and be lost to the plants, because the furrows act as drying ditches. Nevertheless, Mae still wants the drying ditches. She says this gives the impression of order and also makes it easier to get to the strawberries without fear of crushing them.

Rasmus takes the shovel again—its handle quite burnished with use—and he heads for the strawberry patches. The furrows have, in fact, risen higher than the level of the patches. That's strange indeed, he thinks. Such a thing certainly wouldn't catch my eye without cause. He thrusts the shovel into the soil but the earth is resilient and resists, so that the steel forces itself to a depth of only a few centimeters. There certainly shouldn't be anything growing here, thinks Rasmus, and strikes it again. Now a white wound becomes visible in a soil root—a light little notch. Rasmus pries the root loose so that he can grasp it with his hand, and he begins to tug the root out. It is long: it stretches and stretches together with the risen soil crust and meshes its own moist, tickling, fibrous roots around his forearms. Actually, roots shouldn't be torn out of the earth in this manner, but since he's already begun, there's no escape, for the root has been damaged in any case.

The root leads Rasmus down what was previously a garden furrow to the nearest cherry tree. He intends to chop it loose from the trunk and prepares to get an ax, but the root catches around his legs and Rasmus stumbles. Almost falls, in fact. As is typical of such an instance, he's a bit resentful. Rasmus seizes the root; he's certain he'll simply tear it out, but the root is tenacious. Shaking it only lands dirt particles in his eye, so that Rasmus isn't able to see anything for a long while.

Finally Rasmus gets an ax from the basement. He splits the root with a single stroke and disinfects the gleaming wound with nitrophene. Following this, he comes into the room to wash up. Nitrophene is a tobacco-colored insecticide quickly absorbed by the skin and impossible to get off afterward. "What in the world are you doing there?" inquires Mae. Rasmus explains wearily that a root got in his way.

Perhaps it's due to the nitrophene that Rasmus's head eventually begins to ache and he feels sluggish. He thinks, never mind about those strawberry patches. Mae comes over to him beside the armchair and caresses him, crawls under his shirt. Rasmus is somewhat happy. "What if we sold the house and got an apartment?" he says.

Initially Mae remains motionless under his shirt, then she slides out. She says pensively, "I was born here." This disarms Rasmus, and their conversation stops at that, for it isn't their custom to quarrel. "What if we actually did replace the green wallpaper with another," Mae agrees. "That beige one you bought."

The summer has been filled with sunshine and occasionally damp as well. At least once a week the house needs to be heated. In July, Rasmus discovers that the coal storage room has filled with fibrous roots. They used to use peat briquettes—had the roots come from that peat, perhaps? The roots have even pressed between the foundation joints and furrowed out a mixture of some sort there; some of them have also seized hold of the cement ceiling.

Rasmus tears the roots loose and burns them. But they constantly grow anew. This will probably be long and time-consuming work, he thinks. I'll have to find the mother root—I won't get rid of this bother otherwise. He is still not quite convinced of the existence of a mother root, for peat has nothing like this, peat roots grow evenly. Besides, the storeroom is still half-full of coal, so that he couldn't even get near it.

During free moments and on warm days, they stay mostly outside. They even eat there, for in the fresh air the appetite is better. And they sleep in a tent erected on the lawn. The children are crazy about this, and it's probably good for toughening them up. In fact, Rasmus and Mae spend the night in a sleeping bag right out under the open sky. In clear weather, this is very exotic. Rasmus has taken it upon himself to locate the stars on the firmament precisely. Sometimes he and Mae chatter until early morning, until the stars grow dim. "That's definitely Cassiopeia over there," says Mae, and Rasmus argues that Mae is no doubt thinking of Kefeus, which is located between the North Star and the Swan, for Cassiopeia is actually located between the North Star and Andromeda. After this, they search the heavens for Andromeda, but they don't find it.

"Maybe it isn't visible now," Rasmus conjectures. They don't know very much at all about astronomy yet.

Life in the house comes to a standstill in various ways. They even avoid being there. At the beginning of August, Rasmus discovers that the floorboards have been forced up in some places. When he bends down to examine the situation more closely, he sees that there are tiny fibrous roots between the cracks in the boards. The roots have gone quite mad, he thinks. He goes back out and tells Mae that as well. His wife is in the raspberries with the children; they're searching for late berries together. "The cherries will be ripe soon, too," says Mae. "See how many of them there are!" And, following this, "Perhaps the cherries should be covered with nets so that the birds can't get near. This year there are a tremendous number of thrush." Rasmus brings nets from the basement and does the job. With a feeling of regret, it occurs to him that many a bird could get caught in there and break its wings. But what's to be done, the children are impatiently waiting for cherries.

"We should probably renovate after all," says Rasmus later. "The house is getting out of control."

And Mae, "Perhaps we really should."

They lie on the grass, but not to sunbathe. The August sun is no longer suitable for that. They simply lie there with their clothes on. "This is a good place to live after all," says Mae. "Everything's so beautiful."

It's unlikely that Rasmus would be able to convince her otherwise, and sometimes he himself also finds that it's beautiful, although thoughts of a different nature also occur to him. "We'll probably never get control of those weeds," he says. He takes a dandelion that has already bloomed, blows its seeds into the air, and makes a whistle from its stem. At that honking sound, Eesek immediately comes over to him, but the boy has no success in whistling.

Rasmus and Mae locate the stars in the order they become visible on the firmament. It occurs to Rasmus that sometime long ago he might have been a good seaman.

In the latter part of August, the nights are already cooler and they draw a plastic cover over the sleeping bag. The membrane retains warmth well, although the sleeping bag within it has a tendency to grow damp. But then again they don't have to carry it on their backs the next day like hikers, who avoid each additional ounce. They have time enough to dry the bag.

"Perhaps we should move inside," Rasmus suggests. He doesn't care for this dampness at all.

Mae says that she'd like to stay out a few more nights, and the children agree with her—they're already quite stalwart and fit, not even sensitive to the cold anymore. "To think they haven't even had the sniffles," says Mae. That's amazing: winters, the children are sick constantly and always at the same time, for when one gets sick, the others catch it too. Perhaps, with this toughening up, they'll be more resistant to a flu epidemic. "When the cherries have been picked, we'll go." Mae finds a subterfuge and Rasmus agrees: the cherries will soon be ripe; in fact, they're already half-red in the cheek, a week at most.

The seven days pass quickly: in the morning an alarm clock rings in the grass, Rasmus goes to work, and when he returns another day is nearly past, for evening time vanishes unnoticed. Vanishes perhaps because they have internalized within themselves a sense of joy, although they have worries too. But they simply don't think about these, they don't let the worries eat at them. Only once in a great while is Rasmus seized by a vague restlessness. As before, he thinks they would have fewer cares in a publicly owned apartment. He thinks, what if I . . . But it all ends at that.

Then the cherries ripen. Rasmus places a ladder beneath the tree and goes inside to get some cans. The rooms are now completely full of roots: they've wrapped themselves around the furniture and some of the larger ones are in fact dangling from the candelabra. Actually it's beautiful how those naked, white roots have wrapped themselves everywhere. They've enveloped the house as if they were protecting it. But would it also be possible to live in such a room? The roots don't consider that. No, Rasmus definitely doesn't want to be in this house any longer. He'll never overcome the feeling of being a son-in-law living with his wife's parents. A city apartment would be a neutral place; there he and Mae would be equals. If Mae won't come, I'll go alone, Rasmus decides. And suddenly his spirit is freed of its shackles: he'll go, Mae will follow with the children—what choice does she have?

Rasmus prepares to depart, to make his decision known to Mae, and at that very moment the roots seize hold of him. Without Rasmus being able to resist, they've wrapped themselves around his hands, feet, and face. He does indeed try to wrest himself free, but the roots are tenacious; they do not break or give way. They stretch toward him from the ceiling, the curtain rods, the walls, and from beneath the rug. Then, Rasmus feels the roots growing into his flesh. For some reason this isn't even painful, his flesh merely tingles oddly. It occurs to him that he should call for help, but the roots have even bound his tongue and some of them have grown through his vocal chords. But he'd like to call, even to lament a bit: "Ai, ai, ai, the roots are at me!" Only his eyes remain open, although the roots are already stretching toward them too. Rasmus can still see the children caper beneath the cherry tree and eat berries bursting with juice, their mouths completely red.

–1987–

THE ROAD TO ROME

JAKOB WAITED FOR ONE MORE TOURIST GROUP—THEY WERE British, primarily older ladies. He immortalized them on a picture with old Gothic-style buildings serving nicely as a background, gave the guide the studio's card, packed up the camera and tripod, and hastened directly home.

When he arrived, Hubert was playing the piano.

"Home already?" His brother was amazed, for Jakob usually came later.

"Yes," responded Jakob and, sensing that he was disturbing his brother, he crept over to his desk in the corner. They had only one room between them. Jakob was compiling a guide to Tallinn, and he had become so absorbed in this work that he let nothing affect him.

Hubert tried to continue playing, but to no avail. He then went into the kitchen and made some tea. Jakob could hear Hubert clattering dishes in there defiantly. And soon his brother was back. "Well, is work progressing?" he asked. But there was no sign of interest in his voice, and Jakob did not respond. "If you'd only involve yourself in something sensible," said Hubert crossly and set his teacup on the piano with a loud rap. There was still one thing and another he would have liked to try, the ending of the prelude wasn't quite mastered, but, as if out of spite, Jakob gave him no peace.

"And what would that sensible thing be?" muttered Jakob. Behind his back, he didn't see Hubert shrug his shoulders.

"Well, I don't know," Hubert drawled. "I know what isn't sensible." Now he was standing beside Jakob. "Like that monograph of yours about Tallinn's monuments, for instance. It turned out foolish. No wonder a publisher couldn't be found for it." He leaned his hands on the table. "By the way, the photos were good, honest . . . "

Jakob didn't take his brother particularly seriously. Hubert was some ten years younger than he and that explained a good number of things. The fact that Hubert was an acclaimed pianist and the winner of many competitions meant nothing to Jakob.

"And your biography of Marcellanus!" continued Hubert. "Just think about it, you found some sort of unknown scribe, and you're already trying to make who knows what of him!" He seized Jakob's manuscript from the shelf and brandished it in the air.

Jakob didn't understand what his brother had against Marcellanus's story. It was piquant and enticing in every sense. Namely, the poet Marcellanus was said to have borne an unrequited love for the patrician Messalina and drowned himself in the Tiber, whereupon the deities that favor unfortunate lovers turned him into a demon. It was said that Marcellanus had then crept into Messalina, and Messalina became a prostitute. In this manner, Marcellanus, too, received satisfaction. And, in addition, Marcellanus taught Messalina dirty little ditties, which she sang on the street. They'd been dubbed marcellans after their creator.

"And now your Tallinn guide! There've already been scores of them before yours. Where's this going to get you . . . " Hubert paced around the room nervously, but Jakob didn't even seem to notice. He had arranged some pictures and maps in a row on the table, and they absorbed all his attention.

"Oh, I will, I will," said Jakob absentmindedly. "All roads lead to Rome." He had heard only his brother's last words.

"To Rome, to Rome," mocked Hubert. "There's no talking sensibly with you."

Jakob took a magnifying glass out of the desk drawer and set it down on an old map of the city. "Come look," he invited his brother. Hubert was unable to overcome his bad mood, but he went and looked anyway. "You see, here's a tiny street. Ro Street," said Jakob. Hubert looked through the magnifying glass. The name was barely legible, and, in addition, it was precisely at the crease in the map.

"Well, yes, so it is, but a city's supposed to have streets, isn't it," observed Hubert.

However, Jakob continued, now pointing to another map: "You see, there's a building here in place of that street."

Hubert nodded. "It's not surprising that a building was put up to replace that bit of a street," he said.

Jakob then directed Hubert's attention to a third map. "Look, here that house doesn't exist, and it's Ro Street again."

Hubert was at a loss for a moment. "But what's the date of those maps?" he then inquired.

And Jakob enumerated: "The first is dated 1484, the second 1751, and the third 1884."

For some time Hubert again said nothing. "Well," he finally drawled, "maybe that third fellow made a mistake, based his work on the 1484 map or else on one a bit later which, likewise, didn't have that building." Hubert shrugged his shoulders, and Jakob had nothing more to add either.

Hubert then sat down at the piano and drank the tea, which had already cooled. He pressed down on a key, but then gave up wearily. "Is that building still in existence now, too?" he asked, as there was nothing to be done at the piano.

Jakob got up and placed two pictures on the keys in front of Hubert, an old engraving from the eighteenth century on which, among the buildings on Ra Street, that one built on Ro Street was also depicted and a photo he himself had taken of the same structure. "It definitely does exist," he said.

Hubert took only a fleeting glance at the pictures. "Oh, what gibberish," he judged. "No doubt that 1884 fellow made a mistake." Actually that building didn't interest him in the slightest. He tried to concentrate on the notes, but even these suddenly seemed repugnant to him.

"Just like a fairy tale," said Jakob. "Perhaps that street becomes visible every hundred years, on the eighty-fourth year of each century. It's now 1984 . . . "

However, Hubert no longer responded. It was better not to talk with Jakob at all; he always had all manner of foolish ideas in his head.

"For some unknown reason," Jakob added.

The photography studio where Jakob worked was also located on Ra Street. He walked past the Ro Street house every day. A tourist bureau was located there. He dropped in there frequently, for no particular reason; in fact, he himself didn't even know why. He ambled down the long, windy corridors, which didn't have a single window. The employees always eyed him peculiarly, as if they already knew beforehand that he had chanced into the wrong place. Despite this, they made polite inquires about who or what he wanted, and they said that if he was looking for the lavatory, all those rooms were locked. However, because Jakob happened to be standing at his door, a small half-bald man had once asked whether Jakob had come for his Mediterranean passport, and the man had directed him into his office. Jakob had been confused for a moment. He had let the functionary rustle through papers, and thereupon Jakob had announced that actually he wanted to take a few pictures from the window.

The functionary had peered at him questioningly, and then inquired whether his name was in fact Rutmar Salomon. When Jakob shook his head, it seemed the functionary felt a bit sorry for him. "So you're not Rutmar Salomon, in fact?" he muttered to himself. Finally he got up from the desk, and together with Jakob went over to the window. "There is a magnificent view of Ru Street from here," said the functionary, and thrust the window sashes wide open. He inhaled a chestful of fresh air, and then, sighing, he blew out to empty his lungs as if they were filled with dense paper dust. And suddenly he became a new person. "You're so like Rutmar Salomon," he said, sighing and looking at Jakob with a very humanitarian expression. "Think of it—the subtropics. . . . Some people really do have luck." And Jakob didn't comprehend one iota of what he was saying . . .

"A travel bureau's located there, by the way," Jakob said to Hubert, and he had no idea why this had suddenly occurred to him. Jakob took two more maps out of the drawer, the ones dated 1938 and 1977. It's true he had already examined them thoroughly, but that didn't mean anything. The thicket of lines before him concealed within it inexplicable magic, it captivated his glance like a magnet. Inspired, he walked along familiar streets, passed through archways, crossed plazas, or, envisioning the photocopies made in archives, he moved within them together with the changes that had taken place over time.

"Well, where are you going to get this way!" Hubert grumbled again, as if waking him right from sleep. In Hubert's opinion, concentration without a goal was senseless. If one concentrated, it was always with a purpose of some sort in mind. To him, Jakob's Tallinn guide merely signified foolishness. "You used to have shows, you had clout in photography circles, but now?" continued his brother. And Jakob thought, let Hubert grumble. Perhaps he, Jakob, didn't want to get anywhere, in fact. His ventures simply gave him a feeling of satisfaction for no particular reason, even though Hubert tried to convince him that for every person there existed only a single road—one must find it and not wander about in reality's wilds.

THE ROAD TO ROME

Usually Jakob simply let his brother's fits of moralizing pass without even taking the trouble to defend himself. Actually they understood each other superbly, and what's more, perhaps they didn't even know how to exist without each other. And Jakob also liked Hubert's interpretations of music. Hubert chose pieces from the heights of lyricism. The compositions he performed were light and rippling. In Jakob's opinion, however, "the heights of lyricism" and "the wilds of reality" were one and the same. In some respects Hubert agreed, but at the same time he maintained that his choice was based upon the public's taste and not his own, because, after all, people came to a concert to relax, didn't they? And here Jakob caught Hubert deceiving himself. For music must come from the soul; otherwise, even robots could sit down at a piano . . .

Hubert played. It was apparently a prelude, one by Chopin perhaps, or someone else—Jakob wasn't an expert. But there was an irritating undertone to the music, abrupt, tearing chords. Jakob looked at Hubert in amazement. On his forehead there were a few sharp creases. Jakob couldn't comprehend in the slightest how a renowned pianist could have such weak powers of concentration. More and more frequently, Hubert's glance came to rest on the clock, for at about six Jakob usually went to the studio to develop pictures, and then he'd get some peace from his brother.

The studio closed at six, and then only Dore, the compact, blue-eyed woman who assigned jobs, was there. Jakob liked Dore: she was open and talkative, with her you could unwind completely. Both of them talked at the same time and neither listened to the other. They simply chattered, and, oddly enough, all life's cares seemed to flow out of Jakob without his having gained any understanding. But actually, in Jakob's opinion, understanding wasn't always the sole true road, because people with understanding were, for the most part, also burdensome. They wore a scholar's mild expression and always had words of wisdom poised. Understanding exacted a high price.

Afterward Jakob shut himself in the darkroom, and when Dore had left and the film was drying, he sat in the waiting room. It had the feeling of waiting, and Jakob liked that too. Occasionally he also came to the studio during working hours and surreptitiously peered through the door at how clients preened themselves before a picture-taking session, a bit excited, a bit awkward—one liked to pose, another didn't. Or he studied their expressions as they tried to recognize themselves in the photographs they had received, seemingly incredulous that this was indeed the right picture. People were strangers to themselves, and in this way Jakob believed he was glimpsing their true nature. Suddenly they seemed comprehensible and close.

Tired of the waiting room, Jakob settled in to develop photos. He placed the film in the enlarger, sharpened the image, positioned the group, and—there it was. Those bizarre types referred to as tourists. Torn from their natural surroundings, it was possible to discern in their faces many shades of childlike enthusiasm as well as stupidity, excessive animation, and senseless bravado. This wafted everywhere about them to such an extent that it even congealed upon the contact paper, and thus, miraculously fixed, also infected Jakob, who in eyeing the tourists suddenly felt an undefined yearning. He could sit in the darkroom for hours, and when the work was completed, he was seized by an overwhelming sadness . . .

Jakob had often wondered why Hubert didn't find himself a new apartment—he could practice alone there in peace. He need never fear that Jakob would come and disturb him. Or did he, in fact, need such disturbance? Simply to have someone come from time to time. They had already coexisted this way for nine years. Jakob sensed that Hubert sometimes considered him a child, his brother wouldn't just leave him. Although Hubert also had Rhea, a violinist and as beautiful as a model. They were to marry soon, and Jakob couldn't ascertain whether his brother intended to bring his wife into their one room also. No, of course not. That would be odd. How in the world would they live then?

Hubert's concert took place on Saturday. Usually Rhea came to visit them beforehand, as now, and the three of them drank Turkish coffee. They would relax there before departing. Apparently Hubert needed this to calm himself. Previously the two of them used to sit together, but Jakob hadn't been jealous. He too found Rhea pleasing in every respect. The proximity of a beautiful woman was electrifying. Jakob himself had only Priscilla: she wasn't beautiful, she was married, and she had two children; her sole virtue was that her husband was often sent away on business.

Generally they didn't talk very much at all before a concert. Hubert was nervous and perspired profusely. He put on a clean shirt immediately before departing. To relieve the tension, Rhea made a few jokes about their bachelor existence and laughed continuously. Jakob found even her laughter pleasing: it was open and sisterlike. Actually Jakob missed having a sister, for unfortunately he had not been given one. He felt the lack of a woman's daily presence. It was different with Priscilla: everything between them was strangely feverish, as if stolen. Jakob wouldn't have had anything against living with Rhea and Hubert, but in a larger apartment, of course. And Rhea, too, no doubt related to him as trustingly as in a brother. She often talked to him about Hubert, complained about her concerns. These were indeed simple in nature, for actually everything was in order between her and Hubert, but nevertheless. Jakob was particularly pleased about this. The two of them were more than a match for Hubert, he couldn't chide them both at once, and Hubert was forced to yield.

Finally they got into Hubert's car and drove up to the

concert hall. Then Jakob was left alone with Rhea because, immediately before a performance, Hubert wanted to be alone. He went to his dressing room, put on his tuxedo and . . . Jakob couldn't imagine what else he did there. Jakob and Rhea drank lemonade at the café, and afterward they walked about the corridor. Rhea took him by the arm, and Jakob felt as if an electric fish had slipped into his breast—everything whirred so pleasantly. They were always joined by many people, mostly musicians. Thanks to his brother, a bit of honor also fell to Jakob, although he had no need of it. He would rather have avoided those friends and been only with Rhea. Of course, he also had Rhea only thanks to his brother, but that was another matter; it was a private family concern. Some who were less au courant actually considered Rhea to be Jakob's chosen one, and their jealousy was visible. This made Jakob happy, and he didn't have an opportunity to rectify the misconceptions because, of course, the matter was not spoken of directly. Actually, those people themselves should have sensed that such a beauty couldn't belong to Jakob, a roundish, plump little man with sparse hair such as he was. But the eye is king; what is seen is believed.

Then a bell rang and they went into the concert hall. Rhea leaned over to the armrest on Jakob's side trustingly; she didn't ever draw her elbow away when it came into contact with Jakob's. And so the electric fish remained in the latter's breast as before, and when the concert began the music coursed through them simultaneously. Anticipating this, they looked at the audience, and in looking at the audience Jakob was actually looking at Rhea. Then Hubert came on the stage, and with a bow he thanked the listeners for the applause with which they had received him. He sat down at the piano, began to play. Jakob closed his eyes, for this is how he cut himself off from all distraction. Initially there was still Rhea's touch, but even that was soon forgotten. Jakob was alone with his thoughts and emotions. And, strangely enough, he was again rambling somewhere in time, somewhere in a distant space. On those streets he stood before open windows, looked down. The more the music carried him with it, the more unreal his vision became. The music was like a *laterna magica*. Those were perfect moments, and even Hubert understood this when he and his brother chanced to discuss it. For this was music . . .

After the concert, he and Rhea were together once again, because Jakob wanted to walk home and Rhea likewise, but Hubert didn't dare leave the car on the street overnight. Hubert said never mind, he'd stop at a store and buy some cognac. They walked together arm in arm. But actually Jakob was alone, Rhea merely provided a good repose for him, and this forced him to delve into himself. The mood emanating from them was like that of an old house. Of course, they did also talk a bit, but this didn't disturb Jakob in the slightest. Rhea's voice had a pleasant, sad undertone, and, besides, she knew the right time to keep silent.

The evening city was nearly deserted. Dark office windows glowered mutely. "Why don't you write a novel?" asked Rhea. Since Jakob already liked to write. . . . And Jakob responded that he simply didn't know how. At that moment the streetlights went on, and since the streets were empty, suddenly this seemed senseless. Or was it perhaps for them alone? As if someone were secretly shadowing them. "Well, you'll never get anywhere this way," said Rhea, exactly as if Hubert had put the words in her mouth. But Jakob wasn't angry, for Rhea had already put her head on his shoulder and was pressing herself against him apologetically. The woman's frailty canceled out all the disagreeable words.

Tree shadows fell onto the street, and a few tardy sparrows were hopping on the pavement. Jakob asked why a person couldn't simply live for a moment like this one, for instance. But Rhea didn't respond. She drew away from Jakob a bit—had he perhaps gone too far?—and her head inclined a little. She seemed to be weighing what to say. Had

Jakob fallen in love with her? The idea was simultaneously pleasant and not, still she would have preferred not. No, no. Jakob was simply a scatterbrain. A good human being she felt close to.

It seemed to Rhea that, along with Hubert, she had gotten Jakob as well. Actually, she was attached to Jakob. Just as you are to an older brother who always stands by you, genial and well-meaning. And perhaps, without Jakob, Hubert might have become nothing but a go-getter. What of it that Hubert himself didn't want to admit this? Jakob's goodness filtered into him secretly. Actually, she and Hubert were children, and, with his gentle glance, Jakob watched as they acted out their lives. His presence also forced Rhea to stop once in a while and view herself from aside. Yes, Jakob was somewhere up high—somewhere up high and supremely near . . .

Jakob listened to the click of Rhea's high-heeled shoes on the pavement. From somewhere came the sound of distant carriage wheels. Voices. "Where are we going?" asked Rhea, for they had strayed a bit from the way home, and Jakob said, wasn't it all the same where they went, really? And Rhea nodded: beside Jakob perhaps it didn't matter at all, actually. Beside a good person . . .

A bluish gaslight burned in the street lamps, it made the streets seem bewitched. The voices had grown louder. There were clearly distinguishable words, sentences, laughter. . . . Then piano music. (Hubert was self-absorbed, absent.) Afterward, however, came the sound of a powerful round of applause, bursting forth directly from the open windows. Involuntarily, Jakob had seized Rhea's hand, and she hadn't drawn it away. All around, chairs clattered, there was the sound of conversational chatter. That too diffused onto the street along with the chattering people. They were oddly dressed, almost as if it were the turn of the century, in tailcoats, tuxedos, evening dresses. (Where are we going? asked Rhea.) Jakob felt exceptionally fine. Inside, the atmosphere was genial. (We'll see, responded Jakob.) They had come to Ra Street. Two good people. (You'll never get anywhere this way, said Hubert.) And here it was in fact, Ro Street (barely legible and right at the crease in the map—and suddenly Jakob understood that some of the letters were simply missing there.) An endless street. If they wished, they could go down it now. Written so clearly on the corner of the house: Rome Street. "Do you see?" asked Jakob. But Rhea didn't answer. She only pressed herself against him. Completely without cause, completely by chance.

–1987–

THE ROCOCO LADY

SHE PASSED BENEATH OUR WINDOW AGAIN WEARING A DARK brown suit fitted at the bodice, the lower portion of her jacket, together with two flared ruffles, luxuriant on her hips. Her hair was an odd color—grayish-white, arranged in a smooth part on her brow; it fell onto her cheeks and back in coiled ringlets. Beneath her arm she carried a tiny brown purse, and her high-heeled shoes were also brown.

"The rococo lady," said Mother, noticing my captivated glance. The word "rococo" was unfamiliar to me, making it all the more appropriate for denoting this mysterious woman, so different from all the rest. "The rococo lady," I repeated, unable to believe that a word as odd as "rococo" existed and that it, specifically, was used to designate a creature such as that beauty in the brown suit. I didn't even ask Mother what "rococo" meant. I didn't want to ask because there was a bit of derision in Mother's voice, wasn't there?

The beautiful lady lived two houses down from us, in a second-story apartment. Drawn across her windows there were mysterious curtains, different from all other curtains I had ever seen, and Mother had also referred to them with a strange word unfamiliar to me—*Jugend*. And so, there was yet another word bound to this lady I admired, one that referred solely to her.

I rang the bell of the girl next door to invite her out into the yard. These neighbors had moved into our building after the war, and an extra word had also been thought up to specify them—*petsoora*.[1] They, too, were entirely deserving of that special label because they were different from the other people in our building. Among themselves they spoke in Russian, but with me they spoke a peculiar Estonian not exactly like that which we spoke at home. But I did indeed understand their conversation. The *petsooras* had two daughters—Anna and Yevgenia, however they were hardly ever referred to that way. Anna was called Nyura for some reason, and Yevgenia was referred to as Ženya. Their father, a perpetually somber man with a reddish face and sparse, light hair was a captain. He wore officer's dress, drank liquor, and when he had drunk a great deal he fired a revolver in the yard. It was exciting except that his wife, Marusya, always prevented us from watching the captain shoot. After the first shot, Marusya's scream of desperation would sound from the building's direction, and she'd storm into the yard, seize us all into her arms as she herself would begin arguing with the captain in Russian. Then the captain would usually turn the revolver toward us, shout, and his face would turn bright red. Looking terrible and proud, he was absolutely ablaze, but he didn't fire the revolver anymore.

Marusya had a little shed in the yard; the captain had built it together with his soldiers. In the shed lived a goat, Katya, an intelligent, sociable animal that comprehended everything. When Ženya and Nyura weren't in the yard, I went over to Katya, turned her drinking pail upside down, climbed onto the pail in order to reach over into the pen, enticed Katya over to me with bread, grasped her horns, and talked to her. Katya nodded her head and rolled her eyes.

Katya especially liked when I rubbed my nose against her hairy snout, murmuring softly.

Nyura and Ženya had had yet another sister, Lyusya, but she was dead. Sometimes we went to her grave at the cemetery. Lyusya was buried in a place called the children's row, which was in fact filled with little graves. Lyusya, too, had her own little grave with a cement border, entirely covered with tiny little stones. The grave also had a plaque with a name. Some of the letters of the Cyrillic alphabet were even familiar to me: I could read the a's, the m, the o's, the k's. Ženya said that actually Lyudmilla Popkina was written on the plaque because Lyusya's real name had been Lyudmilla.

When the three of us were at Lyusya's grave and no strangers were visible nearby, Nyura usually danced for Lyusya. She whirled among the graves, extended her hands, and raised her tiny feet, humming to herself. Ženya and I sat on the cement border of Lyusya's grave and fingered the little stones. Afterward we all went to look at the bride together. The bride had died right in front of the altar, even before she had been able to say her "I do." The groom had later had the statue of her made. The statue had been placed in a small mausoleum that had windows with iron grating, and the statue stood right at the head of a grave that was probably her grave in fact. There were two more graves there. All three graves in the stone floor were very small. I wondered how coffins had been lowered into such small graves, but Ženya said that the graves had been there first and the mausoleum had been built on top of them.

I liked the bride very much. I looked and looked at her through the window latticework and I wished that she were alive . . . Even when alive, her skin must have been pale, almost white, like the marble statue's, except that on living skin, on the nose and soft arms there are tiny, yellowish-brown freckles. The bride's hair is grayish-white, almost like the rococo lady's, except that it is short and there is a white flower in her hair. The folds of her pale dress flutter around her feet and silver roses adorn her little white shoes. As she comes toward me, she extends her hands through the window lattice and caresses me, but I, with a key obtained who knows where, turn open the padlock on the mausoleum's iron door and let her out. We leave together, holding hands, and behind us come the others, admiring the bride's white beauty.

When I rang, my neighbor Marusya's mother opened the door and invited me inside. The smell of food frying permeated the apartment. Marusya was frying flounder, but because she was a *petsoora,* she wasn't frying with lard, but rather with an oil called *poslamasla.*[2] It had a better smell than lard, margarine, or even butter; from the expression on my face, it must have been apparent how good the *poslamasla* smelled because Marusya took some flounder from a large plate, lifted it in front of me on a smaller plate, and told me to eat. Nyura came into the kitchen. Ženya wasn't at home, but I preferred Nyura actually. She was younger than Ženya, the same age as me, in fact, and she didn't badger like Ženya did. We ate flounder and potato pirogi. Potato pirogi was never made at our home, and when I once asked why, Mother said that Russians eat that. I didn't start to explain that Marusya also made potato pirogi.

Nyura and I went into the yard. I suggested that we go play in the courtyard of the building where the rococo lady lived. Nyura hesitated. When you played in an unfamiliar courtyard there was always the possibility that someone might come and scold. But I promised Nyura that if she'd come, I'd tell her a word she hadn't heard before. Of course Nyura thought I'd teach her a foolish new word, and she did come along with me. I wanted to play in front of the stairs, not on the lawn behind the building or in the yard where it would have been better. But from there it wouldn't have been possible to see when the rococo lady came home. And so we did in fact play in front of the stairs where there was nothing but gray earth, and soon our clothes, hands, and even our faces were soiled.

"Say the word now," Nyura remembered.

I stretched out my neck, conjured up an expression of delicate contempt and said, "rococo!"

"That's it?" Nyura was disappointed. "What does it mean?"

"I don't know."

"Where did you hear it?"

"My mother said it."

"What did she say it about?"

I didn't want to tell Nyura that. "She just happened to say it once."

"Strange," thought Nyura and repeated: "Rococo!"

At that same moment the rococo lady turned in through the gate. That startled me because she might have heard Nyura and no doubt thought that we were talking about her. But her expression certainly didn't indicate that she had understood. She probably hadn't even noticed us. Nevertheless, she turned around on the stairs, looked at me, and said: "Why are you playing here? Go home, wash yourself, and change your clothes! It would be better for you to be reading something." The lady had a slight, somewhat plaintive voice.

I felt so badly and ashamed that tears welled up in my eyes. Nyura didn't feel insulted, however: "She didn't even speak to me. What a rococo!"

"I'm going home," I said. But I didn't even have a chance to leave before in through the gate came a man whom Nyura and I knew because we had often seen him following the rococo lady, also talking to her sometimes. The man was tall, wearing a gray suit, and he was quite nice looking, except that his chin was too large and angular.

The man with the angular jaw went into the rococo lady's building. "Let's follow him," whispered Nyura. We opened the door slowly and peered into the corridor. We could see the man climb up the stairs and ring the rococo lady's doorbell. We snuck over to the stairs and peered through the railing. The door was opened by a cross-looking old woman who lived with the rococo lady. She was said to be the lady's servant, but this was probably not known for certain because no one in our country had a servant any longer.

"Is Ella at home?" asked the man with the large chin.

"No," answered the old woman thought to be a servant. "Ella isn't here, in fact."

"She's lying," whispered Nyura.

"Shhh!" I motioned.

"When is she coming home?" asked the man, and he whispered something else, which I didn't hear.

"I really don't know," said the old woman and slammed the door shut.

Nyura and I burst into a run; with a single breath we ran into our own yard. Then Marusya called Nyura inside and I went over to Katya in the shed. I discussed everything I knew about the rococo lady with Katya. That she was rococo. And a lady. That her skin was almost as white, fragile, and fine as the graveyard bride's, and that she didn't even have freckles. That she had whitish-gray or yellowish-gray hair, but her face wasn't wrinkled. I didn't really understand exactly whether the rococo lady was young or not—she was too unique for that.

I had once heard Father and Mother discussing the rococo lady between themselves; in referring to the lady then, Mother had used strange words. "In her day she was a deputy's lover," Mother had said. That had to have something to do with men. But Mother had noticed me then and asked what I wanted, and I had slipped out into the yard. There was furniture in the yard, someone was moving, a round coffee table stood on the lawn, and Nyura, Ženya, and I ran around it singing a song we had heard somewhere: "Oh we need no clock, Moscow keeps the time in stock!"

That move influenced our lives—into our building came

Vello, a boy Ženya's age. He immediately took an interest in the rococo lady, but even more so in the cross old crone who lived with the lady. "She's a witch," said Vello with conviction and slurped saliva.

"Stupid!" Ženya grew angry.

"You're stupid yourself, get lost *petsoora!*" shouted Vello. "You're stupid and a liar. A liar and a cheat, in hell the devil you'll meet!"

Of course none of us, not even Vello, believed that the old woman was a witch, but we pretended to believe it, and this became an exciting game. We followed the woman, shouted at her: "Old witch! Old witch!" and we made the sign of the cross when she came toward us.

"We must force our way into the witch's cave," said Vello one day. "We have to see what she eats and whether she has tools for witchcraft." Pleasant chills ran down my spine. "You're going!" Vello pointed a finger at me. "Go see what sort of den that is there."

The four of us were in the corridor of our building. I was about to argue, just for effect, when the door sounded downstairs. We rushed down the steps to see who had come. There stood an unfamiliar woman, a scarf on her head, a roll of paper under her arm. She drew a sheet of paper from the roll, took a box of thumbtacks from her pocket, and fastened the paper to the outside door. "Well, children!" she called briskly. "Everyone go vote!" And, banging the door, she left. A large plaque now hung on the door, and on it was a man's picture. The man had curly hair, a broad face, and his glance was gloomy and vigilant.

"Candidate for deputy," Vello spelled out syllable by syllable.

"That can't be!" I said—the word "deputy" was familiar to me.

Vello smirked arrogantly. I went over to the plaque and mouthed to myself: "Candidate for deputy!"

"What's 'candidate' mean?" I asked Vello.

"It doesn't even have an exact meaning; it's just that there's such a man," said Vello evasively.

"Is this man here on the picture the deputy, then?" I asked in a whisper.

"Exactly," affirmed Vello with an air of importance. "The deputy."

And the rococo lady had been the deputy's lover—meaning she liked the deputy. This, then, was the man the rococo lady loved. In my opinion this man was actually uglier than the one with the angular jaw whom the rococo lady apparently didn't want. How must the rococo lady feel, seeing her deputy's picture posted everywhere? The paper roll under the arm of the woman wearing the scarf was quite thick. Then it occurred to me that I should in fact enter the witch's cave—go see what they're like there. Actually I wasn't even very afraid of the old woman; I desperately wanted to see what the rococo lady's home was like, where she lived, the gloomy curly-haired deputy's lover. Besides, it didn't hurt a bit to look brave in the others' eyes.

"Sure I can go," I said to Vello.

"Where?" Vello didn't understand.

"Into the witch's cave," I announced proudly. Nyura and Ženya gasped. "In fact, I'll go this evening."

I went home, washed my ears and neck, put on a raw silk dress Mother had sewn for me from a dress my aunt had had during the Estonian period.[3] The dress even had a beautifully embroidered belt with an identical collar. I put on shoes of fish skin and white socks with bows, so there was no need to wash my feet. This was the aunt who had married a Baltic German and left long ago ("she went when Hitler called" Mother had said once, and I had been amazed that Hitler knew my aunt, that must have been terribly gruesome). I put on multicolored beads left by this same aunt, and on my finger Mother's ring with a green gem. The ring was a bit large; just in case, I pressed it onto my thumb. I poured an ample amount of Red Moscow perfume on the front of my dress. This turned the light beige raw silk bluish-purple, which was exciting to watch, but soon the stain left by the perfume dried up and the dress was again beige. Then I took a book from the shelf. There was an entire series of books there and their title was Novels from the Northern Lands; all of them were different, actually. I pressed the novel to my breast and started off.

Nyura, Ženya, and Vello were waiting in the corridor. When I came out, the girls began chirping around me and my adornments enthusiastically, but Vello ordered them to be quiet and we set off. I walked at the very front, a Novel from the Northern Lands in my hand, surrounded by a cloud of sweet perfume; and behind, keeping a reverential distance, came Nyura, Ženya, and Vello.

"Don't you come into the stairwell," I told them when we had reached the rococo lady's building.

"We will too," said Vello. "How else will we know that you're not bluffing?"

I didn't understand what that meant exactly, but I sensed that Vello had doubts about whether I would really have the courage to go.

"I'm not bluffing," I said haughtily. "You go stand under the window, there where the *Jugend* is. I'll come to the window."

"You're bluffing," said Vello hesitantly, for he didn't know what *Jugend* was.

"Under which window?" asked Ženya.

"Under their big window," I said and stepped into the building. A plaque with the deputy's picture was also posted on the door of the rococo lady's building. For a moment I wavered beneath the deputy's gloomy look, but I had no choice. I went up the stairs.

Inside the door, I pressed the Novel from the Northern Lands more firmly to my breast and rang. The old woman opened the door. Because she didn't notice me immediately, she pulled open the door chain and thrust the door wide open.

"Is Ella at home?" I asked and slipped beneath the old crone's arm into the vestibule.

"Yes, but what do you want?" asked the old crone in amazement.

"I brought the book," I said and thrust the Novel from the Northern Lands under the old woman's nose. "My mother sent it."

"Go on in, then," said the old crone and directed me into the room that had the *Jugend* curtain in front of the window. There was also a large, oval table, beautiful chairs, a buffet, and a small bookcase. Perhaps there was something else as well. I didn't have a chance to see everything because I went immediately over to the window and looked out. In the yard stood Vello, Ženya, and Nyura. They stared at me, frightened.

"Who's there!" the rococo lady's voice called from somewhere.

"A child!" the old woman called in response.

"What does she want, let her come in here!"

The old woman directed me into another room where, on a tremendously large bed with a shiny white satin blanket and two pillows, the rococo lady sat. White closets and mirrors as well as vases with flowers gleamed around her. The rococo lady herself was also in white—in cut-off pajamas of shiny silk. On her shoulders she had a cape of floating swan feathers, a white silk turban was tied around her head, and a wondrously beautiful peacock feather swayed upon it. The rococo lady was holding a large cold cream jar of frosted glass, and she was putting cream on her snow-white thighs. I remember her long, shiny but unpainted fingernails as she patted the cream into her skin. For a moment we eyed each other in silence, and I understood that in fact the rococo lady wasn't very young. She smiled and her chin, the line of her mouth, seemed weary to me. I couldn't contain myself any longer, I ran into the vestibule, stumbling against a closet, and knocked something over. I saw that there was a chain on the door, I pulled open the chain and ran into the corridor. Downstairs, near the outside door, I bumped into someone. It was the gray-suited man with the angular jaw. He took hold of my shoulders, shook me, and asked where I was coming from. "From Ella's!" I shouted, and because the plaque with the deputy's picture was directly opposite me, I pointed to the deputy with my finger and added, "She's his lover." The man with the angular jaw groaned and stormed up the stairs. I saw how he flung open Ella's door; apparently the old crone hadn't had a chance to fasten the chain. I ran away. Somewhere Nyura, Ženya, and Vello joined me. They asked something, but I kept on running. Suddenly, I sensed that my hands were strangely empty. The Novel from the Northern Lands had been left behind at the rococo lady's apartment. I was afraid to go back, but I was even more afraid that I would get scolded at home for having lost the book.

"Wait!" I called to my companions, "I have to go back." I went to the rococo lady's building again. The man with the angular jaw came toward me, but he didn't even acknowledge me. I ran up the stairs and gently tried the rococo lady's door. The door was open. I stepped into the vestibule, the light was on, from the distance came the sound of someone crying and lamenting. I became frightened. Quivering, I snuck over toward the crying sound. The large room was empty, but in the bedroom the rococo lady lay on her back in bed and the front of her white pajamas, the satin blanket, and even the pillows were bloody. She lay clumsily, her head outstretched, her glance directed at the corner of the room. Before her, on the floor, sat the old woman, she was stroking the rococo lady's hand with its long, shiny fingernails and weeping loudly. Strewn on the floor were the cold cream jar of frosted glass and my Novel from the Northern Lands.

For many years, I yearned that someone would love me as

passionately as the gray-suited man with the angular jaw had loved the rococo lady. Only later, in a conversation about that old tale of murder, did I learn that the man in the gray suit had been dangerously insane.

–1991–

THE MILL GHOST

AFTER THE CRITICS HAD LEVELED MY FIRST BOOK, I LEFT MY job and went to the country. Despite the harsh criticism, I planned to devote myself entirely to writing. For living quarters, I obtained a room in quite good condition on the top story of an old water mill. The other rooms in the mill were empty, their windows and doors nailed shut with boards. The first months were spent putting the room in order—I had never had a place entirely of my own and I enjoyed arranging my room. But the disadvantages of living in a water mill became apparent quite soon: the room was damp, the murmur of the mill dam was more irritating than soothing. Because no one lived on the bottom story, my floor was terribly cold; it took me a great deal of money and effort to heat it. Before long, rats appeared in the empty rooms of the mill. Creating a great commotion at night, they ran, squeaked, and, crunching, chewed the wall as they tried to force their way into my room.

Influenced by the harsh criticism, I had obviously taken an exceedingly desperate step, given up amenities, a peaceful job, and a steady income. I had grown shy of people; it seemed to me that everyone knew me as a failed writer. In writing new stories, I tried to take into account the critics' suggestions in order to produce a work that would be sure to win praise, but that didn't seem to be succeeding. There had to be a great deal of blind anger, bitterness, and derision in the depths of my consciousness, the part called the subconscious. I wanted to write about goodness and love, but all the relationships among my characters were transformed into illness. I was incapable of depicting a single positive emotion, of endowing my heroes with nobility and spiritual grandeur. Only pettiness, jealousy, maliciousness, a desire for revenge and betrayal motivated my characters' actions. All those same evils of which the heroes of my first book had been accused by the critics. To the world, I myself must have appeared equally as sullen, gloomy, and evil as my characters—why else didn't I have any friends? The critics had alluded to the similarity between my gloomy, self-assured person and that which I created. Arrogance and vanity were the evils for which the critics castigated me, as these had previously merited castigation in the Bible. My gait, bearing, gloomy derisive laugh, manner of dress—all this spoke contrary to altruism, humanism, and pacifism. A gloomy water mill was deemed the perfect place for the likes of me. It's unlikely that anyone would have believed me had I written about how my heart began to beat wildly upon seeing the bird cherries near the mill in bloom, of how I became intoxicated with their scent, with the nightingales' call, of how my eyes grew moist when, from my window, I saw the caution and love with which a young mother took her little ones across the mill bridge every day, or how a family of ducks splashed and paddled in the water. Surreptitiously, I slipped the birds food.

But they all nodded understandingly and knowingly when I sent a newspaper my new short story in which I described how I poisoned rats in the mill, and how I myself observed their agony. For this purpose, I had had a display window constructed between my own room and the empty mill room. (Let it be stated that I didn't poison a single rat, although I did indeed ask to borrow a stalwart female cat from the village, and this ended the rats' reign of terror within a few months.)

Although I didn't have many guests, nevertheless my novella did entice some of the more curious from among my former circle of acquaintances to the mill (as has been stated, I had never had friends), who, not distinguishing artistic truth from life's truth, wanted to see the display window between my room and the mill room. And why not the rats' agony as well, although they did not mention that. I said that the window was behind the curtain and that the view visible from there was too hideous for those good people. The curtain did in fact exist; it hid the moisture stains on the wallpaper. I didn't allow the guests to touch the curtain, and I noticed how one poetess, who cultivated beautiful poems about love and nature, tried to peek behind it. I shouted at her, she was startled to tears—soon afterward she wrote a poem about a morbid bat, a bloody nocturnal vampire, a clandestine killer. The poem, a new plane in the poetess' artistic creation, was otherwise very lively and figurative, the bat's Dracula-deeds were portrayed with blood-curdling efficacy. The poetess was indeed talented. Only later did I hear that, after the poem was published, the people who came to visit me had nicknamed me the Mill Vampire, which was later replaced by the entirely more tame Mill Ghost, and even that soon went out of use—society was beginning to forget about me.

With the arrival of autumn, I noticed with shock that the money I had received from the book (its amount had been at least tripled in the fabrications recounted by my acquaintances) was almost gone, the excerpts and short stories published from time to time were insufficient to keep body and soul together; given the superficiality of today's reader, cultivation of long prose has always seemed senseless to me and has the unequivocal aroma of facile servitude. I was reminded of what one of my writer friends had said—never in his life, before or after, had he earned as much as he had for one variety show, which was performed throughout the country almost every week and which earned him five to six hundred a month. I could have tried it, in fact, although I had never cultivated that genre. It's true that some of my novellas had been referred to disparagingly as feuilletonistic. Perhaps I should now capitalize on this feuilletonism? But the path from writing to variety show performance would be long and arduous, all the more so because I hadn't even begun a humorous sketch yet. When I had money, I went to the kolkhoz cafeteria and ate a warm lunch to avert ulcers; and when there was no money, I bought some white bread and drank tea, sugar water, or lemonade along with it. Lately, subsisting only on white bread had grown tedious, and it began to affect my health. In addition, I feared I would be thought of as a parasite because I wasn't a member of any organization that would have entitled me not to work. The kolkhoz manager might also begin to regret his kindheartedness one day and realize that the mill apartment would be well suited for some young specialist oriented toward that enterprise.

Of course, I could have gone to work at the manor, a school held classes there now, but after all, I had come here to write. That is why I constantly forced myself over to the desk, rose from there only to get white bread and sugar water or, if not even these were to be found in the house, then to catch some sleep in order to quench my hunger. But the work did not progress. Or, to be more accurate, it did in fact progress, but in a manner diametrically opposed to what I expected. It didn't have the least bit to do with a variety show—feuilletonism had long since vanished from my novellas. They grew more and more morose and brutal; the characters were not only degenerate in spirit but in appearance as well. In them, sly hunchbacks plotted, a ruthless cripple functioned as a thrill-killer, a man with his right cheek disfigured by a large, purple birthmark stood beneath the windows of the women's sauna for days. In the stairways of the old town center and beneath its archways lurked rapists with seared faces; in the graveyard, a drug addict who suffered from elephantiasis terrified people; a cruel epileptic thrust needles under his wife's nails at night; and a blind hunchback sawed through wooden stairs in order to hear people fall and shatter. I tried to banish the demonic beings back into my subconscious. I began to write a story about a beautiful young woman, Linda, who had a nationalistic bent of mind, but already by the second page everything had returned to its old tracks—Linda turned out to be a lesbian prostitute who suffered from an incurable, evil illness and also passed it on to a lecherous leader of the people. The nightmares in my stories grew crazier and crazier. Despite this, from time to time I tried to sell a story. It's true there wasn't much demand for them but, for some reason, the literary editor of one magazine for young people was taken with them, and every six months a small cluster of stories was published there. Later I heard that the magazine had been reprimanded for tenaciously publishing my stories, but, in the literary editor's opinion, the editor-in-chief apparently had prestige and the little tales were printed almost regularly. My concern over money was alleviated.

On the radio one evening I was listening to Schubert's music, which always affects me very deeply, occasionally even makes me cry. Listening to Schubert, I walk together with him in joyful places where nature is even more romantic than in the environs of the water mill. I am seized by anxiety, loneliness. I see pure, softly flowing rivulets, I hear roaring waterfalls, craning my neck I look toward snowy mountaintops, I lie on a scented, summer-warm meadow where thousands of bugs drone. I return to Schubert's lovely, romantic time when everything was beautiful, even death, grief, love's pain.

But that night a sharp knock pierced my Schubert-reverie. Because I had not had any visitors recently, that knock startled me considerably. I turned off the radio, dried my tears, straightened my clothing, and opened the door. At the door stood a man of some sort—medium height, with thick, dark, slightly curly hair. Small, curious eyes peered from between his high cheekbones. The man's face seemed familiar, but I couldn't remember where I had seen him. A khaki backpack was hanging from his hand by a single strap. "Juhan," said the man, and he stepped inside.

In the room he put down the backpack, then, taking long strides, he went over to the radio and turned it on. "Softly my songs beseech . . ." proclaimed a pleasant alto. "Schubert," said Juhan. He sat down in the rocking chair where I had recently been sitting, listening to Schubert, and he grew motionless as he listened. It wasn't appropriate for me to disturb him. We listened until the Schubert was over, although I was no longer able to immerse myself in the music. When the announcer said in a toadish voice, "You have heard the music of Franz Schubert in a well-known interpretation," Juhan turned off the radio and pushed the rocker into motion. He rocked quietly for some time, and I had nothing to say either.

Then Juhan's glance slid to the papers scattered on my desk. "You just keep on writing," said Juhan.

"Yes," I said, "I just keep on writing."

Juhan did not respond. The silence was embarrassing. After all, I could have asked why Juhan had come or whether, for instance, he wanted some tea. I had all kinds of herbal teas gathered and dried—wild thyme tea, chamomile, bearberry, linden blossom, peppermint, thyme, yarrow, caraway, cowslip, rose hips, birch bud, raspberry stem, black currant leaves, nettles, marigold, tansy. But I thought that it would be more clever to keep silent and to wait and see what Juhan had to say.

"And what do you yourself think of your stories?" asked Juhan at last.

"That's for me to know," I responded evasively.

"Are these the kind you want to write, in fact?" inquired Juhan. His little eyes watched me mockingly and slyly.

Suddenly I recognized him, but hadn't he already died long ago? Juhan's question hit the mark and forced me to answer honestly: "No, they aren't, but they come out this way."

"Right, right," nodded Juhan, "they simply come out this way."

Then we were silent again for some time. "Well, why don't you write, time is fleeting," Juhan finally said.

"But it's not proper to write when there are guests," I thought.

"Have you invited me, in fact?" asked Juhan. He knew very well that I hadn't invited him. I couldn't have invited him for after all I didn't know him.

"I didn't invite you," I said, therefore quite angry.

"If you didn't invite me, then you needn't take me into account, either. Sit at the desk, take a ballpoint pen and paper, and start writing."

I thought it over and found that Juhan was right. If he was forcing his visit upon me but demanding no attention or hospitality, it was probably best to act as though there was no one here, in fact, and to go on with my life as usual. All the more so because Juhan really had no business here at my place.

I sat down at the desk, put some paper before me, grabbed a ballpoint pen, turned my gaze to the window, and began to jab my nose. I became engrossed in waiting for an inspiration and forgot Juhan completely. In order to begin writing, I needed a cue. Lately I had constantly been getting cue words like dead-end street, heretic, wart, main sewer line, submarine, Jew's harp, dysentery, swamp, intestinal parasite. From these I then went on to develop one story or another. Now, however, there rose before my eyes lilacs in purple bloom from the yard of my childhood home. There, too, was the scent of the large jasmine bush beneath our kitchen window and little birds hopped among its branches.

I remembered father and mother, sisters, playmates, and sunshine from my childhood glistened around me, warmer and brighter than all that came later. But I did not allow myself to be deceived. How many times had images of lovely places, beautiful memories, good people, noble scents risen before my eyes and entered my imagination, yet when I began to write them down, a heretic who had escaped from a submarine stumbled along a dead-end street, a wart on his neck, and, stinking of his intestinal parasites and dysentery like a main sewer line, he disappeared into a swamp droning his Jew's harp. That's why I didn't hasten to write about the lilac- and jasmine-scented sunshine, but continued jabbing my nose instead and waited for new cue words. "Jaan," I heard, and before my eyes rose my first love, a fair-haired, quiet, intelligent boy from our class. "Childhood, jasmine bushes, sunlight, Jaan," I repeated, but in fact no sensible story formed from these words. "The Alps, trout cavorting in a stream, verdant, fruit-laden orange trees growing beside a white highway, a lark's song, wild violets, Hortus Musicus . . . "[1]

Everything beautiful and good swirled around in my head, and I felt nauseous. I crumpled up the empty paper before me on the desk—not even a line was written on it—and I threw it into the trash basket like a manuscript that had gone wrong.

"It's not coming?" Juhan asked from the rocking chair. I had utterly forgotten his presence. "Why strain yourself," Juhan said matter-of-factly. He got up, took his knapsack, and left, slamming the door shut. The rocking chair rocked, empty. I listened, my ear to the door, and although the mill's old wooden staircase usually creaked with every footstep, I heard nothing. No doubt Juhan was standing behind the door. I thrust open the door in order to catch him unexpectedly, but there was no one on the stairs or behind the door. I ran to the window; Juhan wasn't visible in the yard either. Fresh snow had fallen, there should certainly have been tracks in the snow, but I saw not a single track. Was Juhan in the mill yet, or had he left another way somehow? I ran to the yard, I called, no one answered, I circled around the mill—everywhere, the snow was pure and untouched, no tracks of any sort. I began to feel ghastly. I hastened back inside, locked the door, put on some tea water. I scattered some of my herbs into the pot and drank the strong, intolerably bitter mixture that boiling them yielded. That calmed me a bit. Then I sat down at the desk again to work. Since there is never a surplus of clean paper, I searched in the trash basket for the white sheet I had thrown there in despair at my recent creative slump and I smoothed it out. I remembered precisely that I hadn't written even a line down on the paper, but now I saw that the paper was filled from one end to the other with my handwriting. It was a beautiful, ardent, and slightly sentimental story about childhood sunlight, lilacs, and first love. Just the kind I had tried to write half a year ago. I revised the little tale and sent it to the editorial office of the young people's magazine with which I was acquainted. The editorial board sent back the story (although the board does not return manuscripts), and there was also a brief note: "Incompatible with our readers' concept of your style. Keep on as the Mill Ghost. Respectfully . . . " This was, of course, followed by the literary editor's signature.

I understood that my exile was over. That same day I asked the kolkhoz chairman for a truck, the driver and I piled my things on it, and I rode back to the city to my family. My short stories are having success, they will soon be published as a collection, and I've acquired friends.

—1991—

DISINTEGRATION OF
THE SPIRAL

"PLEASE, TEACHER, DON'T GIVE ME AN UNSATISFACTORY," Artur implored of his literature teacher, a middle-aged, pleasant-looking lady whose name Artur did not recall, however, for he had had very little contact with this instructor.

"You know, dearie, you haven't attended my class at all, how then can I evaluate you," observed the teacher. There was a sad tone in her voice, but the student understood that this was precipitated by a grave matter of some sort known only to the teacher, not, however, from concern about the student.

And so Artur tried to get on that same wavelength and to unite his own fervent appeal with the teacher's sad mood of resignation.

Nevertheless, the teacher did not give in: "No, you know, dearie, I can't. I can't. Now take a look yourself, you've been absent constantly."

"I beg you, teacher!"

The teacher took a long look at the boy beside her desk in the empty classroom.

"Then have you at least read all the books we were assigned?" she asked.

Artur, who sensed acquiescence in that question, a first indication of complaisance, could not but answer yes.

"Well, at least there's that," said the teacher. "We'll be continuing with those works next quarter. Then you'll answer everything nicely, get a very good grade, isn't it better that way?"

"No," said Artur, despairingly.

"Well, how so, don't you want a good grade, in fact?"

"Yes, but not next quarter, I want it this quarter . . . " said Artur, frightened. The teacher began to gather together her papers on the desk, obviously planning to depart. Artur, sensing that he had expressed himself foolishly, made a final effort.

"I'll get a beating, you know," he said, frightened. The teacher fell silent. Her movements froze. Her glance was directed out the window, somewhere far off. At the same time, she began leafing through her diary industriously, as if hoping somehow to find an escape in it.

"But we don't have any more classes this quarter, you know," she said finally. The boy merely looked at her, frightened.

"Well, all right, come see me at the Institute tomorrow, do you know where that is?"

The boy shook his head. The teacher explained to him.

When Artur reached home, he found a letter addressed to him in the mailbox. He had barely gotten inside before quickly opening the letter. Artur read the letter through. My father is a worrywart, he decided. The letter was filled with some sort of sentimental gibberish. Father again asserted that he loved Mother and his son, and held himself solely responsible for everything that had happened.

Does Father really not know, or is he playing dumb, wondered Artur.

The next day, Artur did in fact go to the appointed place. He found the teacher in a room with a glass door and four large tables loaded with piles of books and typewriters.

"Aha, it's you, very good, take this chair and sit down here," instructed the teacher. Artur did as he was told. The teacher gave him a few sheets of paper and requested him to write an essay on the theme: "Ugliness and beauty in V. Hugo's novel *The Hunchback of Notre Dame.*"

"Do you know what he said to me," recounted one of the women who was working in that room. "He said that we women give birth to children, but that counts for nothing with them, it merely interests them insofar as they, for themselves, can find some sort of . . . " The glance of the woman talking fell on Artur. It seemed as if she had only now noticed the boy, and she didn't complete the sentence.

"And that's what he said?" asked the other woman.

"Yes, that's what he said, in fact."

"I wonder what he could have meant by that," a third woman joined in the conversation.

"Well, it's been clear for a long time already, hasn't it, what their thoughts actually are," judged one of the women, and she added simultaneously: "Nevertheless, one wouldn't have expected such vulgar talk."

In a corridor nook, Artur had left a briefcase bulging with the materials he would be needing. But first he must write something in order not to arouse any suspicion. With a swift, small script he began jotting lines down on the paper.

"Beautiful is something which is like this and a bit of something else besides that. On the other hand, ugliness, depending upon how you look at it, you can express it many different ways. In the significant part of the novel, of course, there's something."

Here Artur's pen stopped. By dint of his meaningless sentences, he had tried not to arouse suspicion, but suddenly there weren't even any of those in his head.

As soon as my pen stops, the teacher may glance over at what I've written and then I've had it, the terrible thought flashed through Artur's head.

In the meantime, with more and more intensity, the

women had begun to discuss some problems that had occurred. Artur took advantage of the opportunity and began to write down the women's conversation. Work progressed full force, the conversation did not subside, and Artur saw that the teacher was smiling good-naturedly at his diligence and obvious competence.

Then came the decisive moment. Artur asked for permission to go to the WC. The teacher described its location in a few sentences. Artur quickly hurried over to the briefcase. In a pack of borrowed essays there, he found an appropriate one. Artur also read through it, just in case, then he thrust it inside his jacket and returned.

From the first moment on, he sensed that something was wrong. The room was silent as a grave. Artur sat down to his work. All the women were looking at him with unpleasant glances. Only one of the women was reading a paper of some sort and muttering: "My God, it's base, unbelievable . . . " Artur scowled at the sheets of paper in front of him: his work had disappeared.

"Have you read anything at all?" asked the teacher in dead earnest.

"Yes."

"Well, what's the book about, then?"

"That sometimes the one who's otherwise ugly can be beautiful in spirit, and then again, the opposite as well: someone's beauty is beautiful, but they don't see or understand anything. For instance . . . " and Artur produced convincing arguments to support his position, attempting to alter their girlish vocabulary a bit.

"Well, for heaven's sake, why didn't you write that, then?" finally asked the teacher, who now understood that the boy really had read the book. "A quarter of his grade's at stake . . . " she added, though seemingly to herself. All the women who were in the room stared at Artur as if he were an apparition, something completely unprecedented, an entirely unimaginable being.

But he was like a statue, his head lowered, and he said nothing. He was thinking.

He was thinking that as soon as he got out of this room, he would go to his father and tell him something. He'd tell Father that Mother hadn't left him because he had gotten the car stuck in front of a train and put all their lives in terrible danger. He would tell Father that his explanations, his endless explanations about the fact that the visibility was poor . . .

It really was; although Artur had still been little then, he remembered everything vividly. It had been raining furiously. There wasn't a single star or other point of light in the heavens or anywhere else. And they were in a great hurry, they had to drive as fast as possible in order to make it. Of course Artur hadn't been in a rush, or Father either, probably. And that, in fact, was what Artur would tell Father: that his explanations and observations noting that it had been Mother herself who had implored, as Father kept writing in his despairing letters, who had downright insisted on rushing, were futile because that wasn't the issue at all. And most important was what Father noted in almost all his letters, what had already become the standard introduction and conclusion to his letters, as if required by some sort of etiquette known only to Father himself, namely that the railway barrier had not been lowered but rather had been standing upright. Father can indeed find some kind of relief and excuse for himself in this. Because Father can imagine—and this is exactly what I'll say, thought Artur—that there should be a basic change in Mother's attitude when he establishes that the one who should have lowered the barrier had, against all regulations, kept it raised. And then he, Artur, will make a cheeky quip asking why, in his letters, hasn't Father used excerpts from those regulations and decrees which, in Father's opinion, should have ensured that his wife would stay with him on their mutual, joyful path, despite the fact there was no evidence to show that she would have.

And when he had said all that, then he, Artur, would give

the real reason. He wouldn't even mention that actually Father should be very well aware of this himself and not play the fool. Instead, he would put on an expression acting as if he himself had also discovered the real reason only a little while ago. He would raise a finger and say . . .

"Why didn't you write that, then?" the teacher's irritated voice interrupted Artur's reverie. Reluctantly, he raised his glance. Something must definitely be said. Suddenly a way of salvaging the situation flashed into Artur's head. Why not say what he had just imagined himself saying to his father! Having now thought of this, Artur recounted:

"When I was still small, we once survived an auto accident. I and Mother, in whose lap I was sitting, we suffered only a mild shock, but Father was badly injured. He was in the hospital for many months. At first they thought that he would never begin to walk again, but he made tremendous efforts, and by the time he was released from the hospital, he could already walk, practically without crutches. Before the accident he had a handsome, intelligent air, but as a result of the accident his temporal bone had been crushed. It was replaced with a plastic one and skin was grafted. It may be difficult for you to imagine this, but as a result of the operation, his hairline descended nearly to his eyebrows and that new plastic forehead was, all in all, at a tremendous slant. When Father got home from the hospital, he wanted to cheer Mother up with the fact that he was able to walk on his own. Moving in this manner, his body inclined forward strangely, and he held his hand at his side convulsively, as if he were attempting to rise into flight, but, as a result of the great strain, his mouth remained so open that he looked just like a Moabite;[1] when my mother saw that horrible image, she screamed; you know, I've never heard such an agonized woman's scream, and she ran into the other room. But Father, who it seems didn't comprehend the situation, apparently thought that something had happened, he hobbled after Mother. . . . Well, my mother was a young woman then; of course she couldn't stay with such a person. There-fore I have had to grow up without a father, and whenever I've been asked, by my schoolmates for instance, I've had to say that he's a sailor. Actually, I wanted terribly to have a father . . . "

Artur concluded here because it was clear to him from the teacher's expression that his response had been exhaus-tive. The teacher did indeed understand that the dilemma of beauty and ugliness had passed very near this person's life and left a deep imprint upon his soul. It was no wonder then, either, that he had been incapable of writing down what he knew on that given theme but rather, having evi-dently fallen into great spiritual confusion, he had begun to write senseless and offensive gibberish.

When Artur departed from the Institute he was unable to take his briefcase because, for some reason, the teacher accompanied him to the outside door. Artur was just about to say good-bye when the teacher asked: "Oh yes, I wanted to ask you whether I heard correctly. I think you mentioned the Moabites. Who are they?"

"Why they're the ones who take away pieces from the spi-ral coil of an electric range," responded Artur.

The teacher winced, her glance reflected horror.

—1989—

■ □ ■ □ ■

NOTES

"PHOTOSENSITIVITY"

1. Paide is a town of approximately nine thousand inhabitants in central Estonia, where the ruins of a thirteenth-century fortress are located.

2. Henry of Livonia (Henricus de Lettis, c. 1187–1259), missionary and chronicler. Author of *Chronicon Livoniae,* in which he describes the subjugation of the Livonians, Latvians, and Estonians by the Teutonic knights.

"THE BLACK MOTORCYCLIST"

1. In the Battle of Ümera (1210), the Estonians won a decisive victory over the Germans and their Latvian and Livonian allies.

"HE TRANSLATED"

1. Rossetti wrote this poem in English. The unbracketed variant is his original English verse; the bracketed variant is a literal rendering into English of the story's Estonian translation by this collection's translator.

2. Aleksander Tombach (1872–1944) was on the board of the Estonian National Bank (1926–29), a translator of Shakespeare's *Hamlet* (1910; second trans. 1930), and he also wrote poetry. His pseudonym was A. F. Kaljuvald.

3. Georg Peeter Meri (1900–1983) was an Estonian diplomat, literary scholar, and translator. He translated the works of Shakespeare into Estonian (1959–83). Georg Meri is the father of Lennart Meri, the current president of Estonia.

4. In Estonian phonetics, the quantity of sounds as well as syllables is divided into three durations or lengths: short (first), medium long (second), and extra long (third).

5. In the Soviet Union, reusable glasses rested on ledges beneath the spouts of carbonated water dispensers. Each thirsty person would take a glass, fill it, drink from it, then rinse it and replace it on the ledge.

6. At this time, at least 50 percent of the Estonian urban population did not have a phone at home.

7. *Eugene Onegin* (1833) is a verse-novel written by Aleksandr Pushkin in the 1820s. Contemporary critics called the hero, Eugene Onegin, the Russian Byron.

"TANTALUS"

1. Finnish and Estonian are closely related Finno-Ugric languages. In Estonian, the word *surra* means to die.

"HALLELUJAH"

1. Criminals.

2. Harjumaa and Järvamaa are two counties in north-central Estonia.

3. The approximate equivalent in English is "Open up, fuck your mother."

4. "Yes—yess."

5. "Good evening. Doctor Ulrich."

6. "So. Now I hear you absolutely normally."

7. Konrad Henlein (1898–1945) was a Sudenten-German politician and a proponent of German annexation of the Czechoslovak Sudenten area. During World War II, he held administrative posts in Nazi-occupied Czechoslovakia.

8. "I say to you: if the plutocrats and the Jews drive me to that point, we will march forth to defend German blood and territory even unto the end of the earth."

9. A tinkerer.

10. "What's goin' on?!" "Dammit, an air-raid alarm again?" "The damned Tommies again?!" "Or maybe not . . . ?"

11. Traffic cops.

12. Quick-quick-quick (in Russian, *bystro-bystro-bystro*).

13. Makhorka is an inferior grade of tobacco.

14. "The fucking fascist."

15. "The fucking fascist."

16. Baked pudding.

17. Walter Ulbricht (1893–1973), an East German politician.

18. "I have the honor, my esteemed felt boot driers, to wish you a good workday."

19. Black raven is the slang term referring to the black

enclosed truck in which the Russian state police, the Cheka, transported its prisoners.

20. Bread.

21. People.

22. "Anyone there?" (German).

23. "Anyone there?" (Russian).

24. "Fucking . . . "

"THE DAY HIS EYES ARE OPENED"

1. Nikita Sergeyevich Khrushchev (1894–1971), premier of the Soviet Union from 1958 to 1964.

2. Salvage (*utiil*) operations—state-owned enterprises that collected, stored, and transported scrap metal, old clothes, etc.—were frequently the only places where intellectuals who had been educated in independent Estonia could find employment during the Stalinist period.

3. This refers to the new "underground," mainly of the 1970s and 1980s in Soviet society, when such jobs were often held, either voluntarily or involuntarily, by those who refused to "participate" in society.

4. From the summer of 1941 to September 1944, Estonia was occupied by German Nazi forces.

5. One of many such standard phrases found in Soviet culture idealizing those who brought collectivization and the kolkhoz way of life to small, private farms.

6. In 1942 Velikie Luki, between St. Petersburg and Minsk, was the site of a heated battle between Soviet and Nazi forces where many Estonians who had been forcefully mobilized into the Soviet army lost their lives.

7. From the perspective of the postwar Soviet regime, those who had served in the Soviet forces during the war had been on the "right" side; those who had served in the Nazi forces had been on the "wrong" side.

8. During 1944, Sinimäed [the Blue Mountains] in northeastern Estonia was the site of extensive battles between oncoming Soviet forces and the retreating Nazi forces, which included both forcefully mobilized Estonians and those who had joined to fend off Soviet occupation of Estonia because the Germans refused to allow the Estonians to have their own independent military units.

9. Artur Vassar (1911–77) and Marta Schmiedehelm (1896–1981) were well-known Estonian archaeologists.

10. From June to August 1940, a puppet government with Johannes Vares (1890–1946) as its prime minister was installed in Estonia by the Soviets to legitimize the annexation of the country. Vares later committed suicide.

11. Konstantin Päts (1874–1956), Estonian head of state throughout most of the 1930s and president of Estonia from 1938 to 1940.

12. Nigol Andresen (1899–1985) was foreign minister in the Vares government and minister of education in the 1944 Soviet Estonian government.

13. A purge of leaders in Estonia during 1949–50 included many officials formerly associated with the Vares government, such as N. Andresen mentioned above. Accused of nationalism, many were sent to Siberia and replaced by ethnic Estonians who had been raised in Russia under the Soviet system and were considered more trustworthy.

14. Blue, black, and white are the colors of the Estonian national flag.

15. On June 17–18, 1940, Soviet forces occupied Estonia, and on June 21, 1940, the legitimate government of Estonia was toppled.

16. "Hi mother. Why are you crying? The old man got a child's sentence—"

"THE SWAN-STEALING"

1. Kadriorg is a park surrounding Kadriorg Palace, which was built near Tallinn by Peter the Great in 1718–19 and now serves as the residence of the president of Estonia. The Estonian National Art Museum has also long been situated in Kadriorg.

2. Rocca al Mare (Italian, Boulder by the Sea) is located on the coast of Tallinn. It is the site of the Estonian National Open Air Museum and, formerly, of a Pioneer camp for communist youth.

3. Lasnamäe is a large development of high-rise buildings on the outskirts of Tallinn. It is considered an eyesore.

"THIS SO UNEXPECTED AND EMBARRASSING A DEATH"

1. Rakvere is a town of approximately twenty thousand inhabitants in northern Estonia.

2. *Snegurotska* (Russian): Snow maiden.

3. *Ty moi angel* (correct Russian).

4. *Ya dumal, čto ty ne pridyoš'* (correct Russian).

5. *Ekh, ty moi nekhoroshii* (correct Russian).

6. *Tebe nado vypyt'* (correct Russian).

7. *Ty samyi, samyi khoroshii* (correct Russian).

8. *Svoego mužhika* (correct Russian).

9. *Ty čto* (correct Russian).

10. *ne mogu ikh obizhat'* (correct Russian).

11. *ty menya nepravil'no ponyala* (correct Russian).

12. *ya tebya prekrasno ponyala* (correct Russian).

13. *Nu i bl . . .* (Russian): What a bitch.

"DROOPING WINGS"

1. All-Knowing-Three-Golden-Hairs is a European folktale motif.

2. First published in 1860–64, *Ancient Tales of the Estonian People* [*Eesti rahva ennemuistesed jutud*] is a classic collection of folktales compiled by Friedrich Kreutzwald.

3. "Soviet Estonia" [*Nôukogude Eesti*] was a propagandistic newsreel series. Numerous such shorts were produced every year to be shown before the main feature at movie theaters.

4. *La Légende et les aventures héroiques, joyeuses et glorieuses d'Ulenspiegel et de Lamme Goedzak au pays de Flandres et ailleurs,* a novel by the Belgian author Charles De Coster, published in 1867 and translated into Estonian in 1927, 1947, and 1980. It depicts a small people's struggle for freedom against a large power, and shows how wit and humor can be used successfully to this end. The work has been very popular in Estonia.

5. In the agrarian culture of earlier times, a pig's bladder was used as a plaything, blown up as a ball, for instance.

6. Built in Tartu in 1906, the Vanemuine Theater is the oldest professional theater in Estonia.

7. Juhan Liiv (1864–1913), an Estonian author and poet, is considered a pioneer of Estonian prose realism. Liiv suffered bouts of mental illness.

"the rococo lady"

1. Russians who came to Estonia after World War II were called *petsoora,* the Russian name for the city of Petseri in eastern Estonia, which has traditionally had a large Russian-speaking population.

2. *Poslamasla* represents the Russian *postnoe maslo:* any vegetable oil, typically used during Lent, probably sunflower seed oil. This oil is not customarily used in Estonian cuisine.

3. The period of Estonian independence from 1918 to 1940.

"the mill ghost"

1. Founded in 1972, Hortus Musicus is an Estonian ensemble that plays baroque and fourteenth- to eighteenth-century European music on period instruments.

"disintegration of the spiral"

1. Moab (literally, "from her father") was the son of Lot and his firstborn daughter, conceived after Lot's wife turned into a pillar of salt as the family fled from Sodom and Gomorrah to the mountains. The Moabites, who were forbidden to enter the congregation of Israel, were constantly at odds with the nation of Israel.

BIOGRAPHICAL NOTES

ARVO VALTON (b. 1935), son of a laborer, was deported to Siberia with his family from 1949 to 1954. When he returned, he studied chemical engineering at the Tallinn Polytechnical Institute, where he received his degree in 1959. In 1967, he completed a degree in script-writing at the Moscow Film Institute. His first collection of short stories, *Strange Desire*, was published in 1963. Valton has also published novels, essays, drama, film scripts, aphorisms, and poetry, and has translated literature, primarily from Russian and Hungarian, into Estonian. He became a member of the Writers' Union in 1965. He has recently been serving in the Estonian parliament as an elected official.

MATI UNT (b. 1944), the son of an accountant, received his degree in Estonian language and literature with an emphasis on journalism at Tartu University in 1967. His first book, the novel *Goodbye, Yellow Cat*, was published in 1963, bringing him immediate fame. Unt has written many short stories, though, starting in the 1970s, he began to write novels primarily. He has also written criticism and drama. Unt entered the Writers' Union in 1966, and since the 1980s has been a theater director in Tallinn.

JAAN KROSS (b. 1920), son of an automobile factory journey-man, received his law degree from Tartu University in 1944, and then taught national and international law there until 1946. That year, he was arrested on political charges and spent the next eight years in exile in labor camps in Russia and Siberia. After returning from exile, he became a professional writer. His first work, *Coal-processing Plant,* a book of poetry, was published in 1958, and he thereafter became a member of the Estonian branch of the Soviet Writers' Union. Since the early 1970s, he has primarily written short stories and novels. His novel *The Emperor's Madman* (1978) received the Tuglas Award. Kross has also written criticism and translated poetry and prose from many languages. He has recently been serving in the Estonian parliament as an elected official.

TOOMAS VINT (b. 1944) studied biology at Tartu University and then worked as a director's assistant at Estonian Television while studying painting. Vint has been a professional artist since 1969 and has made his living primarily as a free-lance artist. Vint's first book, *Beyond the Living Fence on Both Sides of the Road,* was published in 1974. He has written many short stories and two short novels. He received the 1979 Tuglas Award for his novella *The Story of Artur Valdez.* Vint became a member of the Artists' Union in 1973 and a member of the Writers' Union in 1977.

MARI SAAT (b. 1947), a scholar's daughter, received her degree in economics from the Tallinn Polytechnical Institute in 1970, then completed her graduate degree in 1979 at the Estonian Academy of Sciences. Her first book was published in 1973. The short story "Catastrophe," which appeared in that book, won the 1974 Tuglas Award. Saat has written many short stories and three novels. The most remarkable of the novels is *Spell and Spirit, I* (1991). Saat became a member of the Writers' Union in 1976. At present, she teaches busi-ness ethics at the Tallinn Polytechnical Institute.

TOOMAS RAUDAM (b. 1947) studied English philology at Tartu University. He has worked primarily as a film director and scriptwriter. His first book was published in 1983. He has published short stories, three novels, essays, and criticism.

ÜLO MATTHEUS (b. 1956) has written two collections of short stories, a novel, *Gleam* (1989), and literary criticism. At present, he works as a journalist in Tallinn.

MAIMU BERG (b. 1945) studied journalism at Tartu University. Although her short stories were already being published in magazines at the beginning of the 1970s, her first book appeared in 1987. She has published a book of short stories and four novels. The most remarkable of the novels is *I Loved a Russian* (1994). She currently works at the Finnish Cultural Institute in Tallinn.

JÜRI EHLVEST (b. 1967) studied mathematics, biology, and theology at Tartu University. His first book of short stories was published in 1995.